W9-CGZ-891

"Git up, boy."

Pardo kicked him in the stomach.

"I said git up, boy," Pardo said evenly. "I swear I'll plain stomp you to death if you don't."

Howie pulled himself up. His head swam.

Pardo studied him in the darkness. "Now, boy—or Howie, I reckon. You got what was comin' and it's over and done with. You ran into a feller tonight that knows who you are and where you came from. He seen you with your pa, once. He knows what happened to your folks. Seems like most everyone east of here does and I ain't surprised. He knows what you did to that Colonel Jacobs feller, too."

Something flashed between them and landed at Howie's feet. He picked it up, and felt Jacobs' pistol and holster.

"We git some time," said Pardo, "I'll show you what to do with it, 'sides struttin' around looking all rough-like. Mean feller like you can likely use some gun-learning."

Other Isaac Asimov Presents titles
published by Worldwide Library:

THE MAN WHO PULLED DOWN THE SKY *(August 1988)*
PENNTERRA *(October 1988)*
AGENT OF BYZANTIUM *(November 1988)*
STATION GEHENNA *(December 1988)*
CALIBAN LANDING *(January 1989)*

ISAAC ASIMOV
PRESENTS

THROUGH DARKEST AMERICA

NEAL BARRETT, JR.

WⓌRLDWIDE.

TORONTO · NEW YORK · LONDON · PARIS
AMSTERDAM · STOCKHOLM · HAMBURG
ATHENS · MILAN · TOKYO · SYDNEY

THROUGH DARKEST AMERICA

A Worldwide Library Book/September 1988

ISBN 0-373-30302-5

First published by Congdon & Weed, Inc.

Copyright © 1986 by Davis Publications. All rights reserved.
No portion of this book, aside from quotes in book reviews, may be quoted
without written permission from the publisher.

All the characters in this book have no existence outside the
imagination of the author and have no relation whatsoever to
anyone bearing the same name or names. They are not even
distantly inspired by any individual known or unknown to the
author, and all incidents are pure invention.

® are Trademarks registered in the United States Patent and
Trademark Office and in other countries.

Printed in U.S.A.

The Bitter End

by Isaac Asimov

Every religion that I know of always has tales of a beginning of Earth and of humanity and of human technology. Some god or other forms the Earth and sky, molds human beings into shape, and teaches them the rudiments of fire, metallurgy, agriculture, and so on. Quite often the gods themselves are described as having a beginning. Zeus was once a baby, for instance.

Christianity is rather different from most in that its creative God is supposed to be eternal. That introduces a great many philosophical difficulties, but we can leave that for theologians to deal with.

It is not so common for religions to picture an end to Earth and humanity. To be sure, we are all reconciled to the inevitability of an individual end for each of us. (We generally palliate the pain of that thought by supposing that transmigration of souls will bring us another life here on Earth, or by supposing there will be an ideal immortality in an imagined heaven.)

But what about an end to everything; to the whole ball of wax?

That, too, is sometimes imagined. The prophetic books of the Old Testament speak of a Day of Judgement in which God brings everything to an end, destroying the vast majority in horrible ways while saving the inconsiderable number who follow the prophet's teaching exactly.

The best-known end, at least in our culture, is contained in the final book of the New Testament, "The Revelation of St. John the Divine."

The first three chapters of the book are routine, but after that is a long, long description of all the endless disasters that are brought upon the Earth by a vengeful God—the sea turns to blood, the stars fall from the sky and so on. I find it all rather tedious and unconvincing. In the end, though, a new heaven and new earth come into being for the inconsiderable remnant who are saved.

A non-Christian ending of violence is in the Norse Eddas, but since the version we now have dates back to about 1000 A.D. it may have been influenced by Revelation. It tells of "Ragnarok" in which the gods and their adversaries battle themselves to mutual destruction and then—a new heaven and a new earth come into being.

Science, too, supplies us with bitter ends—of an astronomical nature. Prior to the 1930s, there was the feeling that slowly the Sun would cool down and Earth would become a lifeless block of ice. Since the 1930s, we realize that the Sun is heating up and someday the Earth will become a lifeless cinder. Both, however, will be billions of years in the future and will be so slow that we will have time to escape (if we haven't died out long before).

For faster bitter ends, there is the possibility of the Sun going nova or supernova, but we now know that the Sun is too isolated and too small for either possibility. In the 1980s we have come to face the possibility of a cosmic impact with an asteroid or comet that might wipe us out just like that, but this isn't very likely in the near future, and if the catastrophe holds off for just a few centuries we may develop the capacity to ward off such an eventuality if it seems to loom ahead of us. All these possibilities have been dealt with in science fiction stories, of course.

Forty years ago, a new possibility came into view. Human technological power, with the development of nuclear bombs and bacteriological warfare reached the point where we can destroy all humanity, or most of it, in a few hours to a few months. We may have a human-caused bitter end.

Almost as soon as the first nuclear bomb, used in anger, had dropped on Hiroshima, science fiction writers began to write post-Holocaust stories, far more grisly than anything the stodgy imagination of the writer of "Revelation" was able to produce.

These are always cautionary tales, the message of which is "Don't let the bombs drop!"

No new earth and heaven arise by magic in such stories, but is there any hope that perhaps, more slowly, the indomitable spirit of humanity will re-create something? Well, read *Through Darkest America* by Neal Barrett, Jr., but remember—

Don't let the bombs drop!

1

When Howie was twelve, Papa took the whole family downriver to the fair in Bluevale.

"Suppose it'll be the same as ever," Papa winked at Howie's mother. "Growler'll dust off his stuffed nigger and 'spect everyone to shell out a copper for it." He chuckled and shook his head. "Like they never seen one before."

Howie's mother gazed out over the river and let her eyes touch deep water. She was a small woman, slim as a girl, and younger than Milo. Web-fine hair fell to her waist in dark disorder, and hid eyes that were feather soft, and sad as ashes. Howie thought she was the most beautiful woman in the world. Papa told her she was, too, and sometimes whispered things to her and laughed his big laugh. Then she would turn away or look down and twine her small hands together and this would make Papa laugh again. Howie liked to watch them together. The things they said, or didn't say, to each other made him feel good inside.

"Milo..." She didn't look at him, but kept her eyes on the water. "I guess Jacob'll be there, won't he?"

Papa's face clouded, then he grinned and squeezed her hand. "Don't you trouble yourself about Jake," he said roughly. He looked past her to Howie and his sister, and ran a big hand through Howie's hair.

"Colonel Jacob'll be on a *horse*, Howie. Now that'll be somethin' to see, won't it?"

His father knew it would. Howie nodded and Papa grabbed up Carolee and set her squealing on the rail of the barge. "You're to have a good time," he said to his wife.

His voice was deep and heavy, but the gentleness was there, like it always was. "That's what fairs are for."

"It'll be new to the children," said Howie's mother.

The day was mild, and a fair spring breeze touched the water. It seemed to Howie as if the whole world had decided to take the day off and laze about in the sun. He leaned over the railing and watched the bargemen dip their long poles into the canal. The poles bent like fine bows with every stroke and he asked one of the men if they might not break in two. The man grinned through his beard and assured Howie this never happened. The poles were stout ash and up to the task.

Young cotton grew nearly to the shore on both sides of the river. He could see women and children weeding the long rows, bent in an easy rhythm. A boy his own age looked up and waved; Howie waved back. He thought the boy must wonder where the barge was going. He wished he could call out and tell him they were going to the fair, and would see a nigger and a real horse, and that Papa had promised him and Carolee they could have red sugar candy. He watched until the fields were far behind and the boy was still following the barge with his eyes.

After noon, the canal made an easy curve and veered south-east. Cotton gave way to young grain and the small shoots nosed out of the rich earth like tiny green daggers. A narrow creek wound into the canal, adding blue water to muddy brown. Its banks were lined with stubby oaks and tall cottonwoods. A trunk had fallen over the shady mouth and a big mossback turtle slept there, just out of the water.

Howie automatically reached for the bow on his shoulder. His mind leaped ahead, feeling the tight hum against his arm as the shaft sped away. He could see the green shell split dead center—the arrow thrumming in dead wood.

The picture vanished abruptly as he touched his neck and remembered the bow was still at home. He felt near naked without it, but Papa said you didn't take weapons to the fair. When Howie asked why, he said you just didn't. Later, though, when the baskets were packed and they were ready to start for the barge, he saw his father slip a small skinning knife in the top of his boot. Howie didn't wonder at this greatly. There were rules for grownups and rules for children and they weren't always the same. Though he was twelve and over, now, and that was near a man.

The barge passed the creek and the turtle slid easily off its perch. Howie wished he could join it in the water. The creek made a quiet pool under the deep shade where it joined the canal and there was a fine swinging tree nearby. That was the only bad thing about going to town, he guessed: you couldn't carry your bow and you had to dress different. His mother had patched his best trousers, which he hadn't worn more than twice and which were too small for him. They pulled at his crotch something awful, but mother said he could stand to look decent for a day or so. He wore his regular shirt, the blue homespun, but she'd starched it until it felt like old corn shucks stitched together. He was certain he'd itch to death before they ever even got to Bluevale.

He looked away from the shore and back to the barge, under the broad canopy strung up across the bow. His heart swelled with pride at the sight of his mother. She had on a new fair dress, one she'd never worn before. It was store-cloth instead of homespun, patterned in tiny yellow flowers on the lightest of blue. She'd made Carolee one exactly like her own. Howie wished she hadn't done that. He felt a twinge of guilt at the thought, but—dang it all—a dress like that should be special! For her, and no one else. So everyone in Bluevale could see just how beautiful she was.

They would anyway, he decided. Carolee was nine and no one was likely to notice her—no matter what kind of dress she wore—not with his mother about. She was pretty enough, he guessed, and looked like a sister was supposed to look. All right, but nothing special.

There was a little trouble late in the afternoon. Howie's father was taking extra stock to market and had three geldings and a mare in the pens at the back of the barge. Two of the bucks had been fixed for some time and were placid enough. The third, though, hadn't been out of action more than a few weeks. He was a short, stocky creature with a barrel chest and thick arms. He'd been a good stud, and easy going—but he was nothing but trouble now.

Howie knew that happened sometimes. And when a stud didn't take to fixing, he was good for meat and nothing more. Which was why he was going to market along with the older geldings. Those two had been fattened up during the winter and would bring a fair price, or make for good trade.

The mare was something else again. She was good stock, barely past sixteen, and had calved three times in four years. Howie's father didn't want to let her go, but there was bad blood in her somewhere. She was smart as a tack and had to be watched all the time.

When they heard the commotion in the pens, Howie and his mother and Carolee all looked at Papa. Papa shook his head and muttered something under his breath. He started to raise himself up, then stopped and looked straight at Howie.

Howie almost knew what was coming and felt the hairs on his neck rise.

"Listen," Papa said easily, like it was an everyday thing, "whyn't you run on back and quiet her down, son?"

Howie wanted to jump up and down, but he checked himself quickly. That's what a kid would do. Instead, he looked as serious as he could manage, and just said, "Yessir, I'll do that, Papa."

Papa unlooped the big stock whip from his shoulder and Howie ambled casually back to the pens. Behind him, he heard his mother say "*Mi*lo..." and could imagine the small hands making nervous circles in her lap.

"It's all right, Ev," said Papa, "the boy's twelve and able enough..."

Howie looked straight ahead, grinning to himself.

The two old geldings squatted in their pens, not looking at anything. Howie walked out on the rampway overhead and the newly fixed buck glared up at him and made noises in his throat. Howie touched the coiled whip on his shoulder, like he'd seen his father do. The buck stepped away, turning his attention back to the mare.

She'd gotten him all worked up, plain enough. And purely on purpose, too, Howie figured. The buck stood in the middle of his pen, shaking his head from side to side. His chest heaved. He stared straight at the mare, like there was something he wanted to understand, but couldn't.

The mare looked up at Howie and grinned out of vacant blue eyes. She saw the whip, but ignored it.

"Just get on back and sit down," Howie told her.

She giggled and looked at the buck. Her hair was wheat-colored, thick and matted. It fell in tangles down her broad back, darkened by the sun.

"Go on, now!" Howie warned. Stock couldn't tell what you were saying, but they were good enough at reading tones. Only this one just plain didn't care. She turned and stood square in front of her pen, as close to the buck as she could get. Watching the buck, she squeezed her breasts and jiggled them purposefully, holding the brown nipples in her fingers.

A low growl stuck in the buck's throat and he threw himself against his bars. The mare grinned, spread her legs, and put one hand between them. Howie flicked the whip along her back and she skipped away. Again, he laid the leather easily over her shoulder, snapping it lightly, so there was more noise than damage. A back full of welts told a clear story to a buyer.

The mare quieted, glanced once more at the buck, and went to the back of her pen to urinate. The recently gelded buck looked up blankly at Howie, touching the spot between his legs where the red scar was still healing. Howie watched them a moment longer, then walked back up to the bow. His father took the whip without comment, but Carolee stared at him, wide-eyed.

Oh, Lordee, Howie thought darkly, if she says anything I'll fair drown her right here, sister or no sister!

2

It was near ten at night when the barge bumped up against the docks at Bluevale and an hour or more after that before Howie finally got to bed. The time didn't matter. He couldn't have slept, no matter what. His eyes popped open every time they closed and his head was full of wonders.

The inn was near the river, just on the edge of town, so there wasn't much to see. A little, though, was plenty for Howie. One glimpse toward the square, lit bright as day. Lordee, more lanterns than you could count, all strung out on wires across the street! Blues, reds, greens, yellows and what all! And people, still up and about. Fiddle music. And laughing.

Somehow that seemed more peculiar than anything. He couldn't remember hearing that many people laughing at one time.

"Couldn't we stop? Just a minute? Just one minute, Papa!"

Papa grinned and laid a big hand on his shoulder. "You'll get plenty of fair come morning, boy." He gave Howie a broad wink. "Does sound like they're having fun, don't it, now?"

His mother, with Carolee asleep on her shoulder, hurried along. "I reckon fun's what you make it out to be," she said coolly.

"They're just feeling their oats and having a good time," Papa told her. "That's what a fair's all about, Ev."

His mother didn't answer. But he could hear them whispering long after they went to bed. They spoke too softly for anyone to listen, though, for the inn was crowded, and there were twenty or so travelers bunked in the big raftered room.

"I SUPPOSE you're going to see it," Papa muttered darkly, "come hell or high water." He shook his head and dug into his pocket for coppers. For a long moment, he brooded over the pile of coins. Like they were covered with bugs or something, thought Howie, and grinned. He loved Papa to act mad when he really wasn't.

When he *was* angry was something else. Papa was a big man, so tall he had to duck to get in most places, and sometimes his broad shoulders scraped both sides of the door. His face was dark from the sun, his long hair a shock of yellow, and his eyes nearly too light to be blue. He and Howie's mother looked like they'd been born on opposite sides of the world. In truth, though, they'd both been raised less than ten miles apart.

Papa reached down and raised Carolee high in the air. "Well, honey, you want to see it too, I reckon?"

Howie's mother showed concern. "Milo, I don't know..."

"Papa-papa-papa-papa!" shrieked Carolee. Her little legs pumped air.

Howie glared at Carolee, then studied the sign above the door. It was painted on cloth in big red letters and nailed to the store front:

SEE THE ANSHINT NIGGER
IN HERE. RIL AS LIFE!

"Papa. I gotta take *her*?" He knew it was the wrong thing to say before he said it, but it just came out anyway.

"Howie!" frowned his mother, "is that nice, now?"

Tears started in Carolee's eyes, which were big and dark like her mother's.

"Howie. Men take care of women."

Howie reddened. Papa wasn't mad-sounding at all, and that made it worse. He looked down at his feet. Papa tousled his hair and dropped two coppers in his hand. "We'll be waiting out here,'' he said. ''I sure ain't gonna see it again. Carolee. You hold on to Howie and don't let go.''

Blankets had been hung inside to form an aisle toward one corner of the room. The rest of the store was empty, but there were bare wooden shelves on one wall, and broken boxes all about. The air was heavy and musty, like the room had stayed wet a long time.

A short man with eyes like a bird took Howie's coins and pointed him toward the back. A farmer was just coming out, and Howie studied him for some clue as to what they might see. If the man felt anything, though, he didn't give it away.

Carolee began to cry the minute she saw it. Howie tried to make her stop, but it was no use. She shrieked all the louder and wrapped her arms around his legs and buried her head. Howie was thoroughly disgusted. It was like walking around with a big rock tied to your foot.

He tried to control Carolee, and look at the stuffed nigger at the same time. In the dim light of the lantern, all he could see was a lean body standing stiff against the wall—leathery, shrunken; pleated features under a gray layer of dust. The eyes were closed, but someone had painted bright staring pupils on the lids. For some reason, that seemed to give real life to the thing, and make it more than something that had been dead and dried out for a long time.

Howie jumped when the short man pulled the blankets aside. He glared at Howie, then at Carolee. ''Listen, you're gonna have to get her out of here.''

''I haven't got to *see* nothing yet!'' Howie protested.

''Out,'' said the man. He threw a finger over his shoulder and held the blanket aside. Howie jerked his sister to her feet.

''You went and ruined it,'' he said harshly, ''I hope you're good an' happy!'' She pulled away and he wrenched her back, hard enough to hurt. Carolee screamed and broke for the door. Howie's mother scooped her up and gave him a questioning frown.

''Howie pulled my arm and broke it!'' Carolee sobbed.

''I didn't do nothing,'' said Howie.

''Son, did you hurt your sister?'' asked Papa.

"I didn't do nothing," Howie repeated. He stuck out his chin to Carolee. "*She* made such a fuss the man threw us right out an' I didn't even get to see the nigger."

Howie's mother soothed Carolee and rocked her gently. "See, Milo?" She looked at her husband through a dark veil of hair. "I said it wasn't something for a girl to see. You just wouldn't pay any mind. She'll have dreams, now, and be up all night."

"Not 'less you tell her she will," Papa muttered. "Let's get on and out of the street. We come to the fair to have fun an' by God we're going to do just that!"

Later, he asked Howie, "Well, what'd you think? About the nigger?"

"I don't know, Papa. It was all shriveled and funny looking. And black." He looked up at his father. "Why's it all black?"

Papa shrugged. "I reckon that's what color they was."

"Why?"

"Don't know, boy. They just was."

"You ever see one? I mean, live?"

Papa laughed. "Godamn, boy that was all 'fore the *War*. Your daddy's not *that* old." He pushed Howie forward and announced they could have sweets if they wanted—red sugar candy or the big loops of blackgum, whichever.

There was more to see than Howie had even imagined. The town was crowded with people. Papa said some had come from as far as High River and across the Ridge at Calliesville and Newpack. Even if there hadn't been a fair, Howie decided, there was plenty to look at. Bluevale's main street was lined with wooden stores, some with another floor stacked on top of the first. And all had been freshly colored in reds, greens, yellows, and bright blues. Howie wanted to stop and look at each one. He hadn't realized you could get paint in anything but white.

There were booths and stalls everywhere. They sold metal knives, and bright clay dishes that had been colored and glazed until they shined brightly in the spring sun. There were strips of glass buttons, bolts of patterned cloth, and a hundred things Howie couldn't even put a name to. Papa bought his mother a fine set of bone and wood forks and spoons, though she flushed and lowered her dark eyes and said she wouldn't know what to do with something that fancy. Papa just laughed his big laugh and said she'd surely figure some way to show them off right.

There were smells Howie had never smelled before. Pepper, cinnamon, thyme, and sage. There were booths offering fresh fruit pies and red candied apples and small cakes with white sugar on top. It made his mouth water just to walk by, but he didn't ask Papa to stop. Carolee, though, wanted one of everything.

Toward noon, his mother took Carolee back to the inn for a nap. This pleased Howie greatly, though he was careful not to show it. Papa was relieved too, he was sure, but he kept his face just as straight as Howie's. Little sisters were all right, as far as they went. But they cried a lot and got tired easy and were always in the way when there were men things to do.

Howie was proud to walk down the long board sidewalks with his father. Papa seemed to know everybody. Howie noticed, too, that most of the men had to look up a little when they spoke to him. He walked close on his father's heels so everyone would be sure and know he belonged with this giant of a man with long yellow hair tied at the neck in leather and eyes that were sometimes blue and sometimes the lightest of gray.

3

If there was a bow, or a set of metal arrowheads, or a bone-steel knife in Bluevale that Howie and his father hadn't seen, he decided it wasn't worth looking for. Papa told him, with a broad wink that said this was not information to be shared with anyone else—meaning his mother—that after the meat market tomorrow there just might be some extra coppers that could go for a few dozen arrowheads, or maybe even that bluebone belt knife Howie said fit his hand like it was made to lie there.

In late afternoon there were contests on the edge of town—archery shoots at wooden targets and the axe throw at a white circle on a big oak. Howie's father said it seemed fair enough if a man wanted to pay good money to show off in front of everyone he knew—or make a fool of himself, as the case might be—but as far as he was concerned these were things a man was supposed to know anyway, and it didn't matter much if someone else knew he could do 'em or not.

Howie wanted to tell his mother all he'd seen in town, but he sensed right away it wasn't a good time for that. You could tell when she had something on her mind; and when she did, it was best to go about your business until whatever it was had run its course.

Howie's father knew the signs, too. And usually what caused them. It was an important something this time, Howie knew, because Carolee was left in his charge while Papa and his mother walked a ways toward the river to talk.

Howie was worried. He was twelve and figured a lot of things out for himself, even when they were things he wasn't supposed to think about at all. This had something to do with the fair, he knew—which his mother hadn't wanted to come to in the first place. And it had a lot to do with what his mother had said on the barge the day before. About Colonel Jacob. Though what that could be, he couldn't say.

A small knot grew in his stomach and stayed there until Papa and his mother got back. They were gone an uncommonly long time and every minute gave him the chance to think about maybe *not* getting to see the rest of the fair—which was the very best part. There was The Gardens, where you ate without cooking anything yourself. People just brought things right to you, whatever you wanted. And then the parade, with government soldiers and real horses. Besides that, there'd be pictures from Silver Island pasted up by the Courthouse. You might even recognize someone you knew, who'd gone there. People from all over won all the time and it might be someone from Bluevale or a farm right next to your own.

Howie decided that if his mother made Papa take them home and they missed everything he'd never say anything to her again no matter what. He took that back right away, though, and told God he hadn't meant it, and not to write it down anywhere.

THE GARDENS was a special place, built for the duration of the fair. There was an open tract across from the Courthouse, between Holdern's Market and the Metalsmith's. The land had been scraped and graveled, and wooden picnic benches set about. A string of colored lanterns added soft light, and there was usually a fiddler or two on hand for the diners.

Papa ordered for everyone. There was a fair cut of meat, charcoaled in the open, generous helpings of potatoes and greens, and a cold fruit punch that had been iced in barrels in the river.

"Seems a waste to pay good money for what you get at home," Howie's mother said wistfully.

Papa stiffened slightly, and his fork paused just an instant. Then he shoved the bite of meat into his mouth and chewed it savagely. Howie busied himself with eating.

His mother was plenty sore about something. They were *both* mad, really—they just showed it in different ways. Nobody had said much of anything to anybody since the walk by the river. Howie had watched them from a window—Papa red-faced and chewing his lip, making a lot of noise when he finally climbed the stairs. And his mother walking real quiet, but with her back straight and her eyes right ahead. Even Carolee, who didn't ever know anything, could tell there was something wrong and managed to keep her mouth shut.

The fiddlers came out of the big tent where the food was fixed and struck up a tune. A few couples sprang up from the tables to dance and everyone picked up the music with their hands. Howie wanted to, but his mother acted like there wasn't any music at all, so he pretended not to hear it, either. He looked morosely at the last bite of meat on his plate. Everything had tasted real good at first; he wasn't hungry, now. He didn't even like the fair anymore. What good was it, if everyone was too mad to even talk to each other?

"Howie..."

He felt his mother's small hand, cool over his own. "Howie," she smiled, "it'd be a gentlemanly thing to ask a lady to dance."

Howie straightened. "Me?" He felt the color rise to his face.

"Yes, you!" she laughed. She swept her long wings of hair into a single dark strand and looped it with a short ribbon behind her neck. Howie tried to glue himself to the bench, but she pulled him to his feet.

"I don't even know *how*!" he protested. His father leaned back and laughed, and Carolee shrieked and spilled punch down her skirt.

She swept him in wide, graceful arcs through the maze of tables. And because she was a striking beauty, and "looked hardly older than her son," they said, the people clapped and formed a circle about them. And the fiddlers moved in so close the bows were nearly singing in Howie's ears.

For the first few moments Howie prayed he'd turn to stone. But his mother's face was whirling about him, flushed with joy, and boyish awkwardness changed in a blink to young man's pride. And then it wasn't his mother who was guiding them through the steps with the small pressure of her fingers, but Howie himself, her hand squeezed tightly in his, a strong arm sweeping the slender waist where he wanted it to go.

The claps and shouts were for the both of them when he brought her through a final turn, and the fiddlers sawed them to a finish.

"Whooooie, Howie!" She laid a hand on her breast and took a deep breath. "You're going to make quite a man." Then she shook her head and kissed his cheek. "No, that's wrong. You're quite a man now!"

"He dances better'n I ever did." His father gave him a mock frown.

"Milo, that's not even sayin' anything at all!"

Everyone laughed. Papa thanked Howie solemnly, shook his hand, and announced that at any further time when dancing was called for, Howie would take over such duties. Later, when the fiddlers did a tune that was some slower, he caught Papa and his mother looking at each other in a certain way, and knew everything was all right again.

Howie and his family stood atop their table to watch the parade, as did most of the people who'd eaten at The Gardens. Howie held his mother's hand, because she didn't like high places. Carolee was in her usual spot, legs wrapped about Papa's broad neck, screaming she couldn't see anything, when she was really higher than anyone.

You could hear them long before they turned the corner at the Courthouse—with drums that sounded like big hearts beating and made the pit of your stomach go tight. The tops of the flags appeared then and brought cheers from the crowd. Howie stood on his toes and yelled until he was hoarse. First the flag of Old America, red and white stripes and white stars on a blue field. Then the White Mountain flag of Tennessee—that brought more hurrahs than anything. Though there were plenty of people from Arkansas

Territory in the crowd, too, and their banner got ample attention.

After that came a whole company of government regulars—all in green denim uniforms that mostly matched. They wore leaf-colored straws set rakishly on their heads and some of the men had stuck long, black-dyed feathers in their crowns. Their captain, a red-faced man with too much stomach, tried hard to keep his troopers in some sort of order, but when they spotted a friend in the crowd or a pretty girl, they'd jerk longbows from their shoulders and wave and shout. The people loved them and didn't mind if they couldn't march right or didn't want to.

Some wore a ragged red patch on their sleeves and that meant they could do more than march straight. They'd been as far west as Colorado and fought Lathan there in the mountains. And come back to tell about it.

The crowd was all but silent, now, and Howie knew what was coming. He watched, struck with both fear and wonder, as the mounted troopers appeared and he saw his first horse. Lord*ee*, Howie shuddered, they were ugly things to be as valuable as Papa said they were! Big barrel frames on long legs, covered with hair all over. And terrible snouts that ended in little mouths, like sucker-fish. Carolee howled and buried her face in Papa's hair. And for once, Howie didn't blame her at all.

The cheers started up again and the noise set the horses skitting about. One reared up on its hind legs and pawed the air. The crowd sucked in its breath and pulled back. The rider laughed, doffed his hat, and made the creature do the same thing again. Finally, the crowd laughed a little at itself.

There was no mistaking Colonel Jacob. There were bigger men in the parade—tall men with proud shoulders, broad chests, and thighs hard as oak posts. Colonel Jacob was lean and spare, and no bigger than a storekeeper. His face was all bone, with leathery skin stretched tight over narrow cheeks and a great beak of a nose. His hair was near white under his cap and everyone knew it hadn't turned from age. The eyes, though, told you who Jacob was—and where he'd been. And when you saw them, it didn't matter anymore how big he was.

Halfway down the street those eyes reached out and picked Howie's mother from the crowd, held for a moment, then flicked away again. Howie saw a shadow cross her face and felt her hand tighten in his. Papa saw it too, but said nothing.

The riders passed directly in front of The Gardens and they were something to see. Each wore the red blood-patch, and blue tabs on their shoulders to show they were officers. Many had hearts cut from purple cloth sewn to their chests. Some had stars over the hearts—meaning they'd been wounded more than once.

Many of the ground troopers wore the same badges and medals, but something else set the riders apart. For each carried a rifle on his back, or a pistol at his belt, and all had broad canvas bands slung across their shoulders. The bands, Howie knew, were lined with brassy cylinders that could kill a man further away than any arrow could travel. He'd never seen a gun before, or the things that went in them, but he was aware they were even harder to come by than a horse.

He wondered what it would feel like to hold something like that in your hand. Maybe that's why the riders all looked down at the crowd with easy smiles. And how they could even sit on a horse without fear. If you had a gun, and some of the little brass things to go with it, there wasn't a man anywhere who could tell you what to do, or stop you from going where you wanted to.

There wasn't much else to see except people from town, mostly boys and young men, who joined the rag-tag end of the parade and laughed and waved their arms and tried to march like soldiers. People were leaving The Gardens and mingling about deciding where to go and what to do. Howie figured a lot of them were going over to look at the pictures from Silver Island.

"Now see, Ev," Papa was telling his mother, "you got to say that was right nice, wasn't it?" He squeezed her arm and patted her shoulder gently.

Howie's mother shifted Carolee in her lap and didn't say anything.

"You want to go on back to the inn and rest up then? You feel better doin' that?"

He looked at her, waiting, and she raised her head and smiled wearily. "Milo. It's all right."

"Damn it all, nothing happened, Ev. Nothin's going to!"

"I guess not, Milo."

"All he done was ride by."

"Yes."

"He rode by and that's all there was to it."

"And looked," she said. "You saw him look."

"I seen him, all right," Papa said fiercely. "Don't guess I can stop him from doin' that."

"Don't guess anyone can stop Jacob from doing what he takes a mind to." She looked up quickly, pain on her face, clearly wishing she could call back the words. Howie saw his father's big fists tighten until they turned white, and he knew they weren't going to be seeing the pictures of Silver Island, or likely anything else at the fair.

4

Just past poortown, near a mile out of Bluevale proper, the high bluff sloped down to the sandy flats of the river and the sprawling site of Ten Creek stockyards. It was a good spot, because the wind usually blew off the bluff and away from town. Also, stock could be brought in easily by barge and processed meat taken out the same way.

Howie and his father walked to the yards just after sunup, along with a rancher from the Territory staying at the inn. The stench was bad, even if you were used to working stock. Not near as bad as it would be, though, Papa pointed out, when the full heat of summer hit the river bed. Howie didn't doubt it, but it was hard to see how something that awful could get worse.

To his left, pit-pens stretched out of sight around the bend of the river. Hundreds of separate hollows checkered the flats, under a network of narrow rampways. Every dozen rows or so, wider ramps had been built to serve the heavy feed carts.

There was a slow, constant motion within the pens—shuffling, incurious. And the sound was one Howie had heard before—an almost visible thing wherever stock gathered—like the dry hum of big, sad bees.

Papa said Bluevale was in a good position between the eastern and western roadways. The river was central to both and there was hardly a time in good weather when ten or twenty thousand head couldn't been seen there. Howie was ready to believe there were a hundred times that many on hand now.

"Over there's the fathering pens," Papa pointed, "and the breed shacks and show barns. And past that—see where the smoke's coming out? That's the processing plant and the dryers and smokers on the other side."

Howie nodded understanding. He was familiar with all these things, and what they were for. Here, of course, everything was on a much larger scale than at the farm. The maze of wooden buildings and sheds tumbling toward the river seemed a fairly big town in itself.

Down the roadway cut through the bluff, Papa led him past the sound and smell of the pit-pens and the noisy mechanical jangle of the cutting plant. They passed under the chute where non-edible organs and parts sluiced down in a tumble of color to four-man wagons, which workers hauled off to waiting barges. From there they floated twelve miles downriver to the fertilizer plant at Harrow Point. Now *that* Papa grinned sourly, had to be the most God-awful smelling place on the face of the Earth! Even birds, he said, wouldn't fly over Harrow unless they had to.

Though he didn't say, Howie knew his father had gotten a good price for the trouble-making mare and the three geldings. He came out of the plant office with a spring in his step, and coins that rang sweeter than copper in his pocket.

There was a tavern leanto set up right on the river under cottonwoods, where the sun brightened the water and sparkled off white gravel. Howie had cold cider while his father drank clear corn and talked to the other buyers and farmers. The reason meat prices were good, they told each other, was that the trouble with Lathan's rebels in the west had gotten a lot more serious than folks figured on. Plenty of towns and ranches had been overrun. Stock west of Arkansas Territory and Missouri had been scattered, stolen, or just plain used up. The army, and the people living out there, needed all the meat they could get.

Howie didn't understand all of it and wasn't given to asking grownup questions. But he'd overheard enough since late winter to know Lathan was someone who'd been important in the army once—like Colonel Jacob—and was now fighting against the country in the west. That was a bad thing, he guessed. Still, if it brought Papa more money for stock, maybe it wasn't *real* bad. He was holding a picture in his head of the bone knife in the window of the store in Bluevale. The one that fit his hand just right, like he'd squeezed it together in his fists out of river clay....

HOWIE FINALLY asked Papa about stock when he was nine— but the questions had been in his head longer than that.

"No reason to get all solemn-like," Papa told him. "Every child there is has to get the wonders out of him. Don't figure you're any different."

He set Howie up on the board fence under the heavy oak that shaded the tool shed and looped his big stock whip on a weathered post.

"Now, just speak what's on your mind," said Papa.

Howie bit his lip and looked down at his feet. "I . . . ain't sure I can do the words right."

Papa nodded understandingly. He'd seen the questions coming, long before Howie knew they were there. "I reckon I can nudge you along a little," he said. "What you got to know, Howie, is lots of things in the world *look* the same, but that don't mean they are. That's kind of what's in your head, ain't it?"

Howie nodded. He didn't want to tell his father what he'd been thinking. He was sure Papa would understand, all right, but the thoughts were real scary and he didn't think he could ever say them out loud. Not to anybody. When it had started, his heart had stopped right where it was and he'd been too frightened to even sleep for three or four days. And after that came the terrible nightmares and he kept his eyes open as long as he could—until sleep caught up with him and he couldn't hold back any longer.

What started it was looking down in the pit-pens one morning. Just watching stock mill about, like he'd done a thousand times before. One of the hands was bringing some colts in for doctoring. He was working alone, because the stock was too young to give much trouble. He waved at Howie and said something, but Howie didn't hear. Because just then one of the colts looked up and stared right at him—that was when Howie felt his heart stop and knew all the blood had gone from his face.

He ran as far as he could, away from the pens and out through the fields. He ran until his lungs quit and he stumbled and buried his face in sweet grass. He kept his eyes closed tight, but the pictures wouldn't go away. He still saw the colt looking up at him, and the terrible thing he couldn't tell anybody was that just then—at that moment—it was like being at the creek and looking down into silver water. And seeing your own face stare back.

Only, that couldn't be.

A boy didn't look in the water and see an animal. Howie had, though. For a quick second, it was the same—and no matter how much he told himself it couldn't be that way, it was.

That was how the nightmares started, and for a while he didn't think they'd ever stop.

"That's how questions come to you, Howie," his father went on. He reached up and pulled a sprig of oak leaves from the branch above. "Things that might *seem* the same is lots of times altogether different."

He turned the sprig of leaves between big fingers and held them up to Howie. "Now suppose you was on that ridge up there," he nodded to the west, "no more'n two hundred yards away. An' I was standing right where I am and I yelled out and said 'Howie, I'll give you a copper if you can tell me what kind of leaf I'm holdin' up here."

Howie grinned. "I'd sure do that!"

"And what kind of leaf is it?"

"It's a oak."

"What *kind* of oak, though?"

"It's a live oak, for sure."

"That it is. But if you was a couple hundred yards up on that ridge and I was to hold up a bunch of *different* leaves— a white oak, say, and then a red oak—what'd you say then?"

Howie frowned. He could see the copper in his father's story vanishing quickly. "I don't know," he said honestly, "might be I couldn't say for sure."

"*Might* be's right," Papa grinned. He rubbed a rough hand over Howie's hair. "They'd all seem the same, wouldn't they? Only they're not. And you don't even have to get up on that ridge, boy. S'pose you didn't live here, and you just come in from somewhere they don't *have* no trees at all. No oaks or pines or maples or elms or anything. And I showed you leaves from a white oak and a red. Reckon you'd know the difference?"

Howie shook his head, imagining a place where they didn't have trees.

"Likely what you'd say is they *seem* just the same. They got the same way of curvin' in and out, and their acorns is about the same. Reckon they *are* the same. Only they're not, are they?"

"No," said Howie, "they're lots different."

"And that's the way it is with people and stock, Howie. They might look kind of alike in some ways, but they're not anywhere near the same. You know why that is?"

Howie thought. "They don't act the same. Or talk or anything."

"That's two things. What else?"

"They're not smart like we are. They don't know hardly anything."

"Right," said Papa, "they don't. And you know why that is? 'Cause they're *made different*, Howie. Their bodies look some like ours, but they're not the same at all. Remember the oak leaves? How they 'peared like they might be the same, but were different altogether? Well there's a lot more difference than that between people and stock. More difference than night and day."

Papa paused, stripping the leaves from his twig and letting them flutter to the ground. He squinted at the sun through thick branches and looked at Howie. "The thing to remember, son, is that what you see on the outside's not near as important as the part you can't see. And that's the biggest difference of all between people and animals. There's other things, but that's the biggest. God gave men a mind to think with and the power to reason out the ways of the world. And he give him something else that's most precious of all, and that's a *soul*. Whatever somethin' might look like, Howie, don't forget that people has got souls. And that's something a animal can't never get. He's got a heart and blood and lots of other things. But in the end, he's still all empty inside."

HOWIE'S FATHER TALKED to the other men under the leanto and drank white corn; then the sun was nearly overhead and Howie wandered over to the pit-pens to watch the feeding. It was a lot bigger job than just slopping a few hundred head. Dozens of the big handcarts rolled out of the cookshed, so heavy it took six men to guide them up the rampways. Long before the carts appeared, though, the stock sensed it was feeding time. They bunched up tight under the edge of the pits, waiting. And those that saw the wagons first made grunting noises in their throats, jumped up and down, and slapped the ground with their feet and hands. Soon, the stock further down took up the cry and the sound swelled toward the bend of the river like rising thunder.

The heaviest carts went to the far end of the yards. The stock there was still being pen-fattened on a rich mixture of cooked grains and cereals heavily laced with meat scraps. The nearest pens got only a handful of the cheapest feed. There was no sense filling bellies that would soon be quartered on the end of a hook, making their way around the heavy plank walls of the cutting room.

The creatures here didn't look as if they could hold another bite, anyway. Some were so fat they could hardly waddle up to the rim. It was a meal most of them would hardly get digested, but hunger was a strong habit and they scrapped up everything that spilled over the edge. Howie knew, from experience, a stockman always had to keep his whip handy, even at the kill pens. Eating was all an animal had to do and sometimes they'd even go after their own wastes, or each other. You couldn't watch them all the time, but you had to discourage them when you had a chance.

THE TRIP WAS NEAR as perfect as you could ask for. There were presents for everyone—a doll for Carolee, the fork and spoon set for Howie's mother, and for Howie, the fine bone-handle knife he'd set his mind to. Papa hadn't forgotten. And Howie knew, from his father's mood and what he'd overheard at the river, that some good trading and studding dates had been set. A lot of hands had been shaken over white corn.

There would be plenty of food for the cold winter, then, and good times for the year to come. Especially if the spring and summer crops were as good as they should be and the frost came when it ought to. Papa was even talking about extra-fine winter barns for the stock.

Everything would have been fine, and Howie didn't even mind missing the pictures of Silver Island. Then the thing at the barge had to happen.

Papa had gone aboard to check on his stock and Howie was just carrying the last sacks of salt and ground meal up the narrow gangway. He chanced to look up and catch his mother's eyes, then saw her face go dead white. He jerked around; Colonel Jacob was right behind him, high on his terrible horse. Howie jumped away, quickly ashamed. The man looked at him and his thin face stretched into a grin.

"I startle you, boy?"

Howie flushed. "No, sir," he said and felt worse because the Colonel knew it was a lie.

The eyes flicked away from him, then, and rested on his mother. "You're looking well, Ev."

"Thank you—Jacob." Howie could hardly hear his mother.

"What's it been," said Jacob. "Eight, nine years? And by *God* you're as pretty as ever, Ev. Prettier, maybe. Your girl?"

Howie's mother tried to open her mouth, but couldn't. She nodded dumbly at Jacob.

"Looks like you. Going to be a beauty, too. Likely have hair fine as silk, Ev. And skin softern' rain."

"Jacob . . . please!"

Howie looked hard at Colonel Jacob, past the fine boots and the big metal gun at his waist. His fingers were hooked in his belt just above the gun, like he sat that way all the time. His smile seemed cut in his face, as if someone had taken a knife to it and sewn it back crooked. Long after, though, it was the eyes Howie remembered. They didn't just look at a person like they ought to—they reached out and touched wherever they wanted. And Howie tightened up inside because he knew plain as day where the eyes were going and his mother couldn't move away, or do anything at all.

Then the man looked down at him and Howie felt the eyes brush over him. "What's your name, boy, and how old are you?"

"Howie, sir. And I'm more'n twelve."

Colonel Jacob nodded. "You look more'n twelve, too. You any good with a bow?"

"Yes, sir," Howie told him, "I guess I am."

Jacob chuckled to himself. "Fine enough. If you're good at something, why, don't mind saying you are—if you've the guts to back it. You thinking on following your daddy's trade, or might you try a spell in the army? You studied on that?"

"No, sir," said Howie, who had thought plenty about just that since he'd seen the parade, "I reckon I'll help Papa."

Jacob looked at him a long moment, then the smile changed some and the blood rose in Howie's cheeks again. It was a funny kind of smile, like he was looking right inside you and knew something you didn't want him to know.

"Ev," he said, the smile still there, "you give my best to Milo, hear? Say I'm sorry I missed him and all..." Then, to Howie: "Take care, boy."

Clucking at his mount, he tossed the reins and turned back up the dockway. Howie could hear his father making his way forward from the stock pens at the rear of the barge as he followed Colonel Jacob until he disappeared in the haze off the river. He didn't turn to look at his mother. And when the man was finally out of sight, he was suddenly aware of an awful aching in his hand; he glanced down, surprised, to see it was curled tight around the bone handle of his new knife. It was a peculiar feeling—good and bad at the same time, and scary, too, because he didn't know what it meant, for certain.

5

Papa said it was the hardest winter in twenty years, that they were just damn lucky they'd been ready for it, and that Howie should remember nothing came to a man that he didn't sweat for.

Howie knew this was so and didn't need to be reminded. He'd heard the same thing a couple of thousand times before. Of course, Papa had a point, like always. Even if you knew winter would come around again, it was awful hard to keep from dreaming through the green days of spring, when the earth smelled deep and alive. There were always lots of things to take your mind off fences and planting and tending stock. Papa seemed to understand all that, though, and where a person might be found if he suddenly wasn't where he was supposed to be.

Some of the stock had sickened and died during the long, bitter months, even in the two big barns Howie had helped build the summer before. But Papa had planned well, and fattened the herd on good feed; the barns, and extra care, had done the job for the most part. On top of that, there was an extra good calving in the spring.

Even the worst stock, now, was bringing prices a man would have been happy to get for prime meat a year before. On the tail of the first good thaw, when wagons could move over the roads again, the countryside swarmed with government buyers. It was much like selling ears to the deaf, said Papa. They'd take anything on two legs that could crawl, walk, or hobble.

News was that Lathan's army had broken out of Colorado, defying winter cold and government troops. They were in a strong position now, and for the first time Howie heard his father and other men use the word *war*. It had been Lathan's rebellion, before, or "trouble in the west." It was more than that now. If Lathan couldn't be stopped, they said, he'd sweep across the plains and down to the Gulf before fall. Then, California would be cut off from the East and the government would have a war on two sides—with a hornet's nest in between.

"There'll sure be hell to pay," Papa said, shaking his head slowly. Howie wasn't sure what that might mean, and didn't want to ask. At any rate, Papa kept everyone working hard as ever, as if they might be close to starving instead of having more real money than they'd ever had before. There was plenty to be done, the war hadn't changed *that* any, Howie noticed. There was summer work and fall work and then another winter, before you knew it. One year seemed a lot like the last, he decided, when you did the same things over and over again.

The spring he turned fifteen, Howie found new things to think about. Things that had seemed important once, didn't matter much anymore. The fair at Bluevale was something that had happened a hundred years ago, to someone who was a different person, and not really him at all. That year, when sap stirred in the big oaks, something stirred in Howie, too. He'd felt it some before, but never quite like this. This was different. Like the whole world was somehow locked up inside him and couldn't get out.

Sometimes, every limb in his body felt like it was full of worms. He'd drop whatever he was doing without saying anything to anybody and run as far as he could, until sweat stung his eyes and the air cut his lungs. Then, he'd fall to soft grass and lay there letting blue sky whirl around him until the storm passed over.

Papa never said much when he came back. Like he understood, maybe, that something was happening that couldn't be helped. And when he just sat under the kerosene lamp at night and stared at the same page of spelling words, his mother pretended she didn't notice.

Sometimes, he woke up from dreams he couldn't name. And there were warm nights when he didn't sleep at all and everything within him came alive. The things that came to his head then were far stranger than the dreams themselves.

ACROSS THE BROAD, flat fields high with summer wheat, the land tumbled away in a line of small hillocks covered with grass. The hills dropped gently to the edge of the woods where the creek was shaded by heavy oaks. Howie lay just inside the forest, his head against a thick trunk. Lace fern touched his cheek and his eyes held the bright bird chattering on the limb overhead. It was a place he came to often, especially when troubling thoughts filled his head. And that seemed to happen all the time, now. Not about any one thing. It was usually a lot of different things that didn't have much to do with each other. It was the way the earth smelled, or how his hands felt gripping a heavy stone, or how willow looked with all the bark stripped. Mostly, though, it was something he couldn't put a name to. Something that made him feel good and bad at the same time; and, worse than that, hard to tell the difference between the two.

Looking up, he decided he'd dozed a minute. The bird was still there, but it was quiet now, moving its head in quick, curious motions. It heard the sound a second before Howie and froze, flattening itself against the rough bark and nearly disappearing.

Howie raised up on one arm, listening. There were voices. Men, and more than one. They were only a few yards away, just outside the woods, in the shade of the tree next to the one that belonged to the bright bird.

For a reason he couldn't explain, Howie didn't stand up immediately, but worked his way quietly through the ferns on his hands and knees. He stopped on the other side of the trunk and moved foliage carefully aside.

Breath caught in his throat. His heart beat against his chest until he was sure they could hear him. There were three men. He knew them, stock tenders who sometimes worked for his father. And a woman, too. She was...Howie's stomach tightened. *Lord God, it wasn't a woman at all—it was a mare! A young mare with yellow hair, and the men were...*

Howie thought his head would split open. The mare lay flat on soft grass. Her legs were spread and she grinned up vacantly at the men. One of them said something to the other. The second laughed and touched himself and rolled his eyes. The third man had already lowered his trousers to his ankles; the big shaft stiffly erect between his legs. In a moment he was down on the mare, hands clutching at her breasts. The mare groaned and engulfed him, thrusting her belly up to meet him. Her eyes were closed and her head arched back until the veins in her throat stood out like blue cords. The man breathed hard, pumping himself into her. His companions watched, laughing and calling out advice.

Howie couldn't hear what they said. He couldn't hear anything. His head throbbed like there were a million bees caught inside.

Help me, he cried out to no one. *Help me, help me!*

The man moaned and thrust himself forward. The mare sucked in a deep breath and her face twisted.

Howie felt his loins swell with unbearable pain; he felt sure he was going to die in the next second or so. Then he gasped and felt warmth flow from his body. *No, no, no!* Blood coursed to his face in shame, tears filled his eyes, and he buried his head in the earth.

The man was still in the mare when the arrow caught him in the heart. The shaft flew with such terrible force the dark feathers buried themselves in blood.

The mare screamed and the two men turned ashen faces in Howie's direction. Howie jerked around; short hairs climbed the back of his neck. Papa towered above him, boots buried in green fern. His face was hard as stone.

"Get up to the house," he said, not looking at Howie. "Get up, and stay there." There was another arrow nocked in his bow, but he released it gently. The two men were making tracks over the hills, into the yellow wheat.

"Get *up*, Howie..."

There was something in his father's voice he'd never heard before. He scrambled to his feet and ran through the woods without looking back. He stumbled, fell. His eyes blurred with tears. Brambles tore at his skin and he relished the sharp pain. Pain was good, and real, and cut fiercely at his heart, scouring out the shame.

Not all of it, though. It could never do that. He was marked, stained, and that wouldn't go away as long as he lived. And he could never, ever look at his father again.

He ran, and prayed hard, and begged God to let him die.

Late in the afternoon Papa came to his room and told him he was to get his boots on and come downstairs. He didn't look at Howie. In the house, or across the field all the way to the place where it had happened.

The two men were hanging from a high branch where Howie had watched the bird. Their faces were nearly black and their tongues were thick and swollen. The third man was on a branch beside them, by himself. He was still near naked, the arrow through his chest, trousers hanging about his ankles.

Howie's stomach boiled, and he turned away. *"No,"* Papa said sternly. He grabbed Howie's head hard in one big hand and held it toward the sight. "You don't turn away from life, Howie. Even if it ain't pretty to see. Not lookin' don't make it go away."

He said nothing more, but walked away down the low hills to the woods, Howie behind him. He stopped beside the creek and settled himself on a big stone. He looked at Howie and Howie sat.

"We had to butcher the mare," said Papa.

"Sir?"

Papa nodded to himself and scratched at the stone with his boot. "Howie," he said carefully, "she might have had seed."

Howie was startled at that. A man was a man, but his seed in an animal...

"You're wrong," said Papa, guessing his thoughts. "We never talked about it. Didn't see no reason. Thing is, that's something where people and animals is alike. Seed don't

know whether it's goin' into man or beast. A *man* knows
where he's puttin' it, though.'' He looked up, nodding toward the edge of the woods. ''Them three, now. Likely they
understand some better about that. Do *you* understand,
Howie?''

Howie swallowed. His mouth was dry as cotton. ''Yes,
sir. I think so.''

''I didn't say *think*, Howie.''

''Yes, sir.''

''What you got to know is there's no sin greater than the
one you saw up there this morning. A man's seed was given
to him by God to plant in woman at the right time. A man's
got a soul, and when he puts that seed in an animal, it's the
same as giving part of his soul to beasts. Do you see that?
And what's the issue from such a thing?''

Papa didn't wait for him to answer. ''Your mother's seen
to it you read the Scriptures. You know this world wasn't
always like it is. Before the War, when God cleansed sin-
ners from the Earth, there were hundreds of different kinds
of beasts roaming the land. The Scriptures tell us that 'man
ate of their flesh, though it was unclean.' Then, there
weren't any beasts such as we eat now, 'which are in the
shadow of man's form, and have flesh that is clean.' God
put 'em here for us, and took all other beasts from the
Earth, leaving only the creatures that fly and those that
swim. And that's the way He wants things to be, Howie.''

Papa was silent for a long moment. Howie listened to the
creek and hoped maybe that was all. Maybe Papa wouldn't
get into the other part.

''You want to say what happened back there, Howie?''

Howie's heart stopped. ''Not...much, Papa. I will, if you
want me to.''

''I think it'd be a good thing, Howie.''

''Yes, sir. I...'' He leaned down and wet his mouth in the
creek. ''I'm not right sure what to say.''

''Just whatever comes to you, boy. Whatever's true and
right.''

"Might be I don't know what's—true and right, Papa." He looked up, meeting his father's eyes. "That's possible, ain't it? That I wouldn't know?"

"I think it is, Howie."

"Well, sir..."

"You afraid of me, son?"

Howie thought about that. "Sometimes. Yes, sir." He looked down at his boots. "Right now I am."

"Well that's a natural thing. I was scared of my Pa. S'posed to be. But—when I needed to say something, he was willin' to listen. Same as I am, Howie."

"Yes, sir." Howie felt all tight inside. Papa was right, but—how could he talk about *that*? What was he thinking? It was terrible, a sin God wouldn't ever forgive him for!

"Papa..."

"All right." Papa nodded and tasted his lip. "You've seen lots of animals breeding, Howie."

"Yes, sir."

"And you seen this. Between man and beast."

Howie's stomach turned over again.

"And what did you think, Howie? Just say it like it came to your head, right when it was happening."

"Well, I..." Howie's voice choked in his throat. "I... *The mare didn't look like a mare. Not then. She looked like a— girl! I wanted to do that to her too, Papa!*"

He buried his head in his hands and felt hot tears burning his eyes.

"Howie..." Papa's big hand covered his shoulder. "Howie, men are weak. They don't always walk the right path. You're a man, now, and no different than other men. What you thought, what—happened to you, ain't too different than what's happened to a lot of men. You know, now, though. You see it, don't you, Howie? It's wrong, and something you got to put out of your head. Now and forever." He lifted Howie's chin and looked at him. "When you was little, we talked about how things could look the same, that wasn't. And that's the way this is. She's *not* the same, boy. Remember that. She was a beast and a beast's got no soul. You thought different—for just a minute, anyway. Not now, though. That's past, ain't it, Howie?"

"Yes, sir," said Howie. "I understand, Papa." And to himself, he prayed that God would take this day, pull it out of his head, and not make him have to remember it forever.

6

Crossing was just that—where the two wagon roads met and crossed one another, then twisted on to nowhere. Once a year, though, the fields on three sides were cleared of autumn bramble, and tents and cook shelters sprang up for the people who would come for Choosing.

Before the big trouble with Lathan, government people from Jefferson would arrive the night before in their big horse-drawn wagons. They'd pull up on the north corner in a wide circle, out would come the hightop tent colored bright red and blue, and the flags of the states and territories. Another, smaller tent was reserved for the pictures from Silver Island.

This year, though, horses were scarcer than ever—even the tired work animals that would have pulled the wagons had been pressed into service as mounts for soldiers fighting in the west. The wagons were lighter than usual, then, and pulled by reserve troopers who clearly didn't like this kind of duty. They cursed and grumbled that they hadn't signed up to pull wagons over bad roads, and said it surely wasn't the proper thing for soldiers to do.

Papa chuckled when he saw them. "Serves 'em right's what I say. Let them fellows in Jefferson see how the other half lives." A few men standing about nodded and laughed with him, but Howie's mother laid a hand on his arm and said someone might hear. Papa just grinned and told her *that* didn't matter to him one way or the other.

Horses were always good for a joke. As long as anyone could remember, the government had been saying it wouldn't be too long before there'd be enough of the big

animals so every farm and ranch could have at least one—
that breeding was going well, and more and more horses
were coming up from Mexico every month.

Nobody believed that, though, and a day didn't pass
during planting season when one neighbor didn't tell another that he shouldn't be pulling his own plow—that
there'd be horses to do that anytime now.

As soon as he finished helping Papa put up their own
shelter, Howie ran across the road to see the pictures.
Bluevale was a long time back and he hadn't forgotten it was
the one thing they'd missed at the fair. Besides, it was a good
time to stay away from everyone. His mother had been
crying again. It made him feel awful to see that—though he
was old enough now to understand why. Choosing was a
good thing and helped everybody, but like Papa said,
mothers had different kinds of feelings than other people.
So did fathers, Howie decided. They didn't show it as much,
but he'd caught a certain look in Papa's eyes.

There were already some people in the tent, but not so
many you couldn't see what you wanted to—and Howie
wanted to see everything. There were drawings and colored
posters and even photographs—pictures where everything
looked as real as if you were there.

Silver Island, he decided, must be an awful lot like
Heaven. Nobody knew what Heaven looked like, of course,
unless they'd died—but he couldn't see how God could
come up with anything much better. There were big white
houses under broad trees. Every window had glass and cur-
tains and the houses came right down to bright blue water.
A smooth, sandy beach circled the island and waves rolled
in from the sea and left sparkling foam on the shore. Sails
colored green, yellow, and cherry red dotted the bay.

It was all truly a wonder. And the biggest wonder of all
was that it never got cold on Silver Island. It was always
kind of like spring or summer, only better. No snow or ice,
and no wood to chop. You didn't freeze your hands and toes
until you couldn't even tell if they were there. Now *that* was
something.

The people, of course, were what everyone really came to see. There were pictures of people from all over the country—people from close by and as far away as California. And it was hard to imagine they'd ever lived anywhere but Silver Island. They didn't look like people you knew. Everyone was smiling. No one was tired or worried or anything. Well, why should they be? Howie asked himself. That's what Silver Island was for. If you went there, you didn't *have* to worry. You had a good life and plenty to eat and you never got cold. He reckoned he'd smile a lot, too.

One picture held Howie's attention a long time. It showed a group of boys and girls on a beach. They were tossing a ball back and forth and laughing. Behind them was a sailboat on a blue-green sea.

As far as Howie was concerned, though, there was no one else in the picture but the girl. She lazed on the beach, away from the others, her eyes closed against the sun. She didn't have hardly any clothes on at all and her skin was tanned the color of raw honey. You could see almost all of her breasts and her legs were long and shiny. He didn't know anyone looked like that—not anywhere!

Howie felt his heart beating against his shirt. Something else was happening, too, and he decided he'd better get out of the tent and back across the road. He looked over his shoulder to see if anyone was watching, but nobody was.

"Will the clown be scary, Mama?" Carolee wanted to know.

Howie's mother started to answer, but Papa grinned and squeezed her shoulder. "Honey, 'course he won't be scary. Clowns are supposed to be *funny*, now aren't they? Isn't that right, Ev?"

"Yes, of course they are. Papa's right, darling." She gave Carolee a quick smile, then turned her around again and ran the long brush through her hair.

"Ow!" Carolee pulled away. Her mother reached out and settled her back.

"You got to look nice, honey."

"Am I gonna *have* to go, Mama?"

"You might not, Carolee. We don't *know* that at all. They don't choose everyone. Just some."

"If I go, will you and Papa come see me?"

"Carolee..." Her mother's lips pressed together in a narrow white line. Howie saw her eyes begin to glisten and his stomach knotted up inside.

"Carolee," she said gently, "no one even *knows* if you're goin' *any*where. Now do they?" She forced a little laugh. "Just hush up and let me do your hair, hon."

"Will Howie go with me?" Carolee let out a deep sigh. "I never get to go *any*where without Howie. I'm closer to thirteen than I am twelve and that's old enough to do stuff by yourself. Mayellen got to go into Callister with the Martins and they aren't even *kin*!"

"Be still, Carolee."

"But Mama..."

Howie saw something move in his father's face. Papa's big frame seemed to get suddenly smaller and, in a minute, he turned and tramped quickly out of the tent. Howie watched, curiously, and started to follow. His mother caught his eye and she shook her head ever so slightly. Howie sat down and busied himself with his studies, though he couldn't keep his mind on any of the words.

THE CLOWN *was* funny.

He came hobbling drunkenly into the big tent, taking quick little steps, arms tight against his sides. Then, suddenly, he tripped over his feet and went sprawling. All the children laughed and most of the grownups.

Parents stood in a big circle, their children cross-legged before them. They'd already heard the speech from the chubby little government man out of Jefferson. He was clearly a man who'd never done anything but town work and they'd all heard the speech before. It was the same every year. How all the parents should be proud to have such fine children—he was certain there wasn't a better looking group of youngsters anywhere. That was no surprise, he said, because there wasn't a heartier looking bunch of men—or prettier women—anywhere in the country.

He told them again what they all knew: That children chosen to go to Silver Island were the luckiest children in the world and that their parents should be more than proud. Silver Island was the beginning of a new America and someday the whole country would be just like that. Because that's what Silver Island was for—to provide citizens to *make* that new America, to give them advantages they couldn't hope to get anywhere else.

It was, he realized, always sad to see a child leave home. He explained, however, that children chosen here and all over the country wouldn't really be gone at all. They'd be the representatives of their parents in a new world of tomorrow. It was a shame that the whole country—children and grownups alike—couldn't enjoy all the advantages of Silver Island right now. But the government believed it had the duty and obligation to do what it could—if not for the many, then for the few. And before long, those few would swell to many again.

He told a little about how we'd been a long time paying for the sins of generations past, who'd near sent the world up in flames. That it was a long road back and we were getting there. He reminded them that there were a lot of countries that were worse off than we were—or weren't even around anymore, for that matter.

There was more. And finally he stopped and the clown in the baggy patchwork suit and lopsided hat came stumbling into the tent. One of the troopers brought out his fiddle so the clown could dance and soon he was twirling about the circle smiling and making faces.

There were children of all sizes in the tent, but each was between nine and fifteen—the limits for being eligible to go to Silver Island. It was the first year Howie hadn't had to sit in the circle and he had mixed feelings about that. It gave him a sense of pride to stand with the grownups. On the other hand, he'd never have a chance, now, to see what Silver Island was like. He thought of the warm sun, the blue water, and the girl on the beach with next to nothing on. There were probably a lot of girls around just as pretty—

though he hadn't seen any. And they sure weren't dressed like that....

The fiddler played, the clown danced about and laughed, and the grownups and children alike followed him with their eyes. Sometimes he'd pause for a moment before one child or another, then he'd waddle off somewhere else.

The fiddler began to play faster and faster, stomping his foot on the hard ground. The clown whirled and leaped about like he'd never stop. You could see the sweat roll off his painted face in different colors. His hat flew off his head and his big mouth opened to gulp air. Finally, he gave an extra high leap, rolled himself in a tight little ball, and flipped over neatly in midair. When his feet hit the ground, a handful of long, silver ribbons was clutched in his hand.

There were a few gasps from the crowd, for they knew what was coming now. Howie saw his mother's hand squeeze Papa's arm until there was nothing but white in her fingers.

The fiddler began a slower, prettier tune. The clown pranced daintily about the circle again, stopping first before one child, and then another. And each time he stopped, he pinned one of the long silver ribbons to the child he'd chosen. He danced until all the ribbons were gone, threw a big kiss to children and grownups alike, and bowed his way out of the tent.

Out of some forty children present, eighteen had been chosen. More than any from Corners in a single year, someone said. Carolee was the fourth child to be picked.

7

Spring came early, after a winter that was more like a cold, bleak autumn than anything else. An old hand who worked for Howie's father said Nature had a way of evening things out and was kind of making up for the bitter season of the year before, which was like two or three winters all bunched together.

For Howie, it meant you had to get outdoors and work when you ordinarily wouldn't. Clear days when there was only a little snow in the air were extra blessings as far as Papa was concerned—days when you could get a head start on spring.

In a way, Howie didn't mind. The things that used to be fun in winter didn't matter now. All his life, cold weather had meant extra good smells in the kitchen, hot fruit pies on special days—and at night, huddling about the big fireplace while the chill wind howled outside. There'd be cider, then, spiced with herbs, and the whole family laughing and telling stories about one thing or another.

Only it wasn't the same anymore. Since Carolee had been Chosen, the laughter had gone out of his mother. Her eyes didn't smile—they seemed to be looking at something far away; and the special things she used to do weren't so important.

Howie missed Carolee, too. She didn't seem so much like a wart, now, and he mostly remembered good things. He thought about her often, having fun on Silver Island, and wondered if she knew the girl who had lain on the beach near naked. Probably she did. There were a lot of people there, but you'd get around to meeting everyone after a while.

The girl had been on his mind a lot since he'd seen her picture at Corners. At night, with the silence outside, he saw her just as she'd been, only she didn't have anything at all on now. Sometimes he imagined touching her all over, and rubbing up against her—doing things that made him sweat and kick the covers aside, even with the chill outside. Then he'd have to stop the pain that filled his loins, though he didn't like to do that often. Stock did it all the time, he knew—bucks and mares alike—but people weren't supposed to. It didn't much matter what animals did; they didn't have a lot in their heads to begin with. But it wasn't supposed to be good for people.

It was funny, he thought. How you saw things different. He could look at the girl on the beach and think about pulling off the little bit of clothes she had and doing all kinds of things to her. Once, though, it occurred to him that Carolee probably went swimming at that very same place, now. Was *she* wearing clothes like that? The idea horrified him. He wondered if the girl on the beach had a brother. Maybe *he'd* look at Carolee the same way. Would that be wrong, if he did? Did that make him, Howie, wrong? It was enough to make a person's head ache—figuring out what was good and what wasn't.

WITH THE EARLY THAW, news of the war came sooner than most people had expected. The mild winter had been good and bad for both sides, they said. It had let the army move against the rebels sooner, but it had also given Lathan a chance to broaden his holdings over good ground, since the earth wasn't churned to mud this spring like it usually was. There was one thing certain, people said, there'd been plenty of chances for fighting and there were a lot of dead and wounded in both armies.

One day a traveler from Bluevale stopped for supper and told Papa there was trouble in town with the army, and likely to be more. After the terrible battles out west, many troopers had been sent back to rest up and lick their wounds.

"They're hungry and most of 'em hurt," the man said. "They got no will to fight Lathan anymore, but there's plenty of mean in them still."

And mean, he told them, meant brawling and burning, and a rape or two thrown in. It wasn't so bad in the countryside, yet—but it would be, soon as the towns got too tough on the troopers.

There was other news, too, that set Papa's jaw and turned his face beet red.

"A War Tax, or that's what they're callin' it," he grumbled. "You're old enough to know what's happening in the country and take some note of it," he told Howie.

The traveler had gone his way and Papa sat with his big fists in his chin before the fire. There was still a chill in the air and wood coals glowed on the hearth.

"Thing is," Papa explained, "it's not what you call something that makes it what it is. You can pin a name on a nettle and call it a daisy, but that don't make it one. An' you can call this tax business what you like—it's the government getting too big for its britches is what it is."

He told Howie that the troopers were going to have to have more food to keep fighting Lathan through spring, because the rebels had stripped the land out west and left nothing but stubble on the ground.

"And we *have* to give it to 'em?" Howie wanted to know.

"Appears that way for now."

"Is it a lot? A lot of food?" Howie had visions of soldiers carrying off everything on the farm, leaving them with nothing at all to eat.

"It's enough," Papa muttered. "*E*nough. And do we have to?" He scratched his beard and looked at Howie. "That's a yes and a no, boy, is what it is. Something that ain't been clear settled. Might be the government'll find they bit off more'n they can swallow 'fore it's over."

"What do you mean, Papa?"

"Just that anybody with good sense knows it's got to stop sometime!" His fist hit the table so hard Howie jumped. "It ain't *just* the war. It's other things, too. Things that give a few folks too much say in other people's business!''

Howie didn't understand a lot about the government, or what it did. He knew there were people like the man who came every year at Choosing and talked about America. That was government and so was the army fighting Lathan. And there were real important people, like the president, who told everyone what to do. But all that was pretty far away. It didn't have much to do with planting crops and tending stock. You couldn't think a lot about things you couldn't see—there were too many real things closer by. Only he guessed the government was going to be close enough to think about, now.

At the end of February the troopers started making their rounds of the farms and ranches in the county, and Howie recalled what Papa had said. It was true enough—a lot of people were thinking the government *had* bitten off more than it could swallow. They worked hard for what they got and didn't take kindly to giving any part of it away for something like a War Tax.

At the Jeffers farm there was a fight between one of Lang Jeffers' boys and a couple of troopers. One soldier got cut up pretty bad and they tried to take the boy in for trial. They didn't get far with that—Lang made it clear the soldiers would have to take him and his other five sons too if they figured on taking one and he didn't think that would be too easy to do. The soldiers were smart enough to see they could easily start their own war right there. They took what Jeffers would give them for the War Tax and went on their way.

There were similar incidents at other ranches. Word got around about what had happened at the Jeffers place and no one was too happy about it. The troopers soon realized they'd made a big mistake backing down once. They were being run off farms now before they got started. And no one was sending anything to the war they didn't want to.

The officer in charge of the troopers was sent back to town and another took his place. The same night that happened Howie and Papa stood out on the porch and watched a red glow light the southern horizon.

"Jess Clayton's place," Papa said soberly. "Can't be anywhere else."

He didn't say anything more, but he stood and watched the fire a long time, and after Howie went to bed he heard Papa and his mother talking. Around midnight, Papa took off walking toward the Claytons.

It was late morning before he came back, and sometime after that before he got around to telling what had happened. Jess Clayton's house and barn were gone. Burned to the ground. Nearly everything he had had been taken off—food and stock alike. Enough to make up for what Clayton's neighbors had held back, it was said. And if any others cared to argue about the War Tax—why, they'd get the same. The country had to come first, now. There was no time for greed and personal wants with good men starving and dying in the west, while farmers stayed snug and happy back here.

That was what the new officer had told Jess Clayton's wife and his boys, Papa said. And he'd told them all this while he made them stand and watch Clayton being hung from a big oak right on his own front yard, where he could see his home being put to the torch. Next to that, the worst thing was that the man who'd done all this was Colonel Jacob himself—who'd grown up right on the land with Jess Clayton and Papa and most of the others.

Papa told that part last. He hadn't wanted Howie's mother to know at all, but it wasn't something you could keep to yourself, he told her, not with the whole county likely to explode over what had happened.

He told it all quietly, without raising his voice or letting his face change at all. And Howie's mother just listened, the dark hair partly hiding her eyes, the small white hands folded tightly in her lap.

And to Howie, that was the worst part of all—to see them both knowing what the other was thinking and not wanting to let anything show. He'd learned that people did that when they had something on their minds so strong they couldn't bring it out in words, or even let it show through their eyes.

If his mother had cried and Papa had pounded something with his fist, it wouldn't have been nearly as bad. As it was, Howie went to bed scared for the first time he could remember.

8

He came up from the field by the woods to the back of the house. The last of the mares Papa needed were hobbled between him and old Jaro and causing no trouble for a change. It was a lot easier to bring stock up near the house than it was to drive them back down. They were curious about people and the things they did, and when their attention was on something they forgot about causing mischief.

"You'd think December was here 'stead of near April," grumbled Jaro. He pulled his jacket about spare shoulders and cast a despairing look at the sky.

"Yeah," Howie agreed, "you would." It was true enough; spring had gone back into hiding for the moment. Gray clouds hugged the ground, dragging a light, chilling rain behind them. Just wet and cold enough to bring a fine ache to your bones before you knew it.

Howie left Jaro to pen the stock and walked to the barn for feed. At least, he decided, the weather fit the day. A lazy morning with the sun bringing green out of the earth wouldn't have seemed right—not with all the somber faces around.

Jess Clayton's hanging had started it all. Papa held a meeting, and a dozen or so ranchers walked in at night to be there. Howie was allowed to sit in, though none of the other men brought their sons, figuring too many people tromping about, even after dark, might get the soldiers to thinking.

"It was a damn fool thing to do," Papa told Howie's mother later.

"Now, I don't see that it was, Milo," she said gently. "Men need to get together when there's trouble."

"Men need to *do* something when there's trouble," Papa grumbled. His eyes turned sullen. "You know what the meeting come to, Ev? Truly? It showed us all together what we were too ashamed to admit to ourselves. That there's nothing *can* be done. That we can talk all we like about what *ought* to be—it ends up we can't do anything at all 'cept what we're told to do."

Papa brought his lips together and looked down at his hands. "'Less we want to get burned out and maybe hung in our own front yards. I'll tell you, Ev, it don't make a man feel too tall...."

They'd meet the War Tax, everyone decided, and not give the soldiers cause for trouble. But that wouldn't be the end of it. They might not be able to undo what had happened at Jess Clayton's—not now, anyway. But there'd be a time. The government had gone too far, and there'd be a reckoning, for sure. Just what that would be, and when, nobody said. But it raised the spirit of the meeting some, and no one went home feeling like they'd been whipped and drug across the ground.

At first, Papa had Howie and the hands gather War Tax goods in the big barn near the house—but it wasn't long before he stormed out dark as thunder telling everyone to get that stuff *out* of his good dry barn—that Jacob and his soldiers could just as well do their stealing off the ground. *He* didn't intend to take care of what wasn't his anymore.

So they hauled the sacks of grain and corn and potatoes, and the bags of stock feed and other items called for, and stacked everything in the open, past the big stand of oaks, fifty yards from the house. The fourteen mares and ten young bucks were kept hobbled in the stock pit near the barn and would be staked out with the rest of the goods when the time came.

Howie knew the moving had made his father feel better. Like he was doing something, anyway—giving in, but letting the soldiers know he didn't want to. It was the only time he ever heard Papa get truly angry at his mother. She remarked that it might not be a good idea leaving everything out in the weather—that they could be asking for trouble they didn't need.

"Damn, Ev!" he exploded, his face turning crimson, "what's a man supposed to do—lie down and let 'em stomp you, then turn over so's they can get the other side? Hell, woman . . ." His hands trembled into big fists. "What you want me to *do!*"

Howie's mother turned ash-white, and her eyes filled with sudden tears. Papa went to her and folded her in his arms, burying her face in his shoulder. Howie left the house quickly and didn't listen anymore, but he knew she cried a long time after that.

"WHEN YOU FIGURE they'll come, Papa?"

Howie stood with his father on the porch and followed his gaze to the dark horizon. There was no sunset—the clouds just darkened to match the night and set a chill in the air.

"I figure tomorrow, maybe," said Papa.

"And Colonel Jacob? He'll be with the soldiers?"

"Stands that he will, son."

Howie thought about that. All he could remember about soldiers were the ones he'd seen in the parade at Bluevale. They seemed like good, proud men; no one you'd figure on burning barns and hanging people. Maybe they were different soldiers—or maybe it was like the stranger who'd come by said; the war and being hungry did things to people, and they weren't the same anymore.

"It'll be over," Papa broke into his thoughts, resting his hand on Howie's shoulder. "It'll be over tomorrow likely, and we can get back to running a ranch like we're supposed to." He laughed in his throat and turned Howie's chin where he could see him. "You figure it's time we took us a day, boy—say, the first good warm morning that comes—and see what's bitin' down to the pool? Would you like that? Just you and me kind of sneaking off for a time?"

"Yes, sir," Howie told him, "I'd like that a lot."

Only, for the first time he could remember, it was hard to get his mind on fishing. His thoughts kept following his father's eyes out past the dark stand of trees, where the soldiers would appear in the morning.

The soldiers didn't come the next day. Or the one after that. Papa's mood grew darker and Howie could hear his big steps moving restlessly about in the room below, long after everyone else had gone to bed.

WHEN THEY DID COME, Howie was looking right at them.

They came silently over the far swell of the land, moving down the furrowed hill against a grey smudge of dawn. He counted twelve mounted troopers in a loose column. A wagon trailed behind, pulled by two more horses—one trooper drove, while another three dangled their legs off the back of the bed. As he watched, Howie saw a man stretch his arms and yawn.

Closer, you could tell these men were nothing like the parade soldiers in Bluevale. They were gaunt, shadow men— hollow faces under grizzled beards. There was no fat about them, only hard planes pushing flesh at awkward angles. Their clothes seemed all alike and no color at all. They rode easy on their horses; it struck Howie they might not even know the mounts were there. If he'd heard that men and horses were all one creature grown together, he'd have taken it for fact.

Howie was aware of Papa standing close behind him, but neither spoke to the other. They watched the men move around under the trees, going about their tasks without talking. The low clouds pressed in upon the earth and swallowed up sound. The day seemed to stop altogether, like the land was caught half between night and morning.

"We got things to do inside," Papa said finally. "Ain't nothing more to see out here."

Neither, though, did more than putter about at things that didn't need doing. And Papa's eyes never moved far from the soldiers under the trees. Howie's mother didn't come down to make breakfast. She was so quiet upstairs it was hard to tell she was there.

IT WAS NEARLY NOON, but for Howie the day seemed no further along. The hours stretched wearily by and even Papa stopped pretending there were things to do. He sat at the big table with his hands in his lap and looked at nothing at all.

When the sun was just overhead, though, he did a peculiar thing—something Howie would never forget. Without a word, he got up and walked out the front door and off the porch and into the yard. Howie followed. At the same time, he saw a single rider move out of the grove and start for the house—as if they both knew the other would be right where they were.

The rider was a copy of the others, but somehow not the same. And no one had to tell Howie it was Colonel Jacob. He rode straight and silent, without looking to either side, letting the horse make its own way. It seemed forever before he touched his reins and stopped just before the spot where Papa stood.

"Milo," he said, "it's been a long while."

"It has," said Howie's father.

There was something in Papa's voice Howie hadn't heard before. Whatever it was, the Colonel heard it, too, and looked at Papa a long moment without moving his eyes. He was an older, thinner man than Howie remembered. A face gone to leather, and a body tight and hard as stone. The eyes, though, were the same—and he remembered how they'd looked at him, and at his mother, and what he'd seen there, even being twelve and not knowing much at all. And when Jacob's glance touched him again, he stared straight back and didn't turn away.

"The boy's grown some," said Jacob.

"He has."

"Looks a little like you in the face. Got Ev's color, though."

Papa didn't answer; Jacob shifted in his saddle and looked up at the low clouds. "The little girl. She coming all right?"

"Carolee went from us," said Papa. "At the Choosing."

"Well, now. That's fine, Milo."

"I guess it is."

Jacob nodded and shifted his gaze to Howie. "You sure have sprung up, boy."

"Yes, sir," said Howie.

"Be big enough to serve, soon. You know that?"

Papa looked up sharply. "If he chooses, Jacob. Don't know as he's given any thought to soldiering."

Jacob shrugged. "Maybe. Might come to something else though, Milo. It's a terrible war out there. Men dying in frightenin' ways. Or gettin' sick and wishing they had a clean bullet in their bellies 'stead of filth and pollution." He shook his head. "You got to see it to know what I'm saying. See it, and wash your hands in a man's blood, and smell his corruption."

Papa stood tall and still, his gaze staying right on the Colonel. To Howie, it seemed as if Jacob's eyes had gone different while he talked—like he'd been somewhere a long way off a minute, and just come back.

"The war," said Papa. "You said somethin' about the war. How it might come to—somethin' different. I don't reckon I understand that, Jacob."

Jacob gave him a weary smile. "Simple as rain, Milo. Soldiers are dying out west faster than boys are joining up. War's got a awful appetite, I'll tell you. Eats up armies like corn in a field."

"Then you might better stop your war, I'm thinking."

"Can't do that. Not now."

"Can't. Or don't care to."

Jacob's smile faded. "You haven't fought," he said stiffly. "You're out of line, Milo, if you ain't been there."

"Maybe," said Papa. "And maybe folks that like fighting so much ought to do as they please. And leave those that don't to themselves."

Jacob stared at him and laughed out loud. "You haven't changed a damn bit, Milo! A simple man with simple answers."

"Suits me well enough," Papa said darkly.

"Suits you, is right. But not the world, not anymore. The world's changing—it's not a simple place anymore, Milo. It chews up simple men and spits 'em on the ground."

"Like Jess, you mean."

Jacob's face went hard and the two men just looked at each other, neither backing away. Howie figured he could measure the silence between them. Finally, Jacob sat back in his saddle and shook his head.

"Lordee," he said, letting out a long breath, "that was a bad thing, Milo. A real bad thing. It ain't easy to do what you have to do. Sometimes, though, a war jus—"

"*Have* to do!" Papa exploded. He stared up at Jacob and the cords of his neck went tight. "Damn, man, what's *happened* to you? You talk like you hung a stranger from that tree!"

"He was a stranger to me," said Jacob.

"He was a man you grew *up* with, Jacob. Jess and you and me and the rest. Right here. The same dirt, the same—"

"No. That's not so, Milo." He looked at Howie's father with no expression at all. "I was a boy here and that's true enough. I grew *up* out there. With men that ain't anything like you and Jess." He seemed to lose himself in thought a minute, then his eyes went tired again. "Hell, Milo. We go back a long way. You know that?"

"We do, Jacob."

"War's hard on a man. You got to understand that."

"I reckon that's so."

"A man don't figure on changing, but he does. It's not something you got much say in. You..." He looked at Howie, and ran a dry hand over his mouth. "You got some cool water in there, boy?"

Howie looked at his father.

"Get him some water, Howie."

"No, no." Jacob held up a hand and raised himself in the saddle. "Reckon I'll walk in with you. Give me a chance to iron out the wrinkles. Ev inside?"

"She's inside," Papa said evenly.

"Well, then..."

"She's feeling poorly, Jacob."

The challenge in Papa's voice was clear enough. Jacob gave him a curious look, then eased back in his saddle.

"You'll tell her I asked, Milo."

"I'll do that."

"Well..." Jacob looked up at the house, then back again. "A lot of years've gone by, ain't they?"

"They have, for certain."

"Things change..."

"I guess they always will, Jacob."

Jacob touched his reins lightly and the mount skittered to one side. "This business, Milo..." He gestured over his shoulder toward the grove. "It's something that's got to be done."

Papa didn't answer. Jacob studied him a moment, then turned his horse smartly, kicking up dust, and galloped back to the grove.

Papa watched him go. He stood where he was until the wagon was loaded, the stock gathered, and the long column of soldiers had followed Jacob back over the hill the way they'd come.

In the afternoon Howie's mother came downstairs and sat at the big oak table. Papa tried to get her to eat some hot bread or take a bowl of soup, but she said she wasn't hungry at all and would just as soon have a little honeywater to sip on. Howie wanted to cry looking at her. She seemed so frail and tired, like all the life had gone out of her. In a little while she asked Papa if he'd mind seeing to supper, something Howie couldn't remember her ever doing before.

"Papa," he asked later, when she'd gone back upstairs, "she's going to be all right, ain't she?"

"Sure she is, Howie." His father forced a smile. "The day's been hard on her, is all. It's over and done with now, and there's nothing more to worry about. She'll see that in the morning."

"For certain, Papa?"

"For certain, Howie."

Howie had a lot more questions about the day, but he could see Papa didn't want to do much talking. He went about his chores, wisely leaving his father to himself and his thoughts.

Everything might be over and done like Papa said, but you couldn't tell by the way he acted. His mind was still out in the high grove of trees and over the dark horizon. Through the long afternoon, he left Howie more than once to stalk about outside. Just standing, out on the porch or in the yard, his face matching the brooding sky.

Late in the evening, after they'd shared a cold supper, Howie went to bed by himself, leaving his father alone. And when he woke deep in the night, he went to the window and found Papa outside, a dark figure listening to the silence.

"HOWIE . . ."

He woke smelling first dawn, heavy with sleep then suddenly awake, seeing his father there and feeling the strong hands on him.

"Howie. Don't talk, boy, just listen."

A cold chill gripped him. There was something awful in Papa's eyes and he didn't want to see it.

"Howie. I want you to get up now and go in real quiet and get your mother. Get her downstairs and out the back. Over the field, Howie, and you can't make no noise at all. You see that? Not any."

"Papa . . ."

"Listen, boy. Take that little gully as far as you can, where you can kinda stoop over good 'till you get near enough to the woods. After that . . ."

"Papa. I can't!"

"Howie . . ." Pap's voice broke. "You *got* to!"

He felt the tears well up and Papa gripped him hard.

"I ain't got time to explain, boy. I just *know.* He let it show right there in his eyes, and I *know,* Howie. I felt it then, an' . . . son, for God's sake!"

Howie moved without thinking. For a moment, his father was behind him, then he was gone. When his mother saw him and what he meant to do, her eyes went wide and

full of fear and he knew she was going to cry out and he'd
have to stop her.

She flailed against him; he pulled her along, hurting her,
and not thinking about that, either. When they were halfway
to the woods through the shallow ravine, he became suddenly aware of where he was and what he was doing. He
didn't dare look at her, then. If he had, he couldn't have
gone on doing what he had to do.

He heard the sound behind him and turned and saw them.
Two men on horses coming fast, gray against the first raw
touch of dawn. He knew there was nothing he could do because they were cutting the angle between the gully and the
woods. He had a quick second to hear the hooves drum over
the soft ground and see the bright flash of fire at the man's
shoulder. He thought his mother ought to be there somewhere but he couldn't be sure....

9

A long time later he'd go through it again and feel it just like it had happened and know that was the time he'd passed being a boy.

But this wasn't the time. There was no feeling or understanding now. It was as if he stood just outside himself and watched another Howie go about his business and do the things that had to be done. Like a little piece of time had been neatly lifted out of the day and set aside on a shelf somewhere. All the minutes and seconds and hours staying just as they were until he was ready for them, the way tiny bits of seed and stone got caught in pond ice, and slept there until the Spring let them go.

THE CLOUDS were breaking up and moving away to the east when he opened his eyes. From the light he could tell it was nearly noon and that meant he'd been out at least four or five hours, maybe more.

When he sat up he felt the pain, sharp and clean like a hot knife. He touched his head gingerly where the rider's bullet had creased a neat furrow across the side of his skull, taking away flesh nearly to the bone. His hair was crusted with blood. There was blood on his face and down his chest but it was all dried and the bleeding had stopped some time ago. He decided he must look pretty awful. Which was probably why they'd left him there and hadn't bothered to make sure he was dead.

He pulled himself to his feet and stood in the ravine, holding to an old root until the nausea went away. He was tired and stiff all over. He stood there a long time just looking anywhere but toward the house. That was when something else took over in his head and, for a while, put everything behind him.

They'd gone quickly through the kitchen, mostly just breaking things and tearing up whatever they could find. There was flour everywhere and sugar grated under his feet. Pots were shattered and the pieces ground into the floor until you couldn't tell what they might have been. He reached down and picked up something white and shiny. It was part of a cup, the one with the flowers painted on it that had been his mother's favorite. He looked at it a minute, then laid it carefully on the table.

In the room upstairs where Papa and his mother slept he found her. Her clothes had been stripped away and her wrists and ankles were tied to the head and foot of the bed with coarse wire. The wire was buried in flesh and he couldn't see it except where it wound around the posts. She had fought a lot, for a while, anyway. The blood made red bracelets around her wrists and ankles and the skin was torn and swollen there. There was blood in a lot of other places, too, where they'd done things to her. He couldn't see all of her face because the long black hair was tangled about her features, but he could see the small dark hole in her forehead, ringed with a faint aura of blue.

He thought about cutting the wires loose and finding one of the sheets or blankets that hadn't been torn too bad and covering her with that. Instead, he turned away and closed the door and went downstairs again.

Papa was halfway up the front steps. He still had on the heavy checkered shirt but his trousers were gone, and Howie saw them bundled up in the yard. He had crawled about ten yards over the hard ground and Howie could look behind him and see the trail he'd made trying to get to the house. He hadn't used his arms, because his hands were pressed tight against his belly where he'd tried to hold everything in long enough to get there. They'd cut him badly. One raw slice across the bowels, deep, from hipbone to hipbone. There were other cuts on his thighs and between his legs where they'd taken everything away.

Howie looked at him, studying the expression on his face for a long moment.

In his own room, he reached up between the eaves and found his bow and quiver of arrows still there. He rolled up his extra work pants and another shirt and his jacket. Downstairs, he picked through the wreckage in the kitchen and added half a loaf of bread and some dried meat to the bundle. Outside he filled a clay jar with water and stoppered it with a dry plug. Then he walked to the grove of oaks where the War Tax goods had been stacked, squatted down, and studied the tracks of men and horses and wagons. He followed the wheel ruts and the hoof prints with his eye and saw they'd gone west, across his father's land, toward the river road. That meant they probably didn't mean to pick up any more goods just now, but were headed for Cotter, which was just outside Bluevale and used a lot by the army.

He looked back once at the house and the barn, then past them to the fields and the stock pits and the green shadow of the woods. There was no sign of old Jaro or any of the other hands. The stock pits were empty. They'd taken everything, as he'd figured. He guessed there were still goods in the barn—there was more there than you could carry away.

He turned and searched the horizon west. On horse a man could go faster, but they had the wagon, which was slow, and the stock to drive along. They'd just make the river, then. They'd have to stop there and rest the stock for the night, even if they felt like pushing on in the dark. He figured he could make it by maybe two or three in the morning. And that would be a good time to get there.

HOWIE KNEW he would have to take care and go slowly. They were soldiers and knew their business; you didn't just sneak up on men like that and figure they'd hold still and line up nice and easy like meat. They'd be fast and alert, and more dangerous asleep than most men full awake.

There were the guns to reckon with, too. A man with a gun had it all over a man with lesser weapons. At least, in a lot of ways he did.

There was a quarter-moon with enough light to see how the low Spring grasses had been flattened where they'd left the prairieland and angled off down the hill to the river. The hollow there was thick with big oaks and cottonwoods. He spotted the red sparks of a dead fire just to the south, twenty yards or so from the river. They'd set up camp in the shadow of the trees, then. The stock would be further down, but well away from the trees so none of the herd could wander off. And since they were on the road, and weren't likely to build pens or dig pits, they'd do what you always did on a drive—keep watch around the meat in shifts.

Howie wasn't sure what you did with horses. But he was near certain you didn't have to watch them or anything. That meant—what? With a herd that size, three men, at least, to stand watch. And maybe two others for the camp itself, if they bothered. And he had an idea they were in the habit of that. Five, six men awake, then. The others asleep. He crawled down the side of the hill and moved quietly through the edge of the forest.

It took a good hour to circle the camp. There were three guards instead of two. Three others watched the herd. Six slept. Colonel Jacob was on the far edge of the camp, away from the fire, and close to the river. The other troopers were dark lumps scattered about him.

Howie stayed just on the skirt of the camp a long quarter hour. Belly flat against damp forest floor, hardly daring to breathe, his eyes taking in every trifle—how the grass bent, and where the dim moonlight touched the ground.

There was a guard between him and the Colonel. He stood just outside the small clearing, quiet and almost invisible against a broad oak. There was a little cover noise from the river, but not enough. He'd never get past the man without being heard. He inched back down the bank, passing the guard and coming up again higher, behind a thick bed of fern.

He lay still on his back a long moment, fitting the arrow quietly to his bow, acutely aware of the man only yards away, and knowing what the slightest sound would do. Coming up slowly, he brought his eyes just over the foliage. For a moment, his heart stopped, thinking the man was gone. Then the body took shape again; he let out a long breath.

Howie knew he had to go for the head or no place at all. Anything less than that and the man could cry out. He didn't let himself think about missing. The bowstring sang and a shadow dropped quietly to the base of the tree. When he crawled forward his hand touched the rifle and a broad cartridge belt the guard had left at his feet. There was a pistol in his belt and he took that and the other things and laid them where he could find them again at the base of the bank. Then he turned back to the clearing and went in for Jacob.

He'd thought about how to do it. He knew even a grown man used to moving fast couldn't stop a quick knife across his throat. Only that wasn't the way it was supposed to be. He knew that, too. It had to be the other way or it wouldn't be right.

A few feet from Jacob a man turned over and groaned in his sleep. Howie froze where he was, part of the earth and shadow, then inched forward until he could touch the Colonel. He slept with his mouth open, one hand across his chest. Howie slipped the bone knife from his belt. He'd already wrapped the butt with thick layers of cloth from his extra shirt. Grasping Jacob's hair with one hand, he brought the padded hilt down solidly, just above the ear. Jacob stiffened slightly, but made no sound at all.

It took nearly an hour to make the thirty yards to the river. When his feet touched wetness behind him he wanted to drop his burden right there and let the feeling come back to his arms and legs. Instead, he pulled Jacob into the water and across to the other side. Then laid him behind high weeds while he went back for the weapons.

There was a clump of scrub oak masking the shore and a sand wash behind that. He stripped Jacob, leaned him against a tree, and wired him securely to the trunk, pulling his feet straight before him and wiring them as well. Then he stuffed the man's socks in his mouth and used his shirt to make a tight gag knotted behind his neck.

He worried about the time. It was a lot lighter now than it ought to be. And soldiers got up early—near as early as ranchers, he figured. He glanced impatiently at Jacob and moved his face up close to the man's nose. He was breathing, all right, but he didn't show any signs of waking. Suppose he *didn't* come to for hours? Then what? Howie shook the thought aside. That wouldn't do at all. That wasn't the way it was supposed to be.

He searched through his bundle, found the clay jug, and emptied it over Jacob. He crawled down to the river and filled the jug again. The water was colder. This time Jacob's mouth twitched irritably and his eyes opened to tiny slits. They looked steadily at Howie, then went wide with understanding. He jerked frantically against his bonds, moaning behind his gag.

Howie ignored him. He straddled Jacob's legs, drew the bone knife from his belt, and started working on the Colonel's bare chest. He went slowly and carefully, making the letters neat like his mother had taught him. It was hard to see in the dim light and he had to keep wiping the blood away to tell what he was doing. Jacob's eyes bulged and sweat beaded his face and Howie could hear the noises he was making but nothing much came through the gag.

When he was through he went to work on the eyes, being careful to do just what needed to be done. He didn't want Jacob to pass out and miss anything, or lose more blood than he had to. He was still conscious, Howie knew, but near out of his head and that was okay. That was the way it was supposed to be.

When he was finished he looked at Jacob and touched the blade lightly against the man's thighs. Jacob jerked uncontrollably, nearly pulling his arms out of the sockets. He knew pretty well what was coming. Howie did the best he could, but the fear and the pain were more than Jacob could handle. He quickly dropped into unconsciousness. That was all right too, Howie decided. He'd wake up and have plenty of time to think about what had happened to him.

ACROSS THE RIVER and below the camp he found where they'd left the horses. There was no guard; he guessed that was part of what the man he'd killed was supposed to do.

He'd thought about the horses. He no longer feared them much, but he wasn't sure he'd be able to handle one right. Maybe horses knew whether you could ride or not. Maybe they wouldn't do anything unless you did what you were supposed to. Anyway, it didn't make much difference now. He had to try. They'd come after him for certain and he wouldn't have a chance on foot. He'd either make it on a horse or not at all. There wasn't time to think about learning how to ride with the sky getting light enough to read by.

The horses were tied to a long rope stretched between two trees. Howie loosened one of the shorter ropes that went over the creature's head and led it away from the others. The horse skittered about nervously and the others answered. Howie knew he had minutes. He strapped his bundle to his shoulders and threw himself over the broad back and hung on. He hadn't even considered trying to use one of the saddles he knew horses wore. There wasn't time and he wouldn't have known what to do with one anyway.

He held on, urging the mount toward the river. When he was across he let the animal do what it wanted to do, which was trot through the trees at a bone-jarring pace until it reached the broad meadow beyond. There it stopped and, to Howie's horror, began methodically chewing grass. He beat at the animal frantically, kicking his legs against its broad sides. He remembered the reins, then, and how he'd seen the soldiers use them to pull and jerk the mounts one way or the other. The reins and the kicking—used together—seemed to work. And when he could see open ground again he closed his eyes and pushed the animal until he could hear wind whistling by over the low, green hills.

BY MID-AFTERNOON he was far to the north, in the midst of deep woods ringed by high, rugged cliffs. He had no idea where he might be, only that he was far from the camp by the river. If the soldiers were after him he didn't know it and, at the moment, didn't much care.

He tied the horse to a tree and stumbled through low brush until his legs gave way and he went shakily to his knees. There was nothing in his stomach, but he vomited bile until his belly felt full of glass.

The tears came, then. And he remembered Papa and his mother and what they'd looked like at the house. He remembered killing the soldier. He tried to throw up again, but there was nothing there. He wished he could crawl away from his own smell only his body wasn't working right.

Howie closed his eyes hard, trying to think of nothing. But his mother was still there. And Papa. Looking surprised at dying. He saw Colonel Jacob and what he'd done to him on the river bank. The hollow eyes and the terrible empty place between his legs. And the bone-deep letters on his chest that would last as long as Jacob and wouldn't ever go away:

HOWIE SON
OF EV AND
MILO RYDER

He knew he couldn't stay there; he had to get back on the horse. And he remembered a whole day had gone by and it was April, now, and tomorrow he'd be sixteen.

10

He halted the mount in a stand of cedars and climbed the few yards to the top of the ridge. He'd been in shadow most of the morning, so he waited to let his eyes get used to brightness and far places.

A raw wind cut steadily across the high crest, the chill going straight to the bone. For a long time, he huddled in the lee of the big stone that capped the far edge of the rim. The thin jacket was nearly useless, but he pulled it tight around him.

It was a good spot, he figured, if you didn't freeze to death. From here you could see nearly every approach to the ridge and all the valley beyond for several miles. If the soldiers were still following, they were being mighty slow about it, or flat out cagey. He hoped to God it was the first. You didn't have to know much about horses to see the animal down below was near done in.

He knew better, of course. Jacob's men hadn't lost him. They were back there somewhere. Likely not too far down the ridge. You could hope all you wanted and wish something different, but that wouldn't change much.

What that was was *child*-thinking, Howie reminded himself. All right for games and daydreaming if you were a kid and could go home for a hot supper when you got tired of playing. Only he wasn't a kid anymore and the soldiers back there didn't have much playin' in mind.

The thought had come to him more than once in the last few days. It was a peculiar kind of feeling. He wasn't real sure what he was anymore. He'd been ripped out of one life—picked up, shaken hard, and tossed down somewhere else. He wasn't a grownup, but he sure wasn't a kid, either. It was something uncomfortably in-between, right where you couldn't do either one real well.

With cold hands, he felt around inside his bundle, grubbed out the last chunk of dry meat, and washed it down with water. The cramping started near as soon as he swallowed. That was happening a lot, now. Eating next to nothing just aggravated his belly, reminding it of what ought to be coming down and wasn't. He had to eat, though. He knew that. Whatever he could scratch up would go down his gullet and his stomach would just have to make do with what it got.

It was different with the soldiers, he figured. They'd been trained to pace their appetites on a hard trail, eating when they could, doing without when they had to. The more Howie rode, the hungrier he got!

There was another thing, too. He had to keep going, no matter what. But the soldiers could send a couple of men out looking for rations without slowing the chase. They'd been close enough at least once in the last six days for him to hear them doing just that.

Lordee—that had been *too* close! He'd been sure the horse would give him away then, but it hadn't. It was trained to travel in silence, a talent that had saved his skin more than once.

He ate what he could, then. Scrambling around at night for nuts left over from the fall before. Stopping on the trail for wild onions, or whatever else grew in his path. He lost near as much as he ate, but enough stayed down to keep him going.

THE SUN PASSED swiftly overhead and shadows crawled down the side of the ridge to fill the valley. Howie lay perfectly still, taking in every inch of the land below. His eyes marked a place where stone turned from one color to another; he could see where water lay under the earth by the way trees would swell up thick and heavy-green one place, and light somewhere else. He knew plants followed the patterns of water, and men did the same. It was the way life moved about. You just kind of naturally followed the way a stream flowed, or a river. He watched where the birds swung in easy arcs over the woods and where they darted and scattered, suddenly aware of something below. It might be nothing at all—but it could be a sign that men were about.

The soldiers were some better in the wilderness, and Howie knew it. But he was no stranger there, either. He was still alive, wasn't he? They hadn't gotten him yet, and that was something. And every day he stayed ahead of them was a day in which he gained trail sense to help him stay alive a little longer. He was learning he knew more than he'd figured. Papa had taught him things he was using without even thinking. That made him proud.

He spotted them late in the afternoon, the sun behind their ragged column, coming east instead of west. His heart sank a little. He'd moved fast that morning, leaving a clear trail that led down through the valley westward, and across onto hard rock again. They'd followed the false trail, but it hadn't fooled them much. They were doubling back now, just as he'd done earlier. Howie felt a sudden chill. They were more than a half a mile away still, but he was certain they could see him plain as day, perched up there on the ridge, squeezed under his flat slab of stone.

He pulled himself up tight in his hole, until cold rock was part of his hide. Squinting right into the sun, it was hard to make a good count—not that a count meant anything. They'd tried that once or twice, too. Let him think the whole bunch was in a column, but keeping a few stragglers behind, or maybe flankers out to the sides.

He was certain that's what they were up to now. Trail sense told him they were coming on too slow and easy—lined up straight and pretty for him to see. The others would be *back* of him, then. Over the ridge. Maybe waiting at the edge of the woods where he'd likely try to break away with the mount. That'd be the normal thing to do—run from the men coming straight on—right into the troopers waiting for him.

Howie gauged the sun again. It was nearly down—another four or five minutes. Once it dropped behind the low hills it'd get dark quick enough. And maybe he'd just give 'em what they wanted.

HE'D JUDGED the horse right enough. It was nearly gone—the ugly head slack against a tall pine, feet spread wide, sides heaving for air. He felt sorry for it. The beast had saved his life, and he'd fair run it to death. That was something that couldn't be helped, though, and there was nothing for it now. And he had one more favor to ask of it. A big one.

It was dark when he led the beast back down the slope. His skin crawled at the idea of getting caught on foot this close to where the pines stopped their march downhill and gave way to the clearing. If the soldiers were anywhere around, they'd be waiting close by. But he had to chance it. If the thing was going to work at all, the soldiers had to know about it. It wasn't any good unless there was somebody there to appreciate what he was doing.

He stood back and let the arrow go without much force behind it, placing it just behind the animal's rib cage. He figured it ought to cause plenty of pain there, without bringing the creature down too soon. The horse screamed and bolted—tearing brush aside and snapping low branches. Howie took off up the hill without looking back. Lordee, if they didn't hear that—!

And by the time they figured what had happened, that he wasn't on the horse, he'd have a fair start. They couldn't trail him until daylight and they'd have a fine time guessing which way he'd gone.

If it was just dark enough, he reminded himself. And if the troopers didn't look too close . . . .

HE WOKE STIFF and cold, hunger growing like something live inside him. For a quick minute he thought he'd died and gone wherever it was people went. The whole world below his branch was draped in a wet blanket of gray. Like the forest had grown a mile high in the night and poked its head right through the clouds.

He thought a while about what he ought to do. The fog would hide him while he climbed down from his perch. But if anyone was close enough to hear. . . .

He stayed where he was, holding himself patiently against the cold. Doing one thing wrong was one too many. It was something he had to keep remembering. Wait. Until everything felt right. Wait until the wind feels easy at first dawn. Until the birds settle at noon. And right now, wait until the fog burns away and there's a chance you'll see whoever's about, 'fore they see you first.

There was a stream in the draw below the trees. Young wild onions were plentiful and he ate as many as he could, knowing they'd tie his stomach in knots again. Further downstream he found button mushrooms—tiny bulbs pale as death clustered under heavy oaks. He didn't worry about whether they were mushrooms or something else. He was proud of himself for that. A town boy from Cotter or Bluevale might not know the difference, but he did. They tasted good and he picked as many as he could find, filling his stomach and his pockets at the same time.

It was a good place and he wanted to stay longer, but he knew better than that. Filling his clay jug with fresh water, he left the green shadows and climbed back up the rise. Where the trees began to thin, he came out suddenly into the full light of morning. And when he looked down through the last tails of fog burning away in the sun he could see the bone-white carcass of the city, stretching clear across the valley as far as the shining river.

11

Who could imagine such a sight? Why, you could've set a hundred Bluevales down there and lost 'em easy! He'd never seen anything like it before, but he knew right off what it was. A City was something you didn't *have* to more than hear about.

After a good half minute he realized he was standing big as you please in bright sunlight—an easy target for any fool who cared to look. Scolding himself soundly for such carelessness, he went to ground quickly.

It was an eerie thing, for certain. Enough to set a chill up the back of your neck. As far as the eye could see, ragged spires of gray stone dotted the dark woods. Like stacks of old bones, thought Howie. The wilderness had come back to claim the valley long ago, but you could still make out where streets had been and how it might have looked before.

A broad river snaked through the far side of the valley, brown and lazy. And that was right enough, he figured— Papa had talked about how towns needed rivers for trade, if they expected to grow and amount to anything. Old Cities were probably no different.

Howie didn't know much about Cities, or what they were supposed to look like. It wasn't something folks talked about. Mostly people just said they'd been bigger than anything ought to be. That there'd been plenty of open country to live in, but that everyone wanted to be close up together. It was a hard thing to understand. Bluevale and Cotter were fun to go to, but Howie couldn't imagine staying there, with that many people about. And those were just towns—not anything like what a City must have been.

Something bad had happened to Cities in the War. Something terrible. Only nobody could say just what. Even the Scriptures didn't go into much detail about that. God had found Men eating the flesh of unclean animals and He had washed the Earth of corruption. Only that didn't tell you a lot. Looking down on the ruins of the City you knew there was more than that. Not something you could see, exactly. More like what you could *feel*, inside.

By noon he was down the side of the mountain and near the edge of the City's beginnings. He hadn't thought much about *not* going, or what dangers he might find there. All the old stories about ghosts and devils and other awful things didn't seem too scary anymore. There couldn't be anything lurking in the City much worse than what was after him already. Still, he kept his mind on the trail ahead and didn't peer too close at the blunt knobs of dead stone all about him. And he was glad enough he hadn't come upon this place in the dark.

THE IDEA had started forming in his head while he was still on the mountain. And the longer he thought about it, the better he liked it. It was one of those ideas you knew was right from the beginning.

He'd been lucky so far, but luck didn't last forever. It had started running out when he'd lost the horse. A man on foot didn't stand a chance, and he knew it. They'd get him sooner or later. Today, maybe. Or next week. But they'd get him. As long as a man left a trail, there was another who could follow it. But the river, now, *that* was something else! As soon as he'd seen it shining in the distance, he'd known that was the way. Get to the river—find something that'd float. Anything. Drift down the current at night, hole up during the day. It didn't matter much where the river took him. It flowed west, away from home where people knew him. Right now, that was all Howie needed to know.

He took a careful, twisting path through the City, watching his tracks and staying to the cracked stone roadways when he could. He watched the sun and knew he was edging toward the river. In midafternoon he holed up in the shell of a building and finished his mushrooms. There was nothing else around to eat. But he could do without, for now. And it was good just stopping a minute and not running. Maybe the City had been a good idea, he decided. Most people stayed away from the old places. It wouldn't stop the soldiers, if they figured he was in there. But he'd gained some time and they weren't around now. The birds told him that. He could rest awhile. Then get to the river, and wait for night to set in. They'd never take him then— nobody'd ever *hear* about him after that.

Jacob's soldiers had kept him on the run, giving him precious little time to more than catch his breath. Still, any chance he'd had Howie studied the guns he'd taken from the trooper. He figured he knew how cartridges fit in the smaller weapon, the one you held in your fist, and what you did to make it go off. That was clear enough from the way it fit your hand. He wasn't too sure yet of the longer one. If he had to, he decided, he could point the handgun in the right direction and fire it.

It was about the last thing in the world he *wanted* to do— and likely would be, if it came to that. That was the thing about guns; you could hit a man further away than a bow'd ever think of reaching. But everyone for miles around sure knew what you were up to.

He didn't mind admitting he was scared to death of the things. How did a man use one without going deaf? Did you ever get *used* to that? Still, he'd never figured on riding a horse, either. And he'd done that, hadn't he? Though his tailbone'd near torn in two the first couple of days. Horses and guns were fearsome things—but they were precious goods to have. Howie had learned that well enough. They made a man faster and stronger than other men. A man with one had terrible power—a man with both could do pretty well what he pleased. Papa and his mother and a lot of other people were dead because they hadn't had either.

Well, it wouldn't happen to him. Not ever. He'd get away from Jacob's troopers, and he would never let another man get the best of him.

THE RIVER RAN SLOW and easy near the shore, swift and certain in midstream. He sat quietly and watched a long branch float by; it bobbed quickly out of sight around the bend and Howie grinned to himself. He'd be long gone when the sun found him in the morning!

It was a safe enough place to wait out the day. The small backwater was studded with high brush and willows, masking him from the river. The log he'd picked was well hidden, but ready to go—the long gun strapped to its side. The handgun was tight against his belt. Howie near itched for sundown. Now that he'd set himself to go, the hours seemed to be creeping by.

He lay on his back in the brush and watched a jay squawk overhead. During the last few days he'd thought about killing one, but something had stopped him. Birds weren't exactly unclean, but you weren't really supposed to eat them, and he never had. He could try for a fish, but that would mean getting too close to the water and he knew he couldn't risk being seen.

He started remembering the canal trip to Bluevale, and Papa and mother and Carolee, and the big turtle on the log, and how Papa had let him handle stock for the first time. He swept the thoughts aside. Those were years gone and over. In a world that wasn't his anymore.

At least, he thought, Carolee was all right. Safe on Silver Island. That was something. He didn't have to worry about what was happening to her. There wasn't anybody left to worry about now. Just him.

The jay hopped to a stone wall and looked at him. Dark brown stained the wall where metal had been. There was probably a lot of iron left in the City, though people had pretty well stripped what they could find years before. Nobody liked the Cities, but metal was worth going after. Sometimes a bargeman or someone else who traveled a lot would show something he said came from the Cities—a coin, maybe, or something out of glass. He'd try to sell it if he could, but no one much wanted things like that. They weren't supposed to bring good luck.

Something stirred in the brush nearby and Howie sat up straight. It moved again, and he searched the foliage without turning his head one way or the other. It was close. Not more than five yards away. He reached for his bow, then turned around slowly—and almost laughed to himself. There it was, green on green and nearly invisible, but plain as day if you knew what to look for. A big bullfrog, fresh from the river and just sitting there, fat as could be, waiting for a fine blue fly.

Hunger came back and set juices moving in his belly. He thought how the frog would keep just fine in the water—and by morning, he'd be far enough downriver for a fire. Bringing up the bow on his far side, he carefully nocked an arrow. There was one thing about frogs—you had to hit 'em square, right in the head, or they'd hop out of sight and die in deep water. Only he was sure his stomach wouldn't let him do a fool thing like that.

The bow sang. It was an easy shot; the frog twitched once, pinned to soft earth. Howie dropped his bow and sprang up after it. He could already smell the white flesh sizzling over coals. He reached down to jerk the arrow and saw the bright flash from the corner of his eye. Sound followed a quick second later, exploding over the water. Lead whined angrily past his ear and chunked into wood. Howie jumped for cover, felt his foot hit the wet frog, and went sprawling into shallow water. The second shot buzzed overhead. Someone shouted. He looked up and saw the two horsemen churning toward him across the river.

He knew he had to move. Keep low, belly fast out of the water, and disappear into the brush. It started just fine. He was close to the bank with a good stand of willow for cover and knew he could make it. Then the riders started firing blindly from the middle of the river. Bullets ploughed up mud around his fingers and clipped the low branches and cratered the rock wall. Fear gripped him hard—jerked him to his feet and set him running. The shot turned him around, slammed him hard into the river.

Howie rolled and cried out. He couldn't believe the pain. He stared down at his shoulder, saw blood turn the water pink.

It's happening, he cried out to himself. *I'm dying! I'm really for sure dying . . . !*

His hand found something hard. A root. He pulled himself toward the bank. Someone yelled nearby and a horse blew water. Howie tried to care, but couldn't.

It was hard to see anymore. There was something—Big. Dark. Blotting out daylight. It came close to him. Howie smelled whiskey and sweat. He knew what was coming, and closed his eyes against it.

WHEN HE WOKE again it was near dark. He was still in the water but he wasn't cold anymore. He didn't feel anything at all now. He was just bone tired clear through. All he wanted to do was sleep for a while. Then he'd get up rested and get on his log and start downriver. On the shore nearby, he could see something dark and terrible squatting in the brush. While he watched, the dark thing lifted a naked man in its big arms, gentle and easy, and took up a silver knife. Then it carefully skinned all the hide off the man's head.

Howie was sure he was dying then. Most likely, he was dead already.

12

Once during the night he woke briefly, saw ground swimming by, and figured he was belly down on a horse. Rain swept over him hard. It stung his neck and coursed down his cheeks and made small rivers to his nose and mouth. Choking, he retched miserably down the animal's flanks.

In the quick flashes of lightning he saw hooves churning up mud. When he turned to see where he was going and who had him, pain knifed him hard and pulled him under again. And in a small moment of relief, he knew that was the best place to be at the time.

THERE WAS fire smell.

Wet clothes and leather.

And food. Honest to God *hot* food on a cookfire.

Howie kept his eyes closed. There were men around the fire; he could hear their voices, low and gruff sounding. He'd been awake long enough to feel dull pain and remember the river. Some of it, anyway. There were pieces missing—things that weren't clear at all.

One thing was certain, though, and that crowded all other thoughts aside. He was still alive. The soldiers had put a bullet in him, but he wasn't dead. Rightly, they should have finished him off and left him in the river. Instead, they'd patched him up and put him on a horse and hauled him off somewhere alive. *And that,* he decided, *had to be a whole lot worse than being dead.*

The big foot caught him full in the ribs. He screamed, sucked in air. The boot found him again and he doubled in pain.

The man laughed. "Hey, our little friend here's waked up, Klu."

Howie opened his eyes and blinked back tears. The man loomed over him like a broad oak. Black-eyed, thick-chested. Dark hair and tangled beard. Light from the fire made his coarse features swim; the flames licked over rocky walls behind. They were holed up in a cave, then. Probably back on the high ridge somewhere.

"You get rested good, did you?"

Howie didn't answer. The man grinned and fingered his beard. "You're right enough, Klu," he said gently, "the lad's some pretty!"

Howie glared up at him. The other man came up behind, a smaller copy of the first. He grinned curiously at Howie, then squatted down close.

"What they call you, boy?"

Howie eyed the man dubiously. They knew his name well enough. The whole bunch had been hard on his heels for more than a week. It wasn't likely they'd forgotten how he left his mark on Jacob.

"Come on, boy. We ain't going to hurt you any."

With a bullet in his shoulder and his ribs near caved, he didn't give much credit to that. If they wanted a new name, though, he'd give them one. "It's Burt," he said.

"Burt what?"

"Just Burt."

"Burt..." The man tasted the word. "That's a real nice name." He turned aside and winked at the man above. The big man gave him back a quick laugh.

"Now then, Burt," the man smiled, "I'm Klu and that big'un up there's Jigger. How's that shoulder of yours coming? Bet it smarts some, don't it?"

"Some," Howie told him.

Klu shook his head and frowned. "Bet it does, too. That was a mighty big slug for a little fella like you. Just a tee-ninsy bit down an' you wouldn't be layin' up in no warm cave with Jigger and me. No, sir. Where you'd be is pushing up river mud like them other *un*-fortunates."

The one called Jigger laughed at that.

Howie studied the man, puzzled. *What* others? Something touched the edge of his mind and he didn't like the taste of it.

"Thing is," Klu went on, "you got to watch them kind of wounds." He touched Howie's arm. "They got a way of goin' bad. You know? Real quick like."

Without warning his finger stiffened and jabbed hard into Howie's shoulder. Howie moaned.

Klu showed concern. "That smart any, Burt?"

"Lordy," Howie gasped, "what'd you do *that* for?"

"You see that, Jigger?" Klu pulled Howie's shirt aside. "Look at that boy's shoulder. Why, it's all festered up."

"It is," said Jigger, squatting down to see. "It rightly is, Klu. What you figure we ought to do?"

"What we got to do first," Klu told him, "is git this boy comfortable." His big fingers worked at Howie's trousers. "Get him out of these soakin' wet clothes an'..."

"Hey, *stop* that!" Howie tried to protest, but every move started the shoulder up again and set his head swimming. He suddenly knew, and understood. His face went hot. Jigger peeled his trousers away and grinned foolishly, big hands searching between his legs. Then Klu was there, too, in another way, and the bile rose in Howie's throat.

No matter what they did or how much it hurt, he was determined to fight them. Even if they kicked loose *all* his ribs he'd—

Klu raised up, then, and met his eyes. Howie went cold all over. He saw something he'd never even dreamed of before. Nobody'd ever told him there were things like that, but it was clear as day in Klu's one look—and he knew whatever they did he'd lie there and take it. That the other thing squatting dark and terrible in the man's head was worse than anything that was happening to him now. It was all Klu was really waiting for; the screaming and kicking and fighting back. He wanted that a lot more than he wanted the other...

"*Jigger! Klu!*"

The two men straightened, pulled back from Howie like he'd turned to fire.

"*Git* your asses over here to me and do it *quick*! Move!"

Howie let out a breath, gripped his legs to stop the shaking. The man stood just past the cookfire, watching. His hair and beard might have stolen color from the flames; he was two heads shorter than the black-browed giants, and spare of frame—but his eyes said more than grit and muscle. They blazed out and seized the two, held them still, and scorched them soundly. If there was anger in either of the men, they held it close and did as they were told.

For a long time, the three squatted by the fire. Klu and Jigger had plenty to say, but it was the red beard who did most of the talking. It was likely about him, Howie figured, but he didn't much care. He was glad for a minute to get back in his clothes. The effort hurt something awful, but he'd decided whatever the soldiers did next, he was by damn goin' to die decent. And *that* meant having trousers on.

Finally, Klu and Jigger swung rain blankets over their shoulders and grumbled out of the cave. They were plain enough unhappy, but they went. Klu shot a dark look over his shoulder in Howie's direction. The red beard spooned a big bowl of stew and walked back to him.

"You're Burt, I reckon. I'm Pardo, if them two didn't tell you. Hungry?" He held out the stew. Howie didn't answer; he scooped up the bowl as soon as Pardo let it go and wolfed it down quickly.

"Hey—" Pardo grabbed his arm. "You git greedy you goin' to lose it all, boy."

Howie looked at him and tried to slow down, but it wasn't easy. Pardo squatted with his own bowl and watched him finish. Up close, it wasn't hard to see what set Klu and Jigger moving. Pardo was plain enough—raw-boned, homely, and pale-skinned—like a lot of folks Howie'd seen with red hair. But the eyes were something else again. Even when they weren't blazing out angry, they looked right through you. Like the man behind 'em knew everything that was going on in your head.

Colonel Jacob's eyes had been like that, too. Only different. Jacob had a meanness in him, and you could read it well enough. You couldn't hardly tell about Pardo. Likely as not, he'd look fierce as lightning without caring one way or the other—and grinnin' all lazy like right before he took a knife to your belly.

"Now," said Pardo, wiping his beard, "I reckon you better tell me just who you are and what it is you're doing here."

"I'm here 'cause them two *brought* me here," said Howie.

Pardo looked disappointed. "Boy, I'm asking plain questions. Likely, you can come up with some plain answers to match 'em." He pulled Howie's pistol from his own belt and balanced it in his palm. "You're runnin' hard, in a place you shouldn't ought to be. Carrying soldier guns. Only you ain't no soldier."

Howie looked bewildered. "You'd sure know I'm not, if anyone would!"

"And why's that?"

"Cause... cause you—you just would, is all!"

Pardo bit his lip thoughtfully. "Soldiers were after you. You got yourself caught, so you figure me an' Klu and Jigger is soldiers, too." He nodded to himself. "Well, it works out right, an' I can see how your thinkin' would go. Only you're plain wrong, boy." He grinned slightly. "About as wrong as you can be."

Pardo could read his disbelief. "Take it however you like," he told Howie. "Only that don't change it none. And seeing as we don't have a lot of time for this kind of business, I reckon it'd be a good idea if you'd *pre*tend that's the way it is. Now I'm askin' you again. What is it you're doing here, and why are them soldiers after your hide?"

"But..."

"But, nothing," Pardo said flatly. He looked straight at Howie. "Don't spend *no* time thinking up answers that ain't goin' to do neither of us no good, all right?"

"Yes, sir."

"That's not too hard to understand, now is it?"

"No, sir. It ain't. I know what you're saying."

"Good. You an' me are going to get along just fine, then."

"You ain't soldiers? For certain?"

Pardo looked at him. "Boy, I *said* we wasn't!"

"Maybe you're not. I just . . ."

Pardo raised a threatening brow.

"All right. I'm—from Bluevale. It's . . ."

"I know where it is."

"Well, that's where I'm from."

"What's your pa do?"

"He runs a store."

"A store. What kinda store? Feed store, whiskey . . ."

"Knives," said Howie. "Bone-handle knives. Stuff like that."

"Knives . . ."

"Yes, sir. Like the one I got. Only I ain't got it anymore. One of your men took it off me."

Pardo nodded, and scratched under his chin. "Your name ain't really Burt, is it?" He looked hard at Howie. "Don't lie to me, now."

"No, sir," Howie looked down at his hands, then at Pardo. "It ain't exactly Burt. It's Jaimie. Jaimie Walters. When I thought you was soldiers . . ."

"All right." Pardo held up a hand. "Let's do some talkin' about soldiers. Like why they might be spending a powerful lot of time chasin' boys from Bluevale around the country when they got a lot better things to do."

"I stole a horse from 'em," Howie put in quickly, "ain't that reason enough?"

Pardo frowned. "You didn't have no *horse* with you . . ."

"No, 'cause I run it too hard and it died on me."

"Truth?"

"Truth, I swear!"

Pardo shook his head and made a face. "Lordy, what a waste. Horses ain't easy to come by."

"And some guns," Howie added. "I stole guns, too. That's why they was after me. They were some mad, I'll tell you, and that's why I was running so hard, and how come I had to use up the horse. I couldn't do nothing else."

Pardo studied him with no expression at all. "That's what happened, is it?"

"Yes, sir. It truly is."

"For certain?"

"Listen," Howie insisted, "You wanted the truth and that's it. I'm not lying!"

"Well, now, I never said you was, did I?" He smiled easily and got to his feet. "I never said you was telling the *truth*, either, or any big part of it, Jaimie—or Burt, or whichever. Most likely, you ain't neither, but I'm not goin' to worry over that. Pardo's a fair man, as anyone'll tell you, an' what I'm going to do is give you a night to sleep off the hurt 'fore we fix up that shoulder, and then I'm going to fill up your belly some; and when you're up to it, we're all going to do a little quiet riding out of here, since you ain't made it exactly a easy place to stay. An' after that, I'm going to ask you to think real hard about who you are an' why you're running from them soldiers. And if I don't care much for what I hear I'm going to give you back to Klu and Jigger for a couple days 'fore I cut your liver out personal." He gave Howie a wide grin. "You git a little sleep now, y'hear?"

13

The trail was an hour old before the sun broke over the ridge at their backs. Howie welcomed the meager heat that filtered through low branches and mottled the forest floor. Frost edged the dark carpet of fern and grayed the trunks of tall pines.

He was hungry. And cold to the bone. If his old jacket had been threadbare to begin with, it was less than worthless now. Klu and Jigger had taken care of that. Nothing he had was worth keeping anymore—trousers, shirt, and shoes were near gone. But he didn't dare toss anything aside. Next to nothing, he figured, was better than going naked.

The handful of hard corn and jerky he'd wolfed down for breakfast didn't begin to fill his belly, and his shoulder was a dull ache that wouldn't go away. If there was something right with the world, he'd be danged if he could see what it was.

Pardo, riding beside him, was no help at all. "You're plain lucky that soldier was so all-fired eager to start shootin'," the man advised him. "It ain't a bad wound, or deep. Best kind to git, s'matter of fact. Come far enough to slow down some and straight on, so you don't have to dig all twisty-like to get it out."

To hear Pardo talk, Howie thought dismally, getting shot and near killed was about the finest thing that could happen to a person. Only it didn't feel all that good if it was your own arm doing the hurting. He was sure his whole shoulder would drop off if the mount stumbled over one more curly root.

And if it did, he'd get no help from the two brooding giants at his back. They'd as soon see his neck broke as not. Pardo wasn't more'n a hair better.

The whole business puzzled Howie more than a little. They'd saved him from the soldiers, patched him up, put a little food in his belly. And for what? They weren't the favorgiving kind, for sure. Whatever they had in mind, he probably wasn't goin' to like it. It *seemed* better to be alive than dead, and feeling another morning when you didn't figure to. But you couldn't trust that kind of thinking. He'd already learned plenty of things could come along to make you *wish* you were deader'n a stone. A couple had already.

Just before noon, Pardo stopped and motioned him forward. "Down there," he pointed. "Just to the left of where the river makes that little bend. You see it?"

Howie wasn't sure what he saw, but he saw something. There was a break in the trees where you could look down on a muddy ribbon of water in a far valley.

"It's Old Chattanooga," said Pardo. "Where you was when them soldiers got you." He gave Howie a smug grin. "Didn't know the name of it, did you?"

"I might of heard it some time," Howie admitted, "but I don't reckon—"

"*Hearing* 'bout something and knowing what it is is *two* different things," snapped Pardo. "Two different things, boy." He flicked his eyes away and kicked the horse forward, leaving Howie to watch his back.

PARDO WAS A HARD MAN to figure. He talked enough when he had a mind to, but mostly about stuff that didn't matter much. When it came to something you *wanted* to know, he was about as wordy as a stump. You might as well be talking to Klu and Jigger.

Pardo was different, though—most of the time, anyway. Klu and Jigger were big, lumbering oaks; Pardo was a tough, gnarly pine. His small frame had been twisted and hardened in the raw winds; his face shaped by hungry winters. There was a power in the man, but it was a thing that came from inside somewhere. The eyes told you that. Klu and Jigger knew it, too. Either of the two could snap Pardo in half like a twig, but Howie was certain that would never happen. Like as not, Pardo could stare down the Devil himself if he took a mind to.

When the sun was straight up, they stopped at the edge of a high meadow and let the horses graze on short grass. There was a hurried meal of bread and jerky, and time to see to your business if you wanted, then they were back on the trail again.

Howie gave up trying to pry answers out of Pardo. Where were they going, exactly? What had really happened back in the City? Pardo replied with interesting facts like what kind of berries you might find near a creek or the best way to tickle a catfish. Still, Howie had guessed a lot on his own, by looking and figuring.

Wherever Pardo was going, he was taking a care about getting there. He sure wasn't looking to be seen, or followed. There was reason enough for that, of course, with two dead soldiers back there in the river. But Howie was sure there was more to it than that. These three had been up to something long before *he* came along.

He'd pieced most of the business at the river together and guessed the rest. Klu and Jigger had been watching him some time before he made that dumb move with the frog and let the soldiers spot him. Why, was easy to figure. They'd made *that* clear enough back at the cave. As to the terrible thing he thought he'd imagined just before passing out in the shallows, that had bothered him more than a little. He didn't see how it could be, though it'd seemed awful real at the time. Well, he had two vivid answers, now. They dangled from Klu's broad belt—long hanks of hair still attached to raw, bloody flesh.

Pardo hadn't been happy about that and he'd let Klu know it. Soldiers got killed all the time, that being part of the trade, he said. A man could lose his life and his horse and his weapons and no one'd think much about it. But a man's companions didn't view trophy-taking too kindly. It made them look all the harder and that wasn't exactly what Pardo wanted at the moment.

Howie shifted on his mount and stretched his sore shoulder. The day was just half over and he was already tired to the bone. He remembered something Papa had said, when he was maybe ten or so. Lordy, could he ever have been *ten*? Papa said men were peculiar creatures to be as smart as they thought they were. The seasons feel the same every year, Papa said, and a man knows this as well as his name, but he gets fooled every time. He welcomes each season for the good it offers and never thinks about the bad. But before it's half finished, he's itching to see it go, ready to take on the next one!

It was true as it could be, Howie told himself. Look at where he was now. Safe from the soldiers after running his heart out—near gettin' killed a hundred times or so. Compared to that bunch, Pardo and Klu and Jigger were almost family! If you could imagine such a thing.

More'n likely, though, what he'd done was just what Papa said: traded one set of troubles for another. He wasn't as bad off as he could be, but that didn't mean it wouldn't *get* that way soon enough. And he sure didn't plan on sticking around long enough to find out.

JUST BEFORE SUNSET Pardo left the others to make camp and disappeared into thick woods. The trail hadn't changed all day. Pardo kept them to the deepest part of the forest; the high ridge to their left, the valley a half mile or so below. The foliage was so heavy here the woods were near dark at noon and the fern beneath the animals' hooves buried all sound in thick blankets of green. A good tracker might have found them—if he knew where to look. But he'd have to be quieter'n breath to do it without ending up under Klu's big belt.

Howie would have bet on any of the three. They were all natural woodsmen and they could sniff out sign in a rainstorm better'n most men could count their toes in bed. It was something Howie could understand, and appreciate. He already knew staying alive in the wilderness was no easy business.

It was dark before Pardo came back, walking and leading his mount. Both Klu and Jigger knew he was coming; their noses came up and their dark eyes switched about. To Howie, though, he appeared like a ghost in the clearing. He looked about once, searching out the shape of things, then gave his mount to Howie and squatted down with Klu and Jigger.

Howie didn't even try to listen. Catching talk from those three was like overhearing the grass sprout up. Later though, after a cold meal, Pardo wiped a sleeve over his mouth and stalked out of camp, telling Howie to follow. He was glad enough to go; most anything was better than riding or squatting. And sitting around with Klu and Jigger made him itch all over. They hadn't tried anything since Pardo'd caught 'em, but that didn't mean they wouldn't if they got a chance to.

Pardo led him a quarter mile through thick trees, then stopped. When his eyes got dark-sense again, Howie could see the forest ended abruptly at the edge of a high, rocky face. The cliff tumbled almost straight down. Below, campfires and lanterns dotted the valley in bright clusters and threw pale light across a broad river.

Pardo grinned at his surprise. "It's a meat camp," he explained. "A big one." He squatted under a broad rock and Howie joined him. "Six, seven thousand head." He laughed to himself in the dark. "If the wind was right, you could smell 'em."

Howie figured that was so. There were enough fires down there to light a town or two. "What they all *doing* down there?" he wanted to know.

"It's what we come for, and where we're going. Or where *I'm* going. There's plenty of old Pardo's friends down there...but there's army buyers in camp, too, for a day or so. And I don't figure it's a good idea for Klu and Jigger to show their pretty faces just yet. Or you, either..."

His words carried a question and Howie was glad it was dark. "You never did say why they was there," he asked quickly. "Seems like a lot of meat just sittin' out where nobody is."

"You ought to get yourself something to keep in that mouth, boy," Pardo said darkly. "It ain't exactly sittin'... it's meat *moving*, 'cept at night. Coming in from all over—bought, sold, strayed, an' stolen—and there'll be two, three times as many before they get out West."

Howie looked up. "It's going all the way West?"

"All the way. If they can," he added wryly. "The government's got a right many soldiers out West with bellies cryin' for meat. Those fellers down there know it and they know the price is climbing sky high every day that passes. Only, you can bet Lathan's boys know a big herd's coming, too. And they ain't going to take lightly to it getting there."

Somehow, that startled Howie. He'd never really thought about just how far the West really was, but it had always seemed a comfortable distance away. He sure hadn't thought about the war, or Lathan's soldiers coming anywhere close to where *he* might be.

"They got plenty far to go, of course," said Pardo. "Through the rest of Tennessee Territory, cross a corner of Old Arkansas, and on into Badlands. The government's strong enough there, though you'll see a raider now and then. But they don't get in close to no stronghold town. Lathan ain't got time or men to waste stealin' liquor and stewpots, which is all that's there except troopers lickin' their wounds."

He shook his head, peering down at the valley lights. "Now, if Lathan wants that meat—an' he does—he'll have to hit it 'bout Arkansas somewhere. But he'll have to go some to get it." He laughed softly to himself and looked at Howie. "There's some mean buggers down there, and more coming!"

Howie didn't pretend to understand everything he was hearing. But that was nothing new, he thought wearily. He'd gotten in the habit of doing stuff he either didn't like, or didn't understand. Trailing along after Pardo, for instance. Looking at meat herds in the middle of the night. He wasn't sure where it was he *ought* to be, but he was near certain it wasn't here.

He felt, just then, like the whole dark sky was pressing right down on him. Was *this* what he had ahead of him, wandering around after someone else, doing things he didn't even want to? If that's what growing up was all about....

"Pardo," he said suddenly. "I gotta ask something. You can answer it or not but I got to say it!"

Pardo squinted at him. "You can *ask* anything you like, boy. Long as you do it quiet like. Sound carries better'n you'd think...and there's some good listeners down there."

"I got to know, Pardo," Howie rushed on, letting the words spill out before he got too scared to call them back. "I got to know what it is you want with me an' what it is I'm *doing* here. I got nothing to do with you or Klu or Jigger or nobody. You just picked me up out of nowhere and I'm grateful for what you done...but now I'm just trailing after the three of you an' I don't even know what for! I know sure you aren't letting me go off anywhere. I don't even have to ask. Only...you keep telling me stuff that's your business and none of mine. Things I don't even know nothing about. Like I was—" Howie stopped; the words quit coming on their own.

Pardo studied him thoughtfully a minute. "Well, you spoke your piece, for certain." He grinned and shook his head. "Men is all different, boy. I reckon you done found that out?"

"I guess I have, but..."

"Like there's lots of kinds of trees and bushes, and they all do something different. Now, Klu and Jigger is made for one thing and I'm made for another. That's not to say they don't do what they're good at better'n most. The thing is, I talk to Klu and Jigger about one thing and I might talk to you 'bout another."

Howie shrugged helplessly. "Why, though? What's that make me?"

"That's what I'm figuring on," Pardo told him. "You. And what kind of bush you might turn out to be."

"I don't see where there's much use in that," Howie said wearily. "Like I was saying..."

"Like *I* was saying, boy..." Pardo reached out and gripped his arm until it hurt. His voice was easy as rain, but his eyes said something else. "What you need to get in that head of yours is that a person don't *have* to know everything at once. You reckon you can remember that?"

Howie nodded, the fingers in his arm bringing tears to his eyes.

"Fine," said Pardo, "and it'll also do you good if you keep in mind I *ain't* forgot you still owe me a real good talkin'...about soldiers and horses? An' names like Burt and Jaimie and what all? Don't you *never* try fooling 'round with my head. You'll sure come to grief doing it."

14

The drive followed the river, winding down through stony canyons under the brow of thick forests. In a few days, the dark mountains gave way to rolling hills and the heavy stands of fir and pine thinned to lowland scrub.

The drivers rested easier; with open terrain ahead a man could see where he was going and who was about. A dozen armies could hide themselves in the Tennessee highlands— you could send out all the flankers you wanted and still not be certain Lathan's raiders weren't grinning down at you from the next dark ridge ahead. There was still danger, and worse to come, but a man didn't feel so bad about what he could see riding at him.

Klu, Jigger, and Howie followed the course of the drive for three days, keeping well out of sight. Then they pushed south, away from the river, making a long loop through open country to meet the drive again from the west. The morning before they let themselves be spotted by the herd's outriders, Pardo wore a bright shell band around his hat— the signal to Klu that the way was clear. For that was Pardo's story: his two cousins and his boy were coming up from the southwest. They'd try to find the drive and join it if they could. Howie wasn't too happy to find a new father in Pardo, but there was nothing for that at the moment.

It was clear the man had wasted no time; Pardo had plenty of followers in camp and was liked and respected by the stock owners. His "relatives" were welcomed; signed up immediately with no questions asked. Howie didn't think there'd have been much trouble if nobody'd ever *heard* of them before. The drive needed all the hands it could get, man and boy alike. And new recruits with mounts *and* fire-arms were doubly welcome.

The days grew warmer, but there was still frost on the ground at dawning and plenty of cause for a fire at night. The drive was moving quickly and the pace was hard on men and meat alike. There were no hungry bellies in the crew, though, for more stragglers died off than even hard-working drivers could eat.

Two more herds joined the next week. Pardo told Howie that, even losing what they were, it was likely the biggest drive ever—close to ten, eleven-thousand head.

At night, the camp was a small city. There were plenty of places for men to spend money they didn't have yet—tents for gambling and playing two-stick and for drinking white corn out of clay cups. There were women, too, brought on the drive by enterprising merchants who also furnished most of the corn whiskey, and backed or broke the gambling riders.

The drive was no secret. Its presence brought visitors from every town and settlement along the way. It was a strange collection: Stolid farmers and their gaunt sons pulling wagons of vegetables and grain for sale. Merchants who knew a driver would buy most anything another man would sell. And people who were just plain curious to see a horse, or a man with a pistol in his belt. All visitors were tolerated, though every man on the drive was sure spies from Lathan's army were openly walking about the camp counting booty to come, dividing up mounts and arms right before their eyes.

Most welcome of all were grain dealers and feed sellers. The drive couldn't possibly carry enough supplies to feed the hungry herd the whole length of the trip. And moving stock burned up a lot more feed than they did penned up. Prices were outrageous, but the owners grudgingly paid them; telling themselves the money they'd already been promised by army buyers would more than make up the difference. If they got where they were going, that is.

"And that's the thing," said Cory Halgood, a driver friend of Pardo's, "you don't never get rich riding herd, but you don't get frightful poor, neither—like ol' Jess here stands to be when Lathan turns him upside down an' lets all that *army* gold run out his boots.''

Pardo and the other drivers laughed, and Jess Blinker turned red and then laughed with them. "Hell's fire," he grumbled, emptying the last dregs of his cup. "I *got* to keep makin' money. Somebody has to buy corn for deadass drivers that don't have the sense to earn it themselves!''

"We're just trying to help," grinned Cory. "No sense leaving all them good barrels of whiskey for Lathan."

The crew grinned, but Jess stared them down. "That just possibly ain't too funny, or far from the truth. The rider that come in from Ozark . . .''

"You can't believe nothing an Arkansawyer says," Pardo put in. "They'll tell you most anything."

"If you'll sit still an' listen," Cory agreed.

Jess eyed them warily. "Trouble is, you *can* believe most anything you hear these days." He filled his cup and downed it with a grimace. "What he says is likely close to bein' true, Pardo. A whole regiment of Lathan's men ain't where they're supposed to be. An' this feller works for the government in Badlands and ought to know what he's saying. If it's not true, it ought to be. If you was Lathan, what would *you* be doin' now?'' He snorted and stamped his big foot. "Why, you'd set loose that regiment—which you could spare easy with no real fightin' going on—and just follow the damn parade drifting in and out of here to gawk. And that'd be that, for certain. Likely enough it will be.''

The men considered that, and looked at their cups.

"Only thing is," Pardo pointed out, "them troopers don't want to lose that meat any more'n you do, Jess. They figure on gettin' here a lot quicker than Lathan can.''

"Figuring and *doing* is two different things," Jess grumbled. "I *figured* on findin' copper pennies growin' on trees up in Ohio country, but I never seen any when I was there.''

HOWIE LIKED both Cory and old Jess. Cory was near twenty or so, but he treated Howie like he was a man doing a man's job—which was more than you could say for some of Pardo's friends. Cory was tall and lean with dark hair and heavy brows. Deep lines were etched about his eyes—the sign of a man born outdoors, who'd seldom slept under a roof. He'd been in the army once and had fought in Colorado, but hadn't liked it much. That was Cory's way, for the most part. When he got tired of what he was doing, he just upped and walked away and did something else and never mind who didn't like it. Still, he hid his face under a heavy beard, now. "Just in case some army feller's got a memory longer'n his nose."

Life on the drive was dreary and hard, but Howie decided it was some better than camping out with Klu and Jigger—keeping one eye open all the time, and one hand on your trousers. One thing galled him plenty, though; Pardo had taken his weapons at the cave and never given them back. Howie hated him for that. He'd rightfully earned those guns, if anybody had. They were his. No one had any call to take them away. If you could *use* 'em, he told himself ruefully, you might still have them.

He vowed that day would come, too. And soon. He wouldn't be caught like Papa had, on foot with no weapons to fend off men who had both mounts and guns. He'd had the strength of half a dozen men and what good had it been? A man on a horse with a pistol in his belt and a rifle on his back—that's who ran the world now.

He was far enough from that at the moment, he decided glumly. On foot, helping tend the smelly herd and running errands for Pardo or whoever could find him. At the end of the day he was too tired to think who he was, much less who he *ought* to be.

JUST BEFORE SUNDOWN, Cory found him above the river at the small stream they used for washing and bathing.

"You git out of there, and make yourself decent," he yelled. "We got things to do!"

"I got about ten hundred hours sleepin' to do," Howie told him, "if I ever get enough stink off to matter." He was up to his shoulders in the cool water, his clothes drying on the bank.

Cory laughed. "Matter of fact, you don't *have* to get too decent, where we're going. Ain't nobody else gonna be."

Howie looked at him. "And where's that?"

"That's for me to know an' you to find out," Cory grinned slyly.

"Then it's likely you'll be goin' alone. I ain't much on surprises."

"You'll take to this one, all right."

Howie studied him. "What I think I'll be doin' is *sleeping*, Cory."

"Not much you won't," Cory assured him.

Howie decided he was drunk. There was no other way to figure the silly, lopsided grin on his face.

"Git out of there," Cory told him. "Too much water ain't good for you. Hear?"

Howie faced him. "Look. I reckon I'll pass up whatever it is. Thanks just the same."

"Oh, you're just as welcome as you can be," said Cory. He moved off the bank and set one big boot in the stream. Howie stared at him.

"I don't recollect ever gettin' a feller your size dressed and all," Cory yawned, "but I suppose I can handle it."

"Now just a damn minute!" Howie retreated upstream.

"The wetter I get," Cory warned, "the madder I'm gonna be . . ."

15

Howie wished he could crawl under a rock somewhere, or die right where he was.

"You are a *fine* looking boy," the girl told him. "You rightly are. Didn't no one ever tell you that?"

She looked at him with dark, lazy eyes and bit her lip in a way that made Howie twist up inside. "Nobody never did, and I ain't no boy," he said bluntly.

She threw back her head and laughed, tossing black hair over bare shoulders. "Well what*ever* you are, I like it. For certain I do!"

Howie scowled at Cory, but Cory wasn't looking. The other girl had perched herself in his lap and was doing something to his ear. Howie could have killed him. Worse than that, he wasn't sure whether he *ought* to be mad. Cory was either treating him older than he was—and a lot older than Howie felt—or else was making a big fool of him. Either way, he wished the girl would leave him alone a minute so he could get his wits back and figure how he felt about *any*thing.

It had all happened too quick to do much thinking. Cory had just dragged him into the big tent where the drivers drank corn and out the other side. No one had paid any attention to them, except one bearded driver who looked up hazily at Howie like he might want to start something. Howie quickly looked the other way and caught up with Cory.

Behind the big one, there were smaller tents with plank and keg tables and an oil lamp. There was a bottle of white corn, and straw pallets in the corner. The girls came out of nowhere, and it was plain enough they knew Cory. It didn't take Howie but a second to figure what was happening. That's when his belly turned upside down and he started looking for things to crawl under.

"Listen, you ain't even told me your name," said the girl. "You know that?"

"Burt," said Howie.

"Well. How do, Burt. We goin' to get along just fine, you know? I'm Aimie, and that's Maye." She laughed and climbed in his lap and kissed him soundly. "Only I can't introduce you 'cause Maye's kinda *occ*-you-pied. Lordee, I guess!"

Howie glanced at Cory, then turned quickly away. Aimie caught his look and laughed out loud. Maye giggled behind him, until Cory did something that made her gasp. Howie felt the heat rise right up to his hairline.

"You don't pay no attention to them," said Aimie, holding his chin firmly. "Just watch what's goin' on *here*." She ran a finger over his cheek. "Where you from, Burt?"

"South."

"South what?"

"Just south."

"Well me an' Maye are, too. Where'bouts?"

"It's . . . kinda small. Don't figure you'd know it."

"I might."

"Uh, it's Clinton."

"Clinton?" She shrugged. "Don't know it. Pardo's your pa, Cory says."

"No, he ain't! I mean, kinda." Howie wanted to bite his tongue. "Why? You know him?"

"*Uh* huh." She raised one brow slightly. "Lord, *ever*-'one knows Pardo. Hey, Burt, don't you like me none?"

"Well, sure I do."

"You don't *act* like it." She showed him a pouty mouth.

"What's a feller sup*posed* to act like?"

"Like you want to be, you know . . . friendly." She studied him a moment, then sat up straight. "Say, you ain't like them uncles of yours, are you?"

"No, I ain't!" He felt himself color again. "I'm nothing at all like them and don't you go sayin' that!"

"Okay, don't get *mad* or anything." She settled back in his lap and leaned her head on his shoulder. Howie had to admit she felt fine enough, laying back like that, her face kind of pushed up into his shoulder. He looked down at her, and smelled the heavy perfume of her hair. He suddenly remembered the girl in the picture, the one on the beach at Silver Island. Lord, that had been a lifetime or two ago! The hours he'd spent wondering what she looked like under those tiny bits of swimclothes. There'd been more than one night when he hadn't been able to sleep, or get her off his mind.

Aimie shifted in his lap and made a small noise. Howie felt himself stirring under her weight. He felt a quick surge of panic. Could she tell what was happening? He was sure she could, and . . . Well, damn, was there anything wrong with that? That's what you were *supposed* to do, wasn't it?

"Aimie . . ." He let his hand run along the curve of her arm. Aimie reached up calmly and slipped her dress off one shoulder. She took his hand and cupped it around her breast.

Howie couldn't breathe. His hand trembled against a softness he couldn't imagine. He didn't believe what was happening—he was touching a girl in places he'd just thought about before. She . . . she was pulling her clothes down and lettin' him *see* her and all and do whatever he wanted to and Lor*dee* he wanted to do just about everything!

"Burt," she said softly, "now you just wait up there." She teased at the buttons of his shirt, grinning with her eyes.

"Aimie. I don't *want* to wait."

"I guess Aimie was wrong," she whispered. "Burt, he's not no boy, for certain. No, sir, he ain't no boy *at* all . . ."

Howie grasped her bare shoulders and turned her on his lap to face him. He pulled down her dress until her arms slipped out of the sleeves and the soft fabric bunched about her waist.

Aimie's eyes were half closed, like she was looking at something real far away. Her lips curved in a lazy smile. Howie's mouth was dust dry. He was vaguely aware of rustling and breathing behind him, but everything except Aimie seemed a thousand miles east of somewhere. He marveled at what he'd discovered—stared at her, eating up all the wonder with his eyes. When he touched her, the feeling ran up his fingers and filled every part of his body. He delighted in the way her skin turned gold under the flickering lamp. He touched the small breasts and watched them swell and wondered if anyone else knew those delicate mounds of flesh were neither soft nor hard, but something in between you couldn't put a name to.

"Burt...oh, Burt!" Aimie's lips were moist, slightly open. He bent to kiss them and his breath came harder. She finished his buttons, let her fingers play about his belt.

"Burt...I reckon we better find us a place to get comfortable."

"Uh huh."

"You want to do that, Burt?"

"Aimie..." Howie couldn't talk anymore. He moved his hand around her waist and down beneath the folds of her dress. He touched the soft skin of her belly and the ache between his legs became an agony. He was sure he'd die right where he was if something didn't happen soon. When he reached out to lift her in his arms she smiled up at him—then stiffened and pushed him away.

"Hey, what you want!" she cried angrily.

He stared at her, then saw she was looking past him. He let her go and turned to see a bearded face blinking in the light.

"You just—go on and git out of here!" he yelled. "St-start moving if you don't want no trouble!" He marveled at his sudden boldness, telling grown men to get up and go and what he'd do if they didn't. The head disappeared and Howie breathed a silent sigh of relief. He'd recognized the face, though. It was the man in the big tent who'd stared at him on the way in. Now what did *he* want? Howie was certain he'd never seen the man before.

"Listen, Aimie, I'm sorry about that. I ain't got no idea—"

But Aimie had already forgotten. She wrinkled her nose at Howie and pulled him toward the straw pallet. When he was down she slipped the dress quickly over her hips and let it slide to her ankles. Howie stared. He fumbled at his belt, wondering why in blazes he couldn't work something easy as a buckle.

"Aimie...Lord, Aimie, you're just—" She looked up at him and he let his eyes start at the long, naked legs and wander on from there. He dropped his trousers, stepped toward her. The room tilted crazily. All the breath went out of him and he hit the ground hard. There was a quick flash of Aimie, eyes wide as saucers, then she was gone.

The tent was behind him; night air filled his lungs. He yelled, and kicked out with his one free leg. Whoever was dragging him 'cross the ground wouldn't answer and didn't care much what Howie hit along the way. Gravel tore at his back and scraped his elbows raw. His head bounced over something hard and he cried out. Then, suddenly, it was over.

He stared up and saw black sky through ragged branches. A hand reached down and wrenched him to his feet. For a quick second, he looked close into Pardo's eyes.

"*Smart* little son'bitch," grinned Pardo. "Oh, you surely are...*Burt!*" Pardo's big fist swung 'round and caught the side of his head. Howie went sick all over. Pardo hadn't dropped him. "Burt, huh?" The hand jerked him close again. "How 'bout *Howie*?" He saw the fist coming but there was no place to go. Hard ground came up to meet him.

Pardo bent for him. Howie rolled away. A boot clamped down to stop him. His hand found a dead branch, swung hard, and heard air whistle past Pardo's head.

Right away, he knew it had been a bad idea. Pardo'd kill him for sure, now.

"Drop that. Do it, boy."

Howie did. His head rang like there was something loose inside.

"You shouldn't oughta done that," said Pardo.

"You shouldn't oughta took my head clean off, neither," rasped Howie. He tried to get his breath and pull his trousers up at the same time. "You didn't have no call for that. No matter what!"

Pardo laughed at him. "Shit. I ain't even finished."

"Listen—"

Pardo kicked him squarely in his ribs. Howie felt something break inside.

"Git up," Pardo said flatly.

"I . . . can't!"

"Git up, boy."

"Pardo—"

Pardo kicked him in the stomach. Howie folded, threw up, and choked on his own bile. He lay on his side, his knees tucked tight under his chin.

"I said get up, boy," Pardo said evenly. "I swear I'll plain stomp you to death if you don't!"

Howie knew he meant it. He fought back pain, brought himself to his knees. "I . . . can't go no further."

"You better."

"What . . . for? So you can . . . hit me again?"

"The hittin's done."

For some reason, Howie believed him. He pulled himself up. His head swam and his knees buckled. But he stayed.

Pardo studied him in the darkness. "Now, boy—or Howie, I reckon. You got what was comin' and it's over and done with and we ain't going to talk about it any 'cept right now. You run into a feller tonight that knows who you are and where you came from. He seen you with your pa, once. He knows what happened to your folks. Seem's like most everyone east of here does and I ain't surprised. He knows what you done to that Colonel Jacob feller, too."

Pardo paused a minute. "Now listen careful and don't git nothing wrong. What you done was right and ain't anyone can take it from you. You ruined him good and I figure you had call for it. Only what you done back there in the hills *weren't* right. You lied to me, boy. An' maybe I can see you had cause, but that don't change nothing. I could have taken you into camp first time I went down, and left Klu and Jigger behind. I thought serious on it, but somethin' told me better. So where'd I be if we'd ridden in with them army fellers still there—and some of 'em maybe the ones after you? Just where'd I be, boy? You answer me that.''

Pardo shook his head and scratched his beard. ''You're just damn lucky you got caught by a feller that's a lot scareder a'me than he is of them soldiers. 'Cause they sure as hell want your head in a sack, boy, and they're willing to pay for it. Reckon I'd be a sight better off if I sold it to 'em!''

''Whyn't you do that, then,'' Howie said darkly. ''Wouldn't surprise me, none.''

''Reckon I won't,'' Pardo told him. ''For now, anyways.''

''And I reckon I'll just get out of your hair so you won't come to no more trouble. That'll suit me well enough!''

''Well, it don't suit me,'' said Pardo. ''Just get that out of your head.''

''Why!'' Howie exploded. ''What you want *me* around for? I ain't anything but trouble, you said so yourself. An' I don't *want* to be here no more'n you want me to!''

Pardo looked off in the dark toward the river. ''Guess you better get down to the creek and wash up and get some sleep. You'll likely be sore come morning, and I don't want you mopin' around none.''

He started down the hill, then stopped. ''I reckon you've earned this right enough. Considerin' how you come by it.''

Something flashed between them and landed at Howie's feet. He picked it up, and felt Jacob's pistol and holster.

''We git some time,'' said Pardo, ''I'll show you what to do with it, 'sides struttin' around looking all rough-like. Mean feller like you can likely use some gun-learning.''

16

Getting cleaned up for bed was about the last thing on Howie's mind. If he could make his body move up the hill and back to camp, he knew exactly where he was going—and it didn't have anything at all to do with working his tail off another day for Pardo.

He felt better about having the pistol back—Pardo, of course, hadn't given him any cartridges for it. He never would, either, Howie figured. That business about teaching him to shoot was so much talking. Pardo was real good at sayin' and not doing, unless it fit his needs.

The idea made Howie so mad he near forgot his aches and pains. Was *that* what Pardo thought? That he'd be so dang excited about getting his gun back he'd just run and hop in bed like a good boy? After near getting beat half to death? Well old Pardo could just think on that some more. Howie didn't intend to be around long enough to care.

The camp was in a small hollow on the far side of the hill, protected from the wind. He was relieved to find both Klu and Jigger off somewhere. Getting by those two wouldn't be the easiest thing in the world.

It didn't take long to gather up his few belongings from the leanto. Most important of all was the good ash bow. He'd kept it wrapped from the weather in his old jacket, and there were even half a dozen good arrows left. And until he could shoot . . .

He wondered what Pardo had done with his rifle. It'd be a good thing to take if he could find where it was hidden. He dismissed the thought, knowing Pardo would have it stashed in a good place. Along with cartridges and other valuables.

He hadn't even thought about where he'd go. It didn't really matter much, long as it wasn't east. Just about everyone seemed to be after him back there. West, maybe. 'Cept there was fighting. And in the north, too, most likely. Maybe he'd head south. Whatever was there couldn't be worse than anywhere else. And it stayed warmer longer in the south. For someone on the run, camping out—

A twig snapped just behind him. Howie froze, then turned quickly and threw himself to one side.

"Lordee, Burt. You sure are a jumpy one!"

Howie sat up, feeling foolish. "Aimie. What you doin' out here?"

"Looking for you, silly. What you think?"

"Listen, that's fine, only..."

Aimie fell down beside him and drew herself close. "Boy, your pa sure was mad. Was it 'cause of me, Burt?"

"It didn't have nothing to do with you. It was somethin' else. Between me and him. And he ain't my pa, Aimie."

"He's not?"

"No. We're not kin at all, and I'm grateful enough for that."

Aimie looked at him curiously. "I don't have no idea what you're talking about, Burt. But I don't much care." Her face brightened. "Thing is, I found you again."

"Yeah. You did that. Only—*ow!*"

Aimie drew back. "Now, what?"

"It ain't nothing you did," Howie explained. He felt his side gingerly. Something seemed to slip back and forth over his ribs. "I just got busted up some, is all."

Aimie looked pained, then thoughtful. "Burt?"

"What?"

"It doesn't hurt...*there*, does it?"

"Oh, Lord, Aimie!" Howie almost jumped out of his skin. Aimie worked skillfully at his trousers. He could feel her breath on his cheek, in quick little bursts like his own.

"You just can't...get a girl all worked up...and then run off and...leave her, Burt..."

"I didn't exactly...go on my own...Aimie.... *Aimie!*"

Laying back, she spread her skirts and pulled him to her. "God, you ain't no boy at all, Burt. Burt, honey, I can't *wait* no more!"

In the dim starlight he could see the flash of creamy skin. His legs met the inside of her thighs, his hardness touched incredibly warm softness, and the whole world exploded in his loins.

Aimie sat up and stared. "Oh, Burt, you didn't!"

Howie swallowed and looked away. "I couldn't help it, Aimie, I just—"

"You just *nothin'* is what!" she snapped, pushing him off. She turned from him briefly, then stood up smoothing her skirts. Howie helped her. His hand brushed against her breasts and she jerked away.

"You done about all the playing you're going to for now," she said hotly. "Such as it was!"

Howie's embarrassment turned to anger. "Listen. You didn't *have* to follow me up here, Aimie. Nobody asked you to. What'd you want to bother with me for, anyway? You got plenty of others to spread out for, the way I hear it!"

He was sorry the minute he said it. He'd lost none of his desire for her at all. If anything, looking at her now, he wanted her more than ever.

"Aimie. I didn't mean that."

"It don't matter." She looked away, down the hill. "I 'spect it's true enough."

"Aimie . . ."

She looked back, faced him. "You want to know why I come after you, Burt? Truly? I wasn't lyin' about . . . what you done to me. I was all hot and ready and . . . I mean it, Burt, it ain't like that with me. Not a lot, anyway. Only it was with you, and . . ."

"And what, Aimie?"

She bit her lip. "And . . . I knew you hadn't had anyone before. I could tell that. And, Lordee, it was something knowin—"

Howie hit her. He didn't want to, but a second before it happened he knew he couldn't stop. And then he was on her, tearing cloth and tossing it aside until she was naked under the sky. He gazed at the awful whiteness of her, loving and hating what he saw, holding her tight against the ground. She stared up at him, eyes wide with fright.

"I ain't nobody's prize fool," he said harshly, "you hear?"

"Burt!"

He slapped her hard, then thrust into her savagely. She cried out and he stopped her with his mouth. He let his hands sink into her breasts. Her nails raked at his eyes, clawed his back. He tore into her again and again.

Aimie fought him. She bit at his mouth and flailed out with her legs. Her hands tore at his flesh. In a moment, though, he knew something strange and different was happening. Aimie still struggled against him, but it wasn't the same. She pulled the pain from him, drank it in thirstily. And when she was certain there was no more there, she triumphantly drew the last he had to give and he exploded in her again. She threw herself up to meet him and he watched in wonder as her mouth opened slackly in a low moan of pleasure.

"Aimie. Aimie, I..."

Her eyes opened and a smile creased the corners of her mouth. "Burt, if you start in tellin' me how *sorry* you are 'bout something or other, I'll...I'll...." She stopped, and her expression made him laugh with her. He moved down to take her up in his arms and she came to meet him.

He held her a long time, not saying anything. He didn't want to talk and spoil the wonder of what had happened there. It was something you just couldn't say right with words. Finally, he bent to kiss her and found her sleeping, a funny smile on her lips. Maybe she was thinking the same thing, he decided. Maybe....

The sound rolled up through the valley and climbed the low hills, cutting the chill night air like a knife. Aimie sat up, frightened. Howie held her close. He felt suddenly tired and empty; visions of riding off on a stolen horse—maybe even with Aimie, now—vanished and fell away. Someone had blown a warhorn at the river, and every driver who heard it knew Lathan was finally on their heels.

17

The rider who stumbled late into camp and started the war-horn wailing killed his mount getting there, but the warning he brought was worth more than a good horse. The rumor was true, Lathan was definitely on the move. A strong element—nobody knew just how strong—had broken out of Colorado, streaked boldly through government territory, and was now less than two-hundred miles away in Old Missouri. Nobody doubted that the big herd was their target.

The news came as no surprise to anyone. Trouble had been expected all along, which was why the army was on its way across Arkansas Territory to meet them. The only real question was: who'd find them first?

"Don't know any other way it could be," Pardo observed stoically. "Lathan's hungry, and there ain't hardly nothing he can do but try an' fill his belly."

Everyone agreed that was so. But even if you knew for certain the river was high and flooding, you could always hope it wouldn't get there.

When the drive began, most of the owners had said that no matter what happened, the herd would be kept together. There was, after all, strength in numbers. Pardo disagreed with this and had made himself heard since joining the drive. Why bunch up and make it easy for Lathan to get all the apples in one neat basket?

"I ain't got no say in this maybe," he told them, "since I don't own anything and won't lose nothin' whether we make it or not. 'Cept maybe my hide, which ain't likely worth much. But it appears to me that it's a sight better to git something 'stead of nothing. Which is what you're *fixing* to do.''

Pardo's friend Jess argued violently against the idea. ''What you're figuring on is exactly what Lathan wants us to do,'' he said. ''Divide one strong force into three or four weak ones, strung out from here to nowhere. Hell, Lathan'd be herding us to the slaughterhouse same as if we was meat!''

Jess fought until he was blue in the face, but nothing came of it. Pardo had done his homework well. Owners and drivers alike respected his judgement. And the truth was, most everyone said, the herd wasn't all that strong anyway—not against trained soldiers who'd all be mounted and carrying firearms and not worrying about fighting and keeping scared meat together at the same time. The only real chance they'd ever had was the one still open to them now. Don't get caught by Lathan in the first place. Nothing had changed that.

At sunup the herd divided into three rough sections. One, loosely guarded, headed straight south, following the eastern bank of the Big River. The south was safe government territory and, though a long march would weaken it, the drivers could turn the herd back north and west as soon as the army made contact with the upper segments.

The other two elements headed west across the river. One of these, led by Pardo, would go straight and fast for the army. The other, with a large part of the herd, would move along a southwesterly route not too far away, with minimum protection, and would join Pardo's group as soon as the army was sighted. This left Pardo with what amounted to a diversionary force: more guards and less meat. It was the section of the herd Lathan would have to hit first, the one with the most strength and the least to lose.

With much to be done, and no sleep for any man on the drive, Howie had little time to think about his aches or bruises, or bemoan the loss of his chance to get away from Pardo. Even Aimie was briefly forgotten. Once, while the herd was moving toward the river, he caught a questioning look from Cory. But Cory didn't ask him what had happened and Howie was much relieved that he didn't.

Near noon, he sat his mount with Pardo and Cory, watching the last of the herd cross the river. The job had taken most of the morning. The river was no more than waist high anywhere, but meat never did like the water. And this morning, the drivers were doing more harm than good, being in a hurry to get moving. Howie thought that meat was sometimes smarter than people gave them credit for; he was sure the herd was spookier than usual because they smelled man-fear all around them.

"Folks say it was some river once," Pardo commented. He leaned over his mount and spit on the ground. "Split the country right down the middle."

Cory shook his head soberly. "Sure ain't much now," he drawled.

Pardo looked at him. "Well, *now* ain't *then*, is it? It was near the biggest there was anywhere once't. Only the War done something to it."

"The War did."

"That's what I said."

"Must of been some War," Cory grinned. "I haven't heard much that ain't been blamed on it."

Pardo pulled himself erect and looked holes through Cory. Then he jerked his mount around and left them in dust. Howie watched him go, keeping his face straight as could be. Pardo wasn't much for jokes, unless he was doing the joking.

Urging his mount through sluggish brown water, he followed Cory across the river. The herd was over and there was no more use watching for stragglers. The only job now was splitting off the last of the sections that would take the southwesterly trail below them. The drivers knew their jobs and the herd was soon on its way.

On the tail end of the drive were the followers they'd picked up along the trek. Most had decided to try the more treacherous route, figuring it was also likely the safest and quickest, if they met the army on time. Anyway, they argued, Lathan was after meat and wouldn't be looking to run down pot sellers and farmers with empty wagons.

There were gamblers with their women in tow, loaded with trail packs and camp gear. Merchants and corn whiskey dealers pulled hastily loaded carts through the shallow water. They were all afoot; few had ever been close to a horse before. Mounts were for fighting men, or whoever could get and hold one of the rare animals for himself. Less than a quarter of the forty-odd drivers in Pardo's group were mounted. And not half of that number had guns. Howie decided he probably ought to feel like something special—even if his horse belonged to Pardo and his pistol couldn't hurt anyone.

Before he splashed up on the far bank he turned and squinted back across. But if Aimie was there, he couldn't pick her out of the dust-covered followers.

At noon, Pardo and Jess had an argument that came near to going past loud talking and hard looks. The land was flat and easy beyond the river and Jess wanted to speed up the herd some. Pardo said he could understand Jess and the others being anxious to get where they were going, but he didn't see any use getting there with three-thousand head of dead meat. Jess flared up and said it wasn't any of Pardo's meat in the first place—dead or otherwise. The end was they did speed up some—then slowed a little—so no one could tell much difference one way or the other.

Howie heard some of it, bringing water bags up to Pardo, but he got hastily away as soon as he could.

"What you think's going to happen?" he asked Cory later. "You figure Lathan'll git here or the army?"

"No way of telling," Cory shrugged. He sat his mount chewing a stick he'd snapped off a scrub tree. "You can't never say about Lathan. He's fooled that old army before, though."

"You didn't like soldiering much, did you?"

Cory chuckled and grinned. "Guess you could say that."

"What's it like?" Howie asked. "I mean, I *know* I wouldn't want to do it either. I don't care much for soldiers."

Cory's face screwed up in a frown. "What it's like is sittin' around waiting to do nothing forever. Gittin' one place, and coming back to where you was. Going here and then marchin' there—and then sitting some more in the cold 'till your ass falls off. And then, all of a sudden like, some fool's throwin' lead at you or coming over the hill screamin' with a big blade flashing and you're wishing to shit you was back doin' nothin' again." Cory sighed and shook his head. "It's some wearin' on the mind and body, Burt."

"Ain't as good as driving, huh?"

Cory held him with one eye. "Lordee, boy!" He spit wood splinters and wiped his mouth. "Where'd you get the idea one piece of work's better'n another? Hell, it's *all* bad!"

Howie laughed. "That what you going to do when we get to Badlands? Nothing?"

"Not if I want to keep eating," he said sourly. He squinted hard at Howie. "You sure loaded up with questions today, ain't you?"

Howie colored and looked at his hands. "I didn't mean nothin' by it. Just talking..."

Cory grunted to himself. "Well... What I figure on doing—after I sober up and get tired of women—is headin' south." He winked at Howie. "Might even go after War booty."

Howie's eyes widened, then he decided Cory was playing with him.

"No, I ain't kiddin' at all," Cory assured him. "There's still booty to be found from the War. Gold and silver and all kinds of metals. Specially copper an' stuff. People find it all the time. There was some fellers in Colorado, right before the war, found a whole building full of goodies. Rain hadn't got in or nothing. Know what was in there? *Coils* of copper. Looked just like rope, they say—big around as your arm. Hundreds of reels of it, all higher'n a man.

The idea intrigued Howie. "What'd they do with it?"

"Huh?" Cory turned on his mount and laughed. "Why, they got rich as old kings, is what they did. Raised all kinds of hell. 'Till one figured he wanted what the other'n had, too, and they blew a bunch of holes in each other. Right smart couple of fellers.''

Cory paused, gazing thoughtfully past the horizon. '''Course, you want to make a *real* find, now. What you want to do is stumble on a whole passle of guns. Lord, I'd rather find me a cache of new weapons than a barrel of gold!'' He laughed. ''So would everyone else. But there's still finds bein' made, an' it only takes one to make a man rich. And it'll be that way until we can make 'em the way they used to . . . and I don't see *that* comin' soon.''

Howie kept his silence a long minute. ''Cory,'' he said finally, ''I'd like to do that. I truly would.''

Cory started to answer, then caught his meaning. ''You would, huh?''

''I surely would.''

''Well, I don't imagine Pardo'd take much to you going off treasure hunting with me, now would he?''

Howie didn't answer. He looked away from Cory and stared out over the herd. ''You know Pardo very long?'' he asked finally.

''Not any longer than he's been on the drive. Knew of him, though.''

''You mean you heard things.''

''Well, sure. This and that.''

''What kind of things?''

Cory looked at him curiously. ''He's *your* pa, Burt. Reckon you know more 'bout him than I do.''

Howie looked straight ahead. Well, he'd done it now. If Cory took it into his head to tell Pardo he'd been asking questions . . .

Cory suddenly seemed to make up his mind about something. He leaned over and gripped Howie's reins and turned him about.

''Listen, boy,'' he said quickly, glancing at the head of the herd, ''what I ought to do is keep shut, but I ain't got good sense and never have. Thing is, I was talking to Maye and she was talking to Aimie. What I'm saying is, you best take a care who you tell your business to.'' He looked hard at Howie. ''Aimie says you told her Pardo ain't your pa.''

Howie felt his stomach drop. "She . . . did?"

"Uhuh."

"Well, maybe I said it. I don't recall."

Cory ignored him. "If he ain't your pa, what is he, Burt? An' if he's not, I can't say I'm real surprised to hear it."

"He's . . . just kind of someone I know, I guess."

"You guess."

"Cory . . ."

"You mean, like a friend."

Howie felt miserable. "Yeah, sort of. I mean . . ." Cory watched him, and he knew there wasn't anything at all he could say that wouldn't turn out wrong. For sure, he couldn't tell the truth. Cory might be about the only friend he had, but there were some things you didn't dare talk about to anyone, no matter how much you might want to.

"Burt," Cory told him, guessing his thoughts, "I ain't sticking my nose in where it don't belong. You're right enough to keep to yourself. Only . . ." He hesitated a moment. "You got any trouble you need gettin' out of?"

Howie looked at him and kept straight as he could. "Everything's fine, Cory. Honest it is."

"Yeah, well that's good." It was plain Cory didn't believe him at all.

"And I'm obliged. About what you said."

Cory shrugged. "Well, that's what friends are for, ain't it?"

Howie felt awful, then, about what he'd been thinking. Maybe it was wrong to try to keep everything to yourself. Maybe Cory was someone he *could* talk to. It was clear he didn't like Pardo. That was a start. And if he ever hoped to get away when the drive was over. . . . It was something worth thinking about, he decided. There was still plenty of time. But he knew he was already sure what he was going to do. It made him feel some better, but it would make the waiting harder, now.

From the corner of his eyes, he caught sudden motion at the edge of the herd, and automatically started his mount forward. Cory put out an arm to stop him. Howie gave him a puzzled glance, then understood. Klu and Jigger had spotted the commotion, too, and were cutting toward the trouble spot.

It was a common enough problem. Several young bucks had edged a ripe mare into their pack, and the inevitable fight had started, spreading like ripples in a pond. In a few minutes, meat fifty feet off were brawling and grunting away without even knowing why.

Jigger plainly knew little about handling stock, but he knew what he wanted done. Using his boots and his big mount to scatter bodies, he cleared a rough path for his companion. Howie knew Klu hadn't the slightest idea which creature had started the business and that he didn't much care. He rode straight into the bunch and right to his choice, like he'd been thinking about it all winter.

The first crack of his big driver's whip dropped the meat to its knees. It tried to rise once, but Klu was good with his weapon. He slashed again and again, keeping his own rhythm, a high, whistling loop from left to right, right to left. Long red stripes patterned the buck's body. Its eyes rolled blankly to the sky; a mouth opened to cry out, but nothing came.

Long after it was dead, Klu kept the carcass hopping about in the dirt—catching an arm or a leg in his thongs, faster and faster all the time, until the whip near disappeared and it looked like the dead thing was crawling bloodily across the ground on its own. Then, as quickly as it started it was over, and Klu and Jigger cut a dusty path back through the herd.

Other creatures passed the body, looked at it vacantly and moved on. A few tried to reach down and dip their fingers in fresh blood, but a driver steered them away. Soon, a butcher from the back of the herd pulled up with his cart and helper to slit the buck's throat and bleed him. The helper tossed him in the cart and the two pulled the meat away; a red trail followed the rattling wheels back to the rear.

Cory sat his horse and studied the situation thoughtfully. "There wasn't no call for that," he said flatly. "Just pure meanness, and waste. A dead stud ain't good for nothing. Tougher'n hell to chew, and he sure isn't goin' to breed no more.'' He looked straight at Howie. "You asked, Burt, and I'll tell you I heard some about Pardo all right, but no more'n you hear about a lot of fellers.'' He glanced back at the herd. "Don't guess you need to hear much, though, seein' what he runs with...."

18

When the Big River was four days behind, even Cory had to admit there was some good to be said for working. If nothing else, it kept you clear of Pardo. That was something worth doing, and more than one driver learned the truth of this, the hard way.

What the trail leader had in mind was anyone's guess. And if you thought you had him figured, ten minutes later you were guessing again. The first day out he kept the herd going so fast drivers and animals alike were dragging belly by noon. Then, he'd slow to a snail's pace and break every hour or so. Or he'd drive everyone to exhaustion for the next eighteen hours and give 'em two to rest up.

If you had complaints or suggestions you mostly saw Klu and Jigger; Pardo had cut himself off from nearly everyone else. Even old Jess, who still seemed to respect Pardo in spite of their differences, was hard pressed to get along with him now.

"It just appears to me we'd fare better," he explained patiently, "if we kept movin' at a *steady* pace, instead of running one minute and crawlin' ass the next. It just seems that way to me, Pardo."

Pardo eyed him like he'd crawled out from under something. "It does, does it? Well, it don't to me."

Jess tried to swallow his irritation. "This ain't my first drive, you know," he said darkly. "I been out once or twice before."

"Figured you had," Pardo said absently.

"Well, you'd best figure on it good," Jess flushed, "'cause if you haven't got some reason for what you're doing..."

"You'll what, Jess? Get yourself a new driver?"

"By God, that ain't impossible!" Jess fumed.

"It ain't likely, neither."

Jess studied him curiously, like he was trying to read what might be going on in Pardo's head. All the anger was out of him, now. He simply wanted to know what in all Hell might be going on, and why.

"I guess maybe I better talk to the rest of the owners," he said plainly, "and get back to you. We're going to have some answers, Pardo. You might as well figure on that." He walked away, feeling the younger man's eyes looking after him.

Not more than an hour later Pardo rode up to him grinning, like nothing had happened between them. "I guess I got off wrong back there, Jess," he said. "There's a couple of things you ain't thinking on, and maybe I should've gone into 'em some."

"Might be you should have," Jess agreed.

Pardo bit a corner of his beard and looked at the ground. "I don't mean to offend none, Jess, but it doesn't matter much how many *drives* you been on, or how much you know about stock. 'Cause this ain't exactly a drive we're on now. It's more like a *e*-vasion than anything else. In army talk that's..."

"I know what it means."

"Uhuh." Pardo squinted at the sun, so all the color went out of his eyes. "Well I ain't real sure you do. 'Cause when you raised all Hell back there about stoppin' and startin' and going this way and that I seen real clear you ain't got much of a head for army thinking."

Jess' brow clouded. He shifted on his mount impatiently. "Pardo, just git on with whatever it is you're trying to say."

"What we're trying to do," said Pardo, "is get from one place to another without meeting Lathan in the middle. Only *you're* forgettin' Lathan wants this here meat pretty bad an' is willing to go some to get it. He knows exactly where we started from, Jess, where we're going, and how long it takes to get there. And if we git there your way, he's going to be *right* on the button." He made his point with a big finger on Jess' chest.

The old man looked down his chin and swept the hand off his jacket. "All right. I see what you're gettin' at. Only..."

"Only I don't figure on being where Lathan wants us to be. Where we'll be is ahead—or behind—the spot he's got in mind."

"Which?"

Pardo grinned sheepishly. "Now that I ain't saying. There's too many long ears and noses in this drive for my liking."

Jess frowned. "You think we got spies?"

Pardo let out a breath. "'Course we do, Jess. You think Lathan ain't covering ever' bet he's got down?"

"Well it ain't me!" Jess snapped. "So you can damn well tell me what you got in mind!"

"I will," Pardo said soberly. He jerked his reins and let his mount skitter away. "Right soon, Jess."

Jess bit off words after him, but Pardo pretended not to hear.

Jess kept grumbling, but mostly to himself. And while he didn't feel much better after Pardo's explanation, he decided there wasn't any use talking about it, either. They were a week into the drive and, whether he liked it or not, they were committed to Pardo's erratic plan. It was too late now to get the herd moving at a regular pace. And, he told himself, if Pardo irritated the Hell out of him, what of it? They'd hired the man because he had a name for outslicking greased eels. If they'd wanted a polite-talking storekeeper, why, they should have got one sooner. He just hoped it wouldn't be too long before they met the army's troopers coming out of Badlands. Jess decided he'd feel a lot better when that happened.

At dawn the next morning a driver came in fast from the south. He announced that the lower herd was turning to join them as quick as they could. That farmers along the way said Lathan had troopers thick as flies nosing through the hills there.

And that, Jess told himself sourly, is all the Hell we need.

Pardo seemed to take the news in stride. "It's your meat, not mine," he told Jess and the owners. "Maybe Lathan's in the south, an' maybe he ain't." Which was all he'd say on the subject, and didn't tell anyone much of anything.

The owners, though, found it hard to take this new development lightly. For one thing, the problem of feed for the stock was growing more critical daily. The addition of the southern herd didn't help matters. A long, overland drive simply wasn't the way to make money on meat. Not ordinarily, anyway. What you did was fatten up a herd and send it lazily downriver by barge. That way, stock didn't use up energy faster than you could feed them. Still, unusual times called for unusual measures, as Jess put it. And when you were being paid seven or eight times what a side of meat was worth, a man was tempted to take some risks.

So the herd went on short rations, and foragers rode farther and faster to find grain to add to the stores. Stock that died or lagged behind was slaughtered and ground into feed on the spot, to give extra energy to the living.

"Way I see it," Cory observed wryly, "is we'll git to Badlands with about half a dozen head. But they'll be the fattest sons of bitches you ever seen!"

ABOUT THE BEST you could say about Pardo, Howie decided, was that you never *could* say, for sure. One day he'd laugh out loud and slap you on the back and tell you what a fine lad you were; and the next he'd likely ride up and knock you clean off your mount for nothing at all. It made a person jittery, wondering what was coming next, and he was sure Pardo did it for just that reason. He was certain nothing Pardo could do would surprise him, but he was totally unprepared for the shooting lessons.

"Time you learned how to handle arms, boy," Pardo announced suddenly. Howie was rounding up two young mares that had wandered off with a buck, and Pardo simply pulled him away and stuck another driver in his place.

"No sense carryin' around weapons you can't use," he said. "They ain't no better than clubs unless you know what to do with 'em."

Howie hid his shock—and excitement. He'd learned the wisdom of concealing both.

Pardo was a good teacher and Howie was eager to learn. He caught on quickly to the basics, and even Pardo was plainly impressed. "You got a good eye," he said simply, "a real natural feel for it."

Howie sensed there was a lot he wasn't saying. He knew, right off, that he was good, and that Pardo knew it, too. He never was sure how hard firing and hitting a target was supposed to be. It seemed like the most natural thing in the world, same as breathing. It wasn't a matter of just figuring distance, taking aim, and squeezing off a shot. You *felt* all that—like your eye and your arm had reached out past the barrel of your weapon and touched the target. You knew that was where your shot was supposed to go and it did.

After they'd been out twice with the pistol, Pardo gave him back his other weapon, the rifle he'd taken off one of Jacob's troopers. With his first few shots Howie shattered a row of small wood chips Pardo lined up for him. Then he threw sticks in the air and solemnly announced Howie was to hit them before they fell. Out of eight tries, Howie split six.

He was disappointed, and showed it. "I reckon I'll get better with some practice," he muttered.

Pardo eyed him narrowly. "Yeah. Well I sure do hope so."

On the way back to camp that evening Pardo took a bright red neckerchief out of his pocket and gave it to Howie. "It's for you," he said. "Wear it 'round your arm."

Howie was puzzled. "What for?"

"Well, godamn, just 'cause I said so!" Pardo snapped.

Howie shrugged and did as he was told. It was better than getting knocked flat, which he figured Pardo was about to do.

"If you don't know what it means I'll tell you," Pardo grumbled. "Where I come from it says a boy's learned his arms, and ain't a boy no more." He looked hard at Howie. "That all *right* with you? That I give it to you?" He slapped his mount, not waiting for an answer, and left Howie behind.

ONCE, SOMETHING PECULIAR happened that Howie didn't forget. They had left their mounts and walked up a narrow gully looking for targets. The land was dry and featureless with little to see except scrub and stone. Suddenly, Pardo froze and grabbed his arm tightly.

"Look, right over there," he whispered. "By that shady bush to the left."

Squinting, Howie could see nothing for a moment. There was a bush and a sandy-colored rock. The rock seemed marbled, like some other kind of stone veined through it. He looked questioningly at Pardo. Just then the rock twitched, found legs, and skittered away down the gully.

"Lor*dee*!" Howie gasped.

Pardo grinned, showing yellow teeth. "Rabut. They're coming back. Slow like. An' some of the others, too. Only you don't spot 'em much 'less you get down past the border."

"But . . . what in the world was it?" Howie wanted to know.

Pardo looked pained. "I told you, boy. Rabut. It's a animal."

"There ain't any animals," Howie said flatly. "'Cept one."

"You seen it, didn't you?"

"I . . . think so."

"Think so, nothing. You did or you didn't."

"Well . . ."

"Then there is animals, if you seen one. Not many, but they sure didn't all die out, like folks'd have you think." He looked mischievously at Howie. "I eat one once. In Mexico."

"Pardo!" Howie sucked in a breath, horrified. "Don't you know they're—"

"Uhuh. *Un*clean. Only at the time I didn't have no Scriptures to eat instead, an' my belly'd been rubbing my backbone for 'bout a week. It sure seemed tasty at the time." He patted his flat stomach and laughed. "So far, I ain't growed no horns or nothing. And don't figure I will."

IF THE ARRIVAL of the southern herd created problems for the drive, it solved one for Howie. He discovered that Aimie was neither lost, strayed, nor stolen. She and Maye and the half dozen other girls in their party had followed their employer along the southern route. Seth DeGuire was a businessman, and he'd decided at Big River that while there'd be fewer customers for his girls, white corn, and games of chance on the lower route, he'd also be less likely to meet Lathan's raiders or government troops. A little profit was better than none, and armies—no matter who they belonged to—had a habit of forgetting to pay for what they got.

It was a subject that Aimie reluctantly mentioned to Howie. "You come and see me all the time, and...you don't never bring me nothing."

"Like what?" asked Howie. He knew very well what she meant, but it was a subject he'd put out of his mind. The idea that Aimie bared all that wonderful flesh to others—and got paid for it—was something he refused to think about.

"Burt..." She lowered her eyes and ran a finger along his arm. Howie shivered and pulled away. "Burt, I'm *supposed* to. *You* know..."

"He tell you that?" Howie demanded hotly. "That I got to quit coming?" He'd only seen Aimie's employer once, but he hated the man with a fierce anger.

"Seth?" Aimie looked pained and shook her head. "Lord, no. He don't have any idea I don't.... If he did, Burt..."

"He'd what? If he ever hurt you or anything, Aimie..." Aimie said nothing. "I'll...quit comin' if it gets you in trouble."

"No, I don't *want* you to do that, Burt."

"Well I can't do nothing else."

"Just a few coppers or something would—be okay."

"I ain't *got* a few coppers," he said darkly. "Aimie, I don't want to talk about it no more."

"Just anything'd do...."

"And I told you I ain't got anything. If you want me to stop coming, just say so, Aimie!"

He wondered what he'd do if she said just that. She didn't, though, and he kept seeing her, as often as he could. And when he wasn't with her he thought about dark, tousled hair and cream-colored breasts and the way her lips parted lazily. And then he itched all over until he could see her again.

Aimie had opened doors more wondrous than he'd ever imagined, even in his wildest daydreams. Why, you could lie awake hot summer nights for a hundred years, thinking about what a girl'd be like—but it wasn't *any*thing like that at all!

"WHAT YOU'RE GOIN' to do," Cory warned him, "is wear it out the first year you use it. I heard of that happening."

Howie turned away and buried his face in his meal, so Cory couldn't see the color in his cheeks.

Cory laughed. "Well, it's so. Way *you're* going..." He shook his head and grinned at Howie's back. "Kind of like that stuff, don't you?"

Howie didn't answer.

"I'm serious. You watch it, Burt. First thing you know..."

"Cory." Howie turned on him. "It ain't nothin' I want to talk about. You hear?"

Cory read his look, but ignored it. "She give you that pretty red neckerchief?"

"No, she didn't!" Howie snapped.

"Uhuh."

"Well, she didn't!"

Cory looked at him with mock astonishment. "Lordee, you mean you got more'n *one* going? You goin' to kill yourself for sure, boy."

Howie dropped his clay plate. "That ain't so."

"What ain't?"

"About Aimie."

"Where'd you git it, then?"

"I said it wasn't Aimie or no one else."

"Uhuh."

"Damn you Cory, Pardo gave it to me!" he blurted out. "It's for learnin' to shoot good an' I reckon I earned it. I bet I'm better'n you are, too!" He was immediately sorry he'd opened his mouth, but it was too late to stop.

Cory sat down his plate. For a moment his eyes went hard, then the lazy grin bent the corners of his mouth again. "Yeah. Okay, kid..."

Howie didn't know what to say. "Listen. I didn't mean nothing by that."

"Didn't figure you did."

Howie made an effort to finish his meat and beans.

"I was riding you some," said Cory. "And I didn't mean nothing, either. Only... I don't get it about the 'kerchief. How come Pardo did that?"

Howie didn't much want to talk about it anymore, but he explained what Pardo had told him.

Cory made a face. "I never heard of wearin' no red hankie 'round your arm just 'cause you done a little shooting."

"Pardo said they do it all the time, so I reckon they do."

"Uhuh." Cory chewed over that. He scratched his chin and squinted into the low hills. "If he give *me* something, I'd likely check it over real close to figure why. That don't sound like the same Pardo to me."

Howie didn't know how to answer that. "I reckon he ain't hardly ever the same," he said lamely.

WHICH WAS LIKELY RIGHT, Howie decided. After the next shooting ride into the hills, he and Pardo were flanking the herd back to camp when the man suddenly pulled up hard and leaned forward on his mount.

"Lor*dee*!" Pardo made a low noise in his throat. "Now *that's* a fine lookin' animal, if I do say so." He nodded toward a long-bodied mare with high breasts at the edge of the pack. "Bet them legs'd fair squeeze the guts out of a man, you think?"

He looked and caught Howie's expression. A big grin spread his beard. "Now, don't tell me you ain't never rooted meat? An' I thought you was a farm boy."

Howie's mind flashed back to green fern and a high oak. And men hanging stiffly from a stout branch. Pardo read his eyes. "Well don't you git uppity now," he growled. "The one you been studdin' ain't a whole lot better...."

He truly hated Pardo then, more than ever.

THAT NIGHT he sought out Aimie and stayed with her until it was nearly dawn. If Seth or anyone else had interfered, he was certain he would have killed them on the spot. It was a strange, savage kind of lovemaking; much like their first night together. Howie didn't pretend to understand his feelings. He was bewildered and fiercely excited by the things that happened between them. He knew he both loved and hated Aimie, and didn't see how that could be. Aimie's eyes told him she knew a great deal more about what was going through his mind than he did. Howie didn't ask, though—he was afraid to really know what was there.

When he made his way wearily back to the drivers' camp, the sky was gray with the first somber hints of morning. The herd was nearly through Arkansas Territory. Tomorrow, or the next day, they'd likely meet scouts from the army. Even Pardo said the worst was over. Maybe, thought Howie. Or maybe for him it was just beginning. What would he do when he found himself in the middle of government troopers again? Did they know about him in Badlands? Had word gotten that far? He was too tired, now, to worry. He pulled his blankets about him, and was asleep nearly as soon as he hit the ground.

A half hour later the sun tipped the edge of the low hills, and Lathan's raiders hit the herd.

19

A heavy mist still clung to the ground, and the sun was dull copper behind it. The raiders moved in shadow browns and greens, the color of morning. Their horses, trained in war, picked their steps carefully over damp earth. Death rode quietly through the camp, but there was little time to think of dying. Men simply sighed back into darkness with sleep in their eyes, as if they'd come awake too soon....

HOWIE SAT UP straight, wondering if he was truly awake or still dreaming. Figures moved about him like silent wraiths, dark ghosts in a gray sea. Branches scraped behind him and a horse blew air. He turned, saw the tall rider loom over him, the big pistol swinging down to cover him. To his right, a driver kicked blankets aside and brought his weapon up fast. The rider's gun roared and the driver's eyes went suddenly empty. The tall man turned in his saddle and looked down at Howie for a long moment, then jerked his mount aside and trotted quickly past the draw.

Howie didn't look at the dead man. He set his teeth and found his rifle, snapped a cartridge in the chamber and brought the gun to his shoulder. The rider's back covered his sights and he squeezed the trigger gently.

The big fist came out of nowhere and sent him sprawling. Howie's shot snapped wood overhead. He sat up, shook his head. A shadow touched the ground and he stared up at the dark, scowling face.

"Jigger!" Howie's mouth opened in surprise. "Jigger, what—"

Jigger jerked the weapon out of his hand and reached for him with a big paw. Howie rolled away. Jigger took one quick step and pulled him roughly to his feet, tore the pistol from his belt and tossed him aside.

Howie got to his feet in time to see Jigger's broad back disappear in the brush. He stared after the man, bewildered. Now what in hell was all *that* about? Had Jigger gone crazy?

A shot nearby turned him around. Another weapon answered, further away. The sharp smell of powder stung his nostrils. Down the draw, a man cried out.

Then—nothing. A terrible silence fell over the camp, and there was only the harsh round ball of the sun blazing up to burn the mist away.

Howie stood where he was for a long moment, uncertain which way to turn, what to do next. The silence was a fearsome thing. You could almost see it, rising on the morning heat. Where *was* everybody? Lord, were they all dead—raiders and drivers alike—except him and Jigger?

A few steps past the trail he came to a break in the trees and saw the dead scattered up and down the draw. He stood a while and looked at them curiously. Funny, they didn't *seem* dead at all. It was more like they'd just fallen down drunk or something, and didn't care to get up for a while. It wasn't at all like Pa or his mother had—

Remembrance hit him hard, grabbing his belly and bringing bile to his throat. He turned away quickly and shut his eyes to the dead men.

Not anymore. He wouldn't let it happen like that again!

The idea of just walking up and seeing one of the dead faces, knowing right then it was somebody he'd talked to. It was something he couldn't do right now. Maybe not ever. What if it was old Jess, or Cory. He shook his head violently and moved back down the draw. He didn't want to think about that. Anyway, it wouldn't *be* Cory. Cory was all right. They were going to do things together, like finding treasure.

A man called out somewhere to his right. Another answered, closer by. Howie dropped to cover, listened a moment, then moved quietly through the grove, away from the voices. Finally, he went to ground and made a wide circle back past the trees, bringing him up behind where he figured the first man ought to be.

A dozen rebel riders were bunched up by the end of the draw, where the trail twisted into the woods past the main camp. They sat their mounts easy, tall men in earth colors squinting against the sudden brightness of morning. One looked off to the east, where the herd was bedded, and pointed. Another man nodded and rode away.

Howie's heart leaped. Lor*dee*, he hadn't even thought about Aimie! What had happened to her? Was she dead, too, like the others? He decided she was probably all right. It didn't make sense killing girls as pretty and willing as Aimie. The gamblers, now, and the merchants who'd followed them all the way from Big River—that was something else again.

A thought struck him. Maybe he could work his way around the herd, find Aimie, and get her away. And if Cory was still alive—he was ready, now, to admit there was a chance that he wasn't, but if he was, though. . . .

Howie liked the idea. Pardo was likely dead and wouldn't bother him. And Jigger would be hightailing it out, looking after himself. Maybe that's what Jigger had been trying to tell him—in the only way Jigger'd be able to—that fighting back now wouldn't do any more'n get him killed. That the best thing to do was just lie low and wait for a chance to get away.

Only one man who mattered, then, knew he was still alive—the raider who'd had the chance to kill him, and hadn't. Howie was more than a little curious about that, but there wasn't time to let it bother him. Maybe he looked like someone the man knew, a son, or a boy back home where he came from. It didn't much matter. He was alive, and that's what counted. He'd just keep quiet and easy, and wait for the right time to make his move.

The riders laughed about something and Howie raised up cautiously to look. Sun filled the clearing, now, and he could put faces on the rebel horsemen. A dark, bearded man joked with another. The second man drank hastily from his water jug and passed it back to his friend. Howie stared. He nearly came up out of the bushes. *Pardo!* By God, it was! And Jigger, behind him, and Klu—and a handful of other drivers sitting big as you please right square in the middle of the rebels. Laughing and kidding around like nothing had happened!

Howie shook his head. It didn't make sense. Why, if Lathan had taken the herd....

Something cold as winter reached inside and held him. Breath stuck in his throat and faces in the clearing blurred behind hot tears. All he could see were the bright red 'kerchiefs Pardo and Klu and Jigger and the rebel soldiers wore 'round their sleeves. Blood-red, just like his own. Suddenly, he knew why Cory was dead and he was alive, and the understanding filled him with a shame and horror he couldn't bear. The pain carried him into the clearing and brought the awful cry from his throat and the bone-handled knife to his hand. Riders turned to stare. A rebel soldier clawed for his pistol; another yelled something he didn't hear.

It happened so quickly, Pardo could do no more than jerk his mount aside. Howie's blade flashed—the horse screamed and pawed air as steel tore its flesh. Howie stabbed out again and Pardo's boot met his face.

He went down hard, spitting blood and dirt, and came up clawing blindly for his knife. But Pardo was off his mount and all over him. He dragged Howie through the riders and tossed him back in deep brush outside the clearing.

Pardo stood back and looked at him a long time. His face screwed up in a tight wrinkle, like he was trying to decide what smelled bad.

"I jest can't figure..." he started. "I jest...aw, *shit*," he finished, "go*damn* you anyway!"

His eyes flashed dark fury at Howie. His fists trembled at his sides, like he was holding them there by sheer willpower.

"To think I was wondering where you was off to and if you was all right and everything. An' you come on pullin' a stunt like that." He shook his head in disgust. "What I *ought* to do is put a godamn bullet 'tween your eyes and put you out of your—''

Howie went for him. He'd been waiting, watching the man's hands. When the tension went out of his fingers and the fists uncurled, he kicked out hard between Pardo's legs.

Pardo hardly moved. He took the blow off his thigh and deftly whipped a big boot under Howie's guard. Howie doubled up and fought to keep his senses. He was sure he'd felt a rib go.

"You better hug dirt some," Pardo told him wearily. "You done about all the movin' around you can likely handle."

"You *killed* 'em!" Howie yelled. "Cory and Jess and . . . and *ever*'one!" The tears came again and he didn't even try to stop them. "Why, Pardo? Why'd you have to *do* that for? Ever'*one*!"

"Naw, now," Pardo looked pained. "Not *ever*'one, damn it." He sighed deeply, and rolled his eyes to the heavens. "Boy, listen . . ." He squatted down close to Howie. "What you got to understand is I didn't have nothin' *'gainst* any of them fellers. They just wasn't part of the business. Now, can't everyone be, can they?"

"They didn't do nothin' to you," Howie said fiercely. He pulled himself painfully up on one arm. "You didn't have no call for that Pardo. I *liked* him. I liked him a lot!"

"Just shut up, now!" Pardo roared. He grabbed Howie's hair and pulled him straight, so close Howie could see the bright flecks of anger in the man's eyes. "Howie," his voice was deadly calm, now, "you got a lot of learnin' to do yet, and the first thing you better get through that head of yours is that a man ain't got no friends but himself. And the only reason someone *don't* do somethin' to you is he ain't thought of it yet or he don't see no profit in the doing."

"Cory . . ."

"Cory wasn't no different than anyone else. A might slower'n some, maybe. Give him half a chance and he'd—"

Howie pulled away from him. "Pardo, you better do whatever you figure on doin' to me. 'Cause I swear I'm goin' to kill you. Any time I figure I can get the better of you."

Pardo gave him a curious look, then a broad grin spread his whiskered features. "Why, God damn, I believe you will at that!"

"I mean it. I sure as hell do."

"I know you do. I don't reckon I'll let it come between us...it's a natural thing, one feller wantin' to cut up another. 'Course, it ain't real smart *tell*ing a man what you figure on doing to him. Not that I haven't known what *you* was thinkin' since it come to you. Which weren't today, by the way."

He looked hard at Howie. "A man, now, he wouldn't let me see that, Howie. But a boy hasn't got enough smarts to know what's good for him. 'Stead of fighting, he talks about what's right and what ain't...an 'bout *poor* old Cory, layin' out there cold somewhere in the bushes—"

Howie struck out wildly and Pardo easily slapped him away.

"You're the dirtiest son of a bitch there ever was, Pardo!" His whole body shook, and he couldn't make it stop. "There ain't no man worse than you anywhere! Not even—*not even Colonel Jacob!*"

Pardo shook his head sadly. "See what I'm saying? There you go with that *child*-talk again." He pulled himself to his feet and looked down at Howie. "Boy, you just cry 'bout poor old Cory and Jess and whoever all day if you got a mind to. 'Cause I'll tell you one thing..." He cocked a shaggy brow and pointed a long finger at Howie. "Come this time tomorrow morning you're going to be so *God*amn glad it's him dead out there 'stead of you you won't hardly be able to pee straight."

"That ain't so," yelled Howie. "I'm not ever going to think like that!"

"Sure." Pardo spat solemnly on the ground. "Not 'til tomorrow you ain't." He turned and walked back toward the clearing without looking back.

HOWIE SAT where he was until the ache in his side went away and watched the riders move down the draw toward the herd. The smell of heat and dust and horses was heavy on the air, and as the morning breeze picked up, the stink of live meat wafted up to the clearing.

While he sat there, a strange and terrible thing happened to him. Something cried out for help deep inside him, something that was—and wasn't—a part of him anymore. Howie tried desperately to answer. He knew what was happening, but there was nothing he could do to stop it. The thing inside him faded quietly away and was no more.

A great shame flooded in to replace the awful emptiness, but that didn't help the hurt. There wasn't anything that could make it better. It was gone and it took part of the old Howie with it. And it could never quite come back again.

It was a peculiar thing, Howie thought. Everytime someone took something from him, they gave something back. It wasn't always something bad, he realized. Jacob and Pardo had given him terrible needs, things he didn't want at all, but Aimie had given him something deep and wonderful that he wanted very much. It seemed like what people did taught you what to do back to them.

There wasn't any question anymore about going south or running away or anything else. He would stay. He would stay until he was man enough to face Pardo, and kill him. It wasn't a good thing, but it was something that had to be. And of course Pardo would know that, too.

20

The town of Roundtree clustered about the far bend of a dry river. Time, and hot winds from the Kansas prairie, had warped the plank buildings and turned them dusty gray. They leaned slightly westward, now, like thirsty old men waiting for water to bubble up out of the parched ground.

Fifty or so people had lived in Roundtree before Lathan burst out of Colorado to swallow Danefield, Caravel Keep, and a clear road to the flat country. Now, the rebels breathed down Loyalist necks in Dodge and threatened to cut supply lines all the way to Arkansas Territory. Still, there was a relative quiet in the north and the big fighting to the south had made Roundtree's fortune. Near enough to Dodge, but close to rebel ground as well, it was useful to both sides without really belonging to either. The fifty citizens had swelled to five-thousand and new buildings rose out of the prairie as fast as men could stand raw timber on end.

It was a place where arms of all kinds could be bought, sold, or traded. Black powder and fresh water brought nearly the same price until a fair well was drilled close to town. Good raw metal was worth a quarter of its weight in silver. And a fine horse might be bought in Roundtree one week and sold there twice the next—its interim owners mysteriously missing.

The town was thick with rebel and Loyalist soldiers, though neither appeared in uniform, and none would admit to any interest in the war. Most were disguised as merchants, raiders, or thieves; and in truth, there were few among them who couldn't rise to such roles. In Roundtree they spied honestly on one another, plied each other with whiskey and women, and traded mounts for their respective armies—always pocketing a fair piece of change for their troubles. It was common enough here to buy back your own stolen mounts and more than once a soldier had found himself bidding for arms against a brother officer.

It was in Roundtree that Pardo had made his deal with Loyalist leaders to join the big meat herd and see it safely through Tennessee and Arkansas Territory. And it was here that he had promptly doubled his money and then some by selling the deal back to Lathan's men.

No one was foolish enough to think the raid was any accident—certainly no one in Roundtree. And it was common talk that Colonel Monroe in Dodge had put a price on Pardo's head for it. Double-dealing was one thing—that was part of the game—but the loss of such an enormous quantity of meat had hurt the government badly, and they weren't likely to forget it.

Pardo laughed it off in good humor and said, where everyone could hear, that Monroe was more worried about losing a star on his shirt than any meat herd and that's what was truly getting his back up. To copper his bet, though, Howie knew he'd secretly sent word to Monroe that he hadn't had anything to do with the rebels stealing his meat, that he was out the rest of his own money on the deal, and had been lucky to get away with his hide. He even offered to hire out at almost nothing to take soldiers into eastern Colorado to steal the herd *back* from the rebels. Monroe didn't answer and Pardo didn't expect him to.

Meanwhile, Pardo had his hands full getting an arms shipment ready for Jeb Hacker, Lathan's top trader in Roundtree and the man who'd closed the meat deal. Guns were getting scarcer than ever and Hacker had offered a high premium for every weapon Pardo could furnish. Which gave Pardo the idea it'd be plain foolish to deal solely with the rebels; if Monroe wanted to play the fool, why, there were other government officers who'd be glad enough to get in on the bidding. Especially, he figured, if it appeared like the guns were coming from someone who didn't have anything to do with him directly. That'd work just fine and a little healthy competition wouldn't hurt the price any....

IF THAT KIND of business didn't get Pardo's head on a stick, nothing would, Howie thought sourly. It seemed like the man was stretching his luck as far as it'd go, just to see if he could—like he didn't have enough trouble and had to stir up some more.

At the moment, his mind wasn't on Pardo at all, or the cartload of nothing he was supposed to be watching. Harlie and Ketch hauled the small wagon, with the top tied down real careful, while Howie or someone else who could handle a gun kept an eye out for trouble. There wasn't much thinking to a job like that, but someone had to do it. It seemed plain crazy to worry about raiders hitting one little cart right in the middle of Roundtree with the streets full of people—but it happened, sometimes. It wouldn't if Pardo and the other dealers who had something going would keep all their business in one place instead of putting one piece together here, and another somewhere else. Only that was plain *ask*ing for trouble. The man who put his whole operation under one roof would likely be out of business before the day was out. It had happened more than twice in Roundtree.

If you were in the arms and ammunition trade, you knew better than to bring all your craftsmen together, or to let a man who worked for you know who got the parts after him. That was the quickest way in the world to get a knife in your ribs.

So there were carts covered to look like whatever they weren't passing through Roundtree at all hours of the day; some full of valuable metals or sacks of springs and bores, and some full of nothing at all going places where nobody was. The decoys didn't do much good, because there were enough idlers in Roundtree willing to follow most anything for a copper.

The truth was, as Howie and most everyone else knew, the really important goods went from place to place in a man's pocket or under a woman's skirt. It was less trouble than the business with the carts. On the other hand, the more people you used, the greater the chance they also worked for someone else.

In Roundtree, there were guards guarding guards and watchers watching watchers. There was work for everybody. And for the few, like Pardo, who had the cunning and patience to keep an eye on everything in town at once, there was a great deal of money to be made. If you could only keep alive long enough to spend it.

It was enough to make a man's head hurt, Howie thought irritably. When the cart reached Center Street, he left Harlie and Ketch to play out the rest of the game and disappeared quickly into the noonday crowd. Instead of going directly back to the Keep, he circled through the middle of town past the crowded clapboard shops and narrow stalls that stretched the length of Roundtree's main avenue of commerce. It was a noisy, sprawling street; merchants large and small vied for every copper that lined a passing pocket. They were intense, quick-eyed men, hungry for trade at ever-climbing prices. No one knew how long the war might last. Why, God forbid, it could end tomorrow!

There were vegetable sellers, feed mash merchants, and whiskey dealers by the dozen. A man could buy steel blades, wheat flour, hemp rope, cotton cloth, bone tools, clay kettles, horse blankets, real and false gemstones, and pretty girls no more than fourteen summers old. ("And you'll be the first to touch her, sir, I promise you that!")

Howie passed the butcher shop where a small boy tried vainly to keep clouds of black flies from hanging cuts of meat. Next door, a whole carcass dripped grease over sizzling coals, while the butcher's other offspring kept it turning. It was prime young mare, fat and full of juices. Howie hadn't eaten since sunup and the rich smells assailed his empty stomach. He gave the boy coppers for a meaty rib half as long as his forearm and gnawed it happily through the crowd.

He'd gone no more than a block before he was certain someone else was in his tracks—and more than one, at that. He'd felt vaguely uneasy since morning, when they'd loaded the cart on Dryside past the Keep. The usual watchers were about; Howie knew the regulars well enough. But there was someone else, too. He could have easily dismissed the whole business, but if they were still with him after he'd left the cart behind, that was a different brand of trouble altogether.

Keeping to the busy street, he glanced in stalls and shops for another short block, then turned off the avenue and walked south toward the dry river, and Pardo's Keep. They wouldn't push him until they were ready, only Howie didn't figure on waiting for that. Pardo was right about some things. If the problem was low down and dirty enough, he likely had an answer for it. In this case, it was clear as day. Get square behind whatever's after you.

There were at least two of them. Howie figured three. He'd seen the first two briefly, in the crowd behind him. The third was hanging back, playing shadow out of sight.

Howie moved slow and easy, giving his followers no trouble. At the end of the block he crossed the street, stopped a moment to hitch up his belt, then turned casually into a narrow alleyway. The minute he was out of sight he broke into a fast run, circled the block, and cut back to the crowded avenue. He was right where he'd started, just past the butcher shop, a short walk from the corner. He saw them coming back up the hill, out of breath, the anger in their faces clear a good block away. From their dour looks, neither was anxious to report their failure.

He guessed their path ahead, a line of shops across the street with an alley at the end. He cut through the strollers and circled the short block, coming up on the alley from behind. Howie grinned to himself. The man was where he ought to be, in the shadow of a doorway a few steps from the street, his eyes on the crowd.

Howie moved, letting the street noise cover him. He wasn't anxious to handle three of them; the man's companions would be on him soon. With one motion he turned the man hard against the wall and brought his blade up sharp under the throat. The man stiffened, then let his body go loose. He watched Howie over his shoulder and grinned.

"Don't want no trouble, boy. Just a little talk."

"You'll get it," snapped Howie. "Move!"

He glanced quickly up the alley, then herded his prisoner out the back way, stopping only when he was several turns from the avenue, where Roundtree backed into the dry river. There was no one about. Only the slat walls and the hot glare of the flats. He searched the man quickly, found a long steel knife and tossed it aside.

"Now we'll talk some," he announced. "That's what you was wanting, ain't it?" He jammed his own blade back in his belt and replaced it with the pistol. The man looked at the weapon, then at Howie.

"No need for that," he smiled. "Said I didn't want no trouble."

He was a tall man, spare, with no meat on his bones. He had an easy grin and a lazy, friendly manner that set Howie doubly on his guard.

"You been pushing me all day, mister," he said darkly. "What for?"

"A question or two," the man shrugged. "Nothing more."

"Questions about what?"

The man studied him calmly. "Guess we could start off talkin' about Cory."

Howie blinked back his surprise. The words shook him visibly, and the man knew it.

"Ah, you recall him, then."

"I . . . remember him."

"He was a friend, perhaps?"

"I remember him!" Howie flared. "You follow me 'round all day to ask that?"

"That, and a bit more if you can," the man said gently. "Like what happened out there . . . and how come Cory ain't coming back."

Howie licked his lips to get the dry out. "Cory got it 'cause the rebels come up on us and took the herd. He wasn't the only one, either. Weren't too many that made it."

"You did."

Howie stepped back and raised the barrel of his pistol. "Mister, who the hell are you and what's Cory to you? And, don't give me one of them answers that don't say nothin'!"

The man shrugged bony shoulders. "A friend of Cory's is all. Maybe one of yours, too."

"Yeah, I'll just bet."

"Might be I could *help* some."

"Help who? Me?" Howie laughed uneasily. "I don't even know you and you ain't making much sense far as I can see!"

"'Bout as much as you, boy." The man turned lazy eyes on Howie. "Lordee, isn't anyone in Roundtree doesn't know what happened out there. The rebels got the herd all right . . . but not by them*selves* they didn't."

Howie started to protest; the man held up a hand. "Now I ain't sayin' *I* care one way or the other. What I care about is Cory and what happened to him."

"And I just told you," Howie said irritably.

"Ah, you did and you didn't," said the man. He wagged a long finger at Howie. "You said he *died* and I know that. What I'm huntin' for is *how*."

"I already said he—"

"—Died when the rebels took the herd," the man nodded. "And I'm certain that's so. What I don't know is whether one of them did the job, or someone else." He gave Howie a sly wink. "Pardo himself, maybe? Or one of the others? You recall right off which it was?"

Howie stared at him. "You got to be crazy. Or figure I am."

"No," the man blinked at the sun and scratched his scrawny neck. "Don't guess it's either of us, boy. It's the times, mostly. Good men are dying and them that did 'em in are walking the streets with pockets full of silver. Peculiar things are happening everywhere and more'n one man has got hisself tangled in other folk's affairs deeper'n he'd like to be." He grinned affably at Howie. "It is some *hot* out here, you know? Looks to me like friends could talk better in good shade over a drink or two, without pistols and such between 'em."

The man took a slight step forward. Howie backed off warily and waved his weapon. "I told you what happened to Cory," he said harshly. "You can take it or leave it, mister. I got nothing else to say."

"No. Didn't figure you did, right now." The man gave him a tired, curious smile. "Might come to it, though. Can't never tell." Without another word, he turned and started back toward the center of town.

"Hey, now just a damn minute!" Howie yelled after him.

The man didn't answer. He just kept walking, as if Howie wasn't there. Howie stood in the sun with the pistol hanging from his hand, feeling like a plain fool.

21

Howie tried hard to put the whole business aside, but it wouldn't go away. He knew he'd handled it badly. He'd had it all over the skinny little stranger and the man had gotten the best of him.

It made him swell up inside just to think about it. If you didn't take care of yourself in Roundtree, someone else'd sure do it for you. He'd learned his lessons well, and had the scars to prove it. Only—this one had called his bluff and walked clean away.

He knew what had happened. All that talk about Cory had taken the fight out of him and made him act just like a kid again. There wasn't a day passed that he didn't think about Cory—he couldn't forget, and didn't want to. Long ago, though, he had put that part of himself away in a special place that didn't hurt so much. It was there, and he could get to it when he wanted to. Only the stranger had come along and found it and brought it right out in the open.

Howie was sure he was going to be sick. The fat, succulent meat he'd eaten earlier was turning heavy in his stomach. He passed a whiskey seller and wondered if a drink would help. Probably just make things worse. He didn't much like the stuff, anyway.

He tried to think about something else. He thought of Kari Ann and wondered if she was back at the Keep. He thought about the way her eyes looked, gray and smoky and kind of half closed all the time. Like she was just getting out of bed, or thinking about going. He brushed the picture aside. It just made him feel worse, in a different way.

Howie wondered again just who the man was and what he was really after. Maybe he was one of Colonel Monroe's people, just fishing around, trying to spook anyone who worked for Pardo and pick up whatever he could. Probably, he hadn't ever even *known* Cory. Finding out what had happened out there wouldn't be any big thing. One of Pardo's crew could've gotten too much corn whiskey in his gut and talked when he should have been listening.

What was he supposed to do—run and tell Pardo all about it and see if *that* would put some fat in the fire? Make Pardo itchy, so he'd pull something Monroe could hang on him? Or maybe he, Howie, was supposed to keep the meeting to himself and let Monroe slip the word to Pardo that you couldn't trust Howie on the street. Howie kicked a big rock and sent it rattling down the alleyway. Lordee, there was sure a lot more thinking to the stealing business than he'd ever figured!

PARDO'S KEEP was a big, sprawling two-story clapboard left over from Roundtree's early days. At one time or another it had served as a hotel, brothel, town hall, dry goods store, and, finally, a warehouse for stock feed. It still smelled strongly of the latter. Now, it housed Pardo's immediate band, eight men and assorted females.

Pardo was extra careful about who stayed in the Keep. The riders he hired from time to time weren't welcome there and unapproved visitors were frowned upon. Pardo didn't trust the people who lived there, much less those who didn't.

The Keep was on the far edge of town, with no other houses close at hand. It backed up to the dry river bed with plenty of breathing room all around so you could see who was coming before they got there. Lew Renner lazed on the porch with a rifle on his lap. Howie nodded as he went up the board steps and inside. The big front room took up most of the lower floor. There was a kitchen in back with rough cabinets for foodstuffs and cooking gear. Boxes, crates, and straw mattresses littered both the main room and the kitchen. A few patched chairs and broken stools were scattered about, but there was no real furniture as such. The

Keep was a place that kept other people out while you slept, ate, had a woman, or made plans to go somewhere else. No one pretended anyone lived there, or cared to.

Howie tripped over a box of trash, cursed, and kicked it aside. Glass and broken pottery clattered across the board floor; the noise brought Klu stomping halfway down the stairs. The big man glared at him.

"Where the hell you been, boy?"

"None of your godamn business," Howie told him.

Klu muttered something to himself. "Well jest turn your little ass 'round and get it back where you come from. Pardo wants you to haul out to Kearney's right quick and fetch Yargo. He's got a deal goin' on them mounts."

Howie didn't look at him. His foot had gone right through the trash box and left him with grease clear to his ankles. He squatted on a crate and scraped meat tallow from his boot with a stick.

"Listen," said Klu, "you hear me?"

"I hear you, but I ain't in no hurry to go horse ridin' in the hot sun. Reckon you better get someone else."

Klu seemed to think about that. "He didn't say no one else. He said you."

Howie stood and faced him. "It don't make no difference who runs out to Kearney's. Ben Yargo'll be dirt crawlin' drunk and ain't going to have no idea who come after him."

Klu just stood there, looking at him. Howie could hardly see his eyes; they were tiny black points lost under heavy brows. Klu was wearing dirty cotton pants and no shirt. The tangled hair from his beard flowed into the thick mat that covered his powerful chest and shoulders. "Well," he growled finally, "Pardo said you was to do it."

"I ain't *going* to do it, though," Howie explained flatly. "So it'll have to be Lew or Jake or *who*ever."

Klu's face reddened. His big fists tightened and, for a moment, Howie thought he might leap right off the stairs. Instead, he shot Howie a look of open disgust and thundered down the steps and past him. Howie heard his great voice roar at Lew, then the man scrambled off the porch for his mount.

Even a few weeks before it might have been a different story. Klu could still squeeze the life out of Howie—that hadn't changed. But Howie wasn't the same anymore and Klu seemed to sense it. He'd seen it long before anyone else, including Pardo and Howie himself. There was more man there now and less boy. He was quick with a knife and better than Pardo with a pistol.

Klu didn't fear him—there wasn't anything moving the big man was scared to tackle. But Klu was closer to the earth than most men; he took a lot more stock in things he smelled on the air or felt in his gut than he did in the thoughts that came to his head. And the thing he knew about Howie was that you'd likely be dead about one fine hair *before* you had any idea Howie meant to put a neat little hole between your eyes. More than that, he'd let Howie have his way this time because he was certain Howie himself had no idea just when he'd decide to kill a man.

Howie checked his boots again and glanced disdainfully about the room. He was dead sure what his mother would've said about Pardo's Keep, and she'd be close to right, too. Anyone who didn't know better would figure stock lived there instead of people. He hitched his belt and moved up the stairs to his room.

"Well, *hey* now."

The voice turned him around. Kari Ann stood against the kitchen door, watching him. She was a tall girl, slim and lean as a sapling, with skin as sun-dark as Howie's. Her hair, wet from washing, hung in black strands about her shoulders. The man's shirt she wore near swallowed her up, and she made no effort to keep buttons where they belonged. Howie pretended not to notice there was nothing under the shirt except Kari Ann. Kari saw him and gave him a look of quiet amusement.

"Baby, old Klu is going to *jump* you good one of these days. You know?"

"He might."

Kari made a face and laughed to herself.

"What's that supposed to mean?"

"Nothing."

"Well, what?"

"*Noth*ing!"

Howie scowled and muttered to himself. "Anything you say ever mean somethin'?"

"Sometimes."

"When? I don't reckon I recall."

Kari pursed her lips and frowned thoughtfully. "Leeet's see now..."

Howie shook his head and turned up the stairs. Kari laughed and followed, then passed him, long legs flying. In his room, she dropped down on his straw mattress and crossed her ankles. From her shirt pocket she took a small piece of machined metal and a file no longer than her fingers. Holding the piece close to her eyes, she turned it in the sunlight, studying every angle intently. Finally, she ran the file over the tiny plane for a full minute, stopped, turned the piece slightly, then started on another. She worked in quick, short strokes. The frown lines deepened between her eyes and her tongue darted between white teeth to worry the corners of her mouth. When she was satisfied, she laid the file aside and started polishing the piece carefully with the corner of her shirt. The harder she polished, the more the shirt revealed of Kari Ann. Kari didn't notice, or care to.

Howie groaned to himself and looked away. He dipped his head in the clay basin in the corner of his room and scrubbed his face vigorously. He didn't dare turn around and face Kari now. She'd know right off what was happening to him.

Any other right-thinking girl'd get all excited and start crawling all over him, he thought grimly. Not Kari Ann, though. *She'd* likely roll over and kick her legs in the air and laugh herself sick. Howie knew plenty of girls in Roundtree—and he didn't have trouble getting them in bed, either. All except Kari. Who lived right under the same roof and wouldn't let him do anything but look. And hell, she let everybody do that. Kari didn't seem to care one way or the other whether she was neck deep in a fancy dress or half-ass naked.

Just looking drove him plumb crazy, but he couldn't stop. He'd never known a girl like Kari. She didn't talk like anyone else and she sure didn't do anything girls were supposed to do. Kari flat *belonged* under a man, but he was certain there wasn't anyone in Roundtree getting to her. Looking was about all he'd ever get, he decided, unless he plain took what he wanted—and there'd be hell to pay for that. Pardo didn't give a damn who laid who, but he'd kill Howie or anyone else who hurt Kari or scared her off. Pardo needed Kari Ann and wasn't about to lose her; because no matter what she *looked* like, Kari knew more about guns than any man within five-hundred miles of Roundtree. She could take any weapon apart, fix it, and put it back together. If the right part couldn't be found, why, she'd just squint up her eyes funny and figure out what *ought* to go where something wasn't, and make one up out of her head.

It sure wasn't proper work for a girl, but she was damn good at it, Howie had to admit. Even Klu and Jigger, who didn't have much use for females of any kind, gave Kari a grudging respect.

No one knew where she came from, or how she learned all there was to know about weapons, and nobody much cared. Except Howie. And he wanted desperately to know everything there was to know about her. Most of all, he wanted to get her in bed so bad it hurt just to think about it.

"What kind of thing is that you're working on?" he asked her. The sun from the window had dried her hair. It looked all fuzzy and bright around the edges.

Without looking up, Kari said, "You know anything about trigger assemblies for the .38 calibre revolver?"

"No," Howie admitted.

"Then it won't do much good to tell you what I'm working on, 'cause that's what it is."

Howie felt himself redden. Kari looked up and winked mischievously. "Howie. You going to stand there all day?" She patted the bed beside her. "It's *your* room. You can sit down whenever you want."

"I'm . . . just fine here," Howie lied.

Kari studied him with one eye. "You're standing, because you like to look at me," she announced gravely. "And you can see things better standing up. That's the real reason, Howie. Why don't you just *say* so? I don't mind you looking . . . just don't stand there pretending you're doing something else."

Howie swallowed. "You . . . make it hard for a man not to look, Kari."

"Do I? How do I do that?"

"You know damn well what you do. You just nearly . . . show everything 'bout half the time."

"*Nearly* everything?" She chewed her lip thoughtfully. "Is that what you want, Howie? To see everything?" She loosened a button or two and let the shirt fall off her shoulders and down her arms. "There. There's everything."

Howie's mouth came open. "Kari . . . My *God*, Kari!" He stared in wonder at the slim, almost fragile body, the perfect little breasts tipped with amber. His throat went dry and he ached so much he could hardly stand it. He let his eyes touch every part of her. He was sure he could circle his hands clear around the tiny waist and the small, flat belly just the color of honey. All he wanted to do was gather up that slight bundle of nakedness and hold it tight against him forever.

Kari watched him and he could see where her eyes were going. "Howie, you want to lay me something awful, don't you?"

"More'n anything, Kari!"

"Hmmmm." She put one small fist under her chin and studied him coolly. "Yeah, I guess you do. I wondered, 'cause you never asked . . . all you do is look."

"Can . . . can I, then?" He could hardly believe what was happening.

"No," she said absently, "you can't, Howie." She slipped the shirt back over her shoulders and picked up the metal part and the file.

"God *damn*, Kari." Howie's legs turned to water. "You can't do things like that. It ain't right!"

Kari ignored him for a long moment, then looked up curiously. "I was wondering, Howie. Why do you stay here with Pardo? You don't *really* belong in Roundtree, you know?"

"Huh?" Howie stared at her. "What . . . what you askin' something like *that* for?"

"Just wondering," she shrugged. She held the part up to the sun and squinted at it. "Why don't you kill him, Howie? You want to. Bet you can just about taste it."

"What do you want to do," he said harshly, "watch?"

Kari put her hands in her lap and considered. "I don't know . . . I don't guess I ever thought about it. Not really. I might, though . . . ."

22

Lew Renner didn't come back that evening from his ride out to Yargo's. It was only an eight-mile trip each way over easy country and there was no reason to spend the night. Unless, someone suggested, Ben Yargo had gotten Lew drunk on white corn and they'd both forgotten about the horse deal.

Pardo was mildly annoyed, but said nothing. He had more on his mind than trading a few mounts, what with the big gun deal with Hacker underway. In the morning, though, he sent Klu and Jigger out to look—riders were easy enough to come by, but a good horse was something else again.

They found Lew in a dry creek not three miles from town. There were cold embers nearby, and bootprints that didn't belong to Lew. From the looks of him they'd started at his feet and worked up, using the fire to heat their blades. They quit carving just above the waist, and didn't leave much below. Lew had either died on them, or they'd found out what they were after.

"Most likely he just give out," suggested Jigger. "Whoever done it sure weren't much good."

Klu and Jigger carried the body into the front room of the Keep to show Pardo. Jigger touched it scornfully with his boot and shook his head. He thought the whole business had been handled badly. There were a lot better ways to make a man talk and most of them didn't take all night, either.

Pardo didn't say anything. He studied the body thoughtfully a moment, then took off for town, taking Klu and

Jigger with him. Howie helped bury Lew back of the Keep. The day was turning hot and the job was done quickly without ceremony.

The minute it was over Howie climbed to his room and shut the door behind him. He couldn't forget that it might easily have been him out there under the hard earth, if he hadn't stood his ground with Klu. He thought again about maybe telling Pardo of his encounter with the stranger. For certain, the skinny little man was in some way responsible for what had happened to Lew.

To hell with it, he decided. Pardo had gotten the message plain enough: someone was pushing him hard, and wanted him to know it.

Howie dozed through the whole morning, ignoring the stifling heat rising off the plains. When he woke near noon he felt worse than ever. His body was covered with sour sweat and his head was full of dark dreams. Lew Renner was there, staring up blindly out of death. Only sometimes it was Cory's face on Lew's ruined body. Once, he was on a bright beach with Kari Ann, and he knew right off it was Silver Island, because his sister was there—only it wasn't his sister as he'd ever seen her. She was Kari's age, a breathtaking young girl with swelling breasts and laughing eyes. Her face, though, was just the way he remembered. When he looked at her, Howie was ashamed of what he was thinking, but she winked at him mischievously and slipped Kari's oversized shirt off her shoulders—and showed him the raw, ugly wounds on Lew Renner's body...

In the kitchen, he poured cold water over his head, scrubbing his chest and arms until he could stand to smell himself. He was hungry, but there was nothing in the cabinets worth eating. He wandered through the main room and out to the porch. There was no one around except Harlie and Jake, and neither had anything to say. He could go upstairs, see if Kari was in her room...

He cast the thought quickly aside, and was angry at himself for even thinking about her. It was mostly *her* fault he felt as bad as he did. Getting him all worked up and everything, then just leaving him hanging. A man couldn't take stuff like that, not without going plumb crazy. And if Kari didn't know what a girl was supposed to do when she took her clothes off, there were plenty of others in Roundtree who did. He'd found two or three without any trouble and they damn sure knew what he wanted. And by sunup, when he'd dragged himself back to the Keep, he swore wearily that he didn't ever want to even *see* a female again.

That had been last night, though. He could hardly remember the girls in Roundtree, but Kari was right back in the middle of his head again.

Lordee, what was a man to do, he thought miserably. What if he didn't *ever* get her, what then? That wouldn't happen, though, he promised himself. He'd have her. He just had to.

PARDO'S ARRIVAL tore the lazy afternoon wide open. Harsh war cries shook the Keep's foundation and brought armed, half-dressed men stumbling down the narrow stairs. Pardo, Klu, and Jigger grinned up at them from under a ponderous collection of crates, casks, cotton sacks, and crockery jugs. The three looked more like traveling junkmen than seasoned raiders, and it was plain they'd sampled the clay jugs more than once along the way.

Pardo took one look at the bewildered faces and threw back his head and howled. Klu and Jigger near fell to the floor.

"Go*damn* if you all ain't somethin' else!" Pardo roared. His smile suddenly faded and he scowled fiercely at the crew. "Why, we could've burned the place down and wouldn't one of you woke up to see the fire! Ain't I taught *any* of you *noth*in'? Jerry? Bo? How 'bout you, Jon?"

No one spoke for a long minute. Then Pardo's grin broke through and they all laughed with him.

"*All* right," he said sourly, tossing the sacks at their feet, "you lazy bastards kin dig in and eat 'til you pop a gut fer all I care, but I'm tellin' you straight . . ." he held up a warning finger, "you best get yourselves movin' proper by sundown, 'cause I'm going to work you *all* night and ride your asses off come morning!"

Nobody understood for a moment, then the whole crew burst into a loud cheer all at once.

Pardo showed his teeth. "Didn't figure you'd *mind* too much, seein' as how you're ever' godamn one going to be rich as Old Kings 'bout this time next week." He punched Jigger harshly in the ribs. "Git that stuff out where we can see it man, and let's hop on it!"

The party didn't take long getting underway. Free food and whiskey was news in Roundtree, the same as anywhere else, and it wasn't fifteen minutes before a curious crowd had gathered in front of the Keep. No one got in who wasn't supposed to, which meant riders who worked full-time for Pardo, and whatever women were available. But there was plenty to eat and drink and more on the way. Soon there was just as big a party outside as in.

Good white corn was on hand for the asking and a few special crocks aged in the barrel, if you knew the right people. There were sacks of new potatoes to toss in the big pot over the kitchen fire, fat loaves of hot bread, and green heads of cabbage brought in from Rebel country, east of the mountains. Best of all, there were great baskets of fresh, hot meat, some of it young colt no more than three or four years old, roasted whole on the spit. Not one slice of that cut found its way out of the Keep and into the crowd.

Howie knew something was up, for certain. When Pardo treated everybody in the Keep and half of Roundtree, you could bet somebody else'd be paying for it soon.

He glanced up once and saw Kari at the head of the stairs. She took one look at the brawl in progress below and fled back to her room. Howie wished glumly that he could join her. Not that anything'd come of it, but at least he'd be out of the mess downstairs. He tried his own room, but one of the crew had already taken a girl in and locked the door behind him. For a moment, he thought about rousting them both out and giving the man what for.

Instead, he wandered down to the kitchen and found himself a hot slab of meat and a piece of bread. Most everyone had gotten their fill and the kitchen was empty, so he settled down behind a big barrel to chew his meal. The noise came in loud as ever, but at least all the people had drifted out to the other room. The eating time was over, and serious drinking was getting underway. It'd last until the whiskey was gone, or a good fight put everyone on the street.

Again, Howie wondered what in all hell Pardo was thinking about. Maybe he *had* gone plumb crazy, filling half of Roundtree with food and whiskey. By sundown, everyone in town would know they were riding out in the morning and no one would have to guess what they were up to. Colonel Monroe and every Loyalist trooper in the Territory'd be just licking their chops and waiting. Then, what? Howie thought miserably. He felt vaguely sick inside and knew it wasn't the meat. The whole business gave him the shivers.

23

The steep trail twisted like a dry river through a tumble of giant boulders worn by wind and weather. From the top of the ridge he could look back and see the long column winding up to meet him. It was hard going and taxed the best that men and mounts had to offer. Loose stone turned slick as ice under a horse's hooves and threatened to send mount and rider sliding off the path. Men below cursed and held their breath as rock and choking dust clattered down to meet them.

Howie decided no one could have mistaken the band for anything but what it was. There wasn't a man afoot in Pardo's hire—only heavily armed raiders on horses. Even the precious cargo of weapons was slung across the backs of a dozen sturdy mounts.

Not one of the riders had ever seen *that* done before—a horse was for carrying a man, and much too valuable for hauling heavy loads about.

But wagons were too slow for Pardo. In this war party a man carried what he needed on his back. When he ran out of that, why, he'd just have to do without.

Harlie reined up beside him and rubbed the mask of sweat and dust from his face. "I'll be godamned if I ain't wishin' I'd of got a lot drunker'n I did," he growled. "Last night I had a right good idea what I come on this trip for, but I sure can't remember what it was."

"You were goin' to be rich as one of them Old Kings," said Howie.

"Oh, yeah, I do recall." He screwed up his weathered face and scratched his chin. "'Bout when you reckon that'll be?"

"I don't reckon nothing 'til I see it, Harlie. And I ain't real sure about it then."

"Uhuh." Harlie thought a minute. "That's sound thinkin' in a outfit like this." He took a long swig of water and wiped his sleeve across his mouth. "Ain't hardly nothin' a man can do but take the breaks as he sees 'em, and hope for the best. But I'll tell you certain, the more I put my mind to it the more I wish I was back under some fine shade in Roundtree with a big, cool cup of corn close by. *Lord*ee!"

Howie laughed. "Harlie, you want to be poor and drunk all your life?"

Harlie looked straight at him. "Shit, boy, it sure beats *dyin'* rich and sober, which is likely what we're in for on this little party." He grinned and whipped his mount away. "Least half of that, anyways."

Howie watched him go. Harlie wasn't thinking much different than anyone else in the crew, he decided. Pardo's riders weren't nearly as excited about filling their hats with gold as they had been the night before. The corn whiskey in their bellies had dried up quick on the hot plains. There was nothing to do now but ride, and wonder where you were going.

Pardo was a tricky bastard, for sure. If you got a man drunk enough, he'd work all night loading horses and packing gear, and take off riding at sunup without asking why. Now, though, like Harlie, they were remembering how they'd left the Keep all stiff and bleary-eyed with half the town up to see them off. Every halfwit in Roundtree knew they were carrying a fortune in guns out to the Rebels. Pardo had done everything but nail up signs pointing the way.

Now, all a man could do was curse Pardo for a fool and keep a wary eye over his shoulder. If there wasn't something after him already, there soon would be.

THE TOP of the ridge was a midday stopping point and, before the tail end of the column reached the summit, the first riders had small fires going to warm their rations. The heat felt good, too. Even under the clear blue sky there was a slight chill to the air. A rider who'd been through the country before told Howie they had left the plains behind and were now on the edge of a great mesa that stretched all the way to the far mountains.

"You *seen* the mountains?" Howie asked him. "For certain?" He'd looked at a picture once, in a real book, and stared at the tall, craggy white towers of stone that seemed to reach clear to the sky. It was hard to believe they were anywhere near. He was sure you could already see anything that big, if you were close enough to talk about them.

"They're there, all right," the man told him. "Taller'n God. Some so high a man can't hardly get all the air he needs on top."

Howie doubted that. There was air everywhere—why wouldn't there be some on a mountain, too?

In the late afternoon he traded outrider duty with Harlie and rode along at the front of the column with Kari. Howie had mixed emotions about her presence on the trip. He was glad she was there, but he knew they were in almost certain danger and didn't like to think of something happening to her. Pardo had felt the same way, for different reasons. Kari was too valuable to risk on the trail. He sure didn't want to think about trying to replace her.

Kari had stood her ground, though—there wouldn't *be* any shipment of high quality arms without her, and she'd damn sure see them through to the finish.

Earlier, Howie had promised himself he wasn't going to let anything show, this time. She could make a fool of someone else if she wanted to, but it wouldn't be him. Not any more. The minute he was with her, though, the whole business started all over again. Everything tightened up inside, like something was fair squeezing the life out of him. He felt hot all over, even in the crisp wind sweeping off the mesa.

He talked about the trail, and the different kinds of rocks, and how cool it was getting, and anything he could think of besides stopping right there and pulling her clothes off and laying her good and proper. Godamn, she looked good, even under the heavy cotton jacket that near covered her

from head to toe! It didn't do any good at all if you knew
what was there.

"Howie...."

"What?"

"Stop it, Howie."

Howie flushed. "Stop...what?"

"What you're thinking."

"You don't have any idea what I'm thinking, Kari."

"Sure I do, Howie."

"You sure as hell don't!"

Kari didn't answer, but he caught the slight corner of her
smile. "You really do like that, don't you? You think I'm
real funny."

"No."

"*Uh*uh."

"I said I didn't, Howie."

"Well...what *do* you think, then? You gotta think
something."

She looked at him a long moment, gray eyes sleepy beneath her lids. "No I don't," she said finally. "I really don't
have to think anything."

Howie felt vaguely uncomfortable. There was something
about the way she looked at him that told him it might very
well be true. And not just about him, either.

AT SUNDOWN the sky turned brilliant red, coloring the mesa
in stark shades of fiery pink. Gray, crimson-topped clouds
hugged the horizon, and Howie imagined they'd reached the
mountains already, though he knew that couldn't be.

Pardo stopped the column at an ancient site, where two
long ribbons of man-made stone crossed each other and
wandered off straight as arrows across the mesa. Everyone
knew they were roads and that machines had used them to
carry people before the War. Just how this was done no one
could say for sure, though there were pictures that showed
what it had looked like.

You could see traces of roads most everywhere; there had
been plenty of them and they usually turned up right where
you were fixing to plow, or dig a stock pen. This one was in

fair condition, with a lot of surface showing. Time had taken its toll, and the stone was cracked and split all over and choked with sand and weeds, but you could still trace its edges with your eyes.

Some of the crew grumbled over Pardo's choice of campsite, not too many liked the idea of spending the night in old places. Pardo ignored them, he had a reason for stopping there. Right at the crossroads there was a gutted building. It had thick stone walls higher than a man, and a narrow doorway. It was here he planned to store the guns overnight. More than that, he explained, if anyone decided to bother the column, why, there was a ready-made fortress right at hand, and it'd be worth a man's life to try to take it over flat ground.

No one argued, but all the riders said they'd just as soon sleep outside in the sand until something happened to bring them inside.

"I WONDER what they looked like?" said Howie.

Kari kicked her boot in the sand and squinted at him. "What?"

"The roads. Before, I mean."

"Just like they do now. Only newer."

Howie shook his head. "You know what I mean, Kari."

"I've seen lots of them. Better than that. Some good as new."

"Where?"

"Where I come from."

"Where's that?"

"That way." She jerked a thumb west.

"Huh?" Howie raised a brow. "You mean the mountains?"

"No, past that."

"California? You come clear from California, Kari?"

That was all she would say, though, and he decided wearily he probably knew more about her than anyone else, anyway.

He watched her make a windbreak for herself in the sand, and spread her blankets down, then he walked around the far side of the old building and made his own bed. No wonder she didn't talk like anyone else. He'd never seen anyone from California before. 'Course, she hadn't come right out and *said* that was it, but he figured it was so.

He wondered, wistfully, if all the girls from California looked like Kari. He decided they didn't. Hell, if that was so, every man in the country would've high-tailed it out there already and there wouldn't be anyone left anywhere else.

With the night, a million stars filled the sky and the real cold set in. Howie pulled his blankets tight around him and tried to sleep. It wouldn't be long before someone'd come by and kick him awake. Pardo had two-thirds of the forty-odd riders doing sentry duty on horseback in a wide circle around the camp. He hadn't said so, but it was plain enough he was more than a little concerned about Monroe and his troopers. They were out there somewhere—everybody knew that. The only question was when they'd try to take the guns. If they had good sense, they'd make their run before Pardo's riders met up with strong Rebel forces.

It was something to think about, and Howie figured every man in camp was wishing he was back in Roundtree, or damn near anywhere else.

Near sunup, he climbed off his horse and crawled half frozen back in his blankets. He was asleep as soon as he hit the ground; it was only minutes later that the scream brought him up straight again. He grabbed his weapons, certain the troopers were upon them.

A dozen riders had bunched up around the far corner of the building and someone had pulled a torch from the fire. A man named Kelsey was on the ground. His eyes were near coming out of their sockets with fear and sweat was pouring like fresh rain down his face. Four men held him down and tried to stop the screaming, while another did something to his head.

The whole side of Kelsey's face was blood-red and swollen, and Howie could see ugly wounds where something had punctured the skin again and again.

In moments, Kelsey was dead, a white foam of spittle ringing his open mouth. The riders covered him quickly, and crowded 'round to take a look at what had done it.

Howie was horrified. Someone had killed the thing, but it still writhed and squirmed blindly across the ground—a long, terrible creature with no legs at all, and big around as his arm. Someone said it was a *snick* and that they'd seen two or three in the mountains before.

God help us, thought Howie. Horses, rabuts, and now snicks. He'd liked it a lot better when there was only one kind of animal around.

24

Hacker and Pardo nearly had it out before breakfast. Howie was sure they'd have killed each other if Klu and some of the Rebel soldiers hadn't stepped in to pull them apart. The two kept their distance the rest of the day—Hacker riding point, and Pardo sticking close to his pack horses.

Everyone in the column had seen it coming. Hacker was storming mad over the way Pardo had pulled out of Roundtree, making a show for the town. And no one blamed him much, either. As Hacker put it, it was a damn fool thing to do. And though he didn't care one way or the other whether Pardo got his own people killed, *he* didn't figure on losing his whole troop over another man's ignorance. That was when Pardo went for him, pale eyes flashing and a big grin spreading his features. Klu wrestled the knife from him before he could sink it half a foot in Hacker's big belly.

Looking at Pardo's face, you could swear the man had lost his senses. Howie knew better than that. The only time Pardo went plumb crazy was when he wanted to, and for a good reason. If he'd figured on sticking Hacker, Hacker'd be kicking up sand right then instead of setting his mount and sulking.

So why hadn't they seen through the *rest* of the business, Howie wondered? He could have kicked himself for not thinking. Pardo never did anything without a reason—and he sure as hell wasn't crazy. If he'd let everyone in town know he was carrying that big shipment of arms to the Rebels—why, that was exactly what he'd intended to do!

Why, though? Where was the sense in it? That was something Howie couldn't figure. The whole thing sent shivers up the back of his neck. He hadn't forgotten his *last* trip with Pardo....

THE COLUMN made camp early, long before the sun was down. Pardo picked a spot where weathered spires of red sandstone capped a small rise in the land. It offered good cover, and was high enough so that the riders had a distinct advantage over any intruders. They could walk the horses up easy, but an attacking force would have to leave their mounts behind and fight on foot over open ground. Even Hacker had no quarrel with the site.

Every man in the column, for that matter, breathed a sigh of relief. Most had figured the Loyalists would hit them sometime during the day and, if they had to fight, they preferred to do it from good cover. A man dragging ass over the flat tableland on a horse was pretty hard to miss with a rifle.

Before the evening fires were lit, the rumor spread through the camp that they'd be meeting the main Rebel forces early the next day. And if that was true, wouldn't Monroe have scouts out like everyone else—and *know* the Rebels were there? If he did, he'd sure try to take the arms while he had a smaller foe to face—and that meant tonight.

"You figure they'll come?" Howie asked Harlie.

"Hmmmph." Harlie nodded through a mouthful of dried meat. "They'll come. Ain't much question 'bout that."

"If they're out there," said Howie.

"Oh, they're out there, all right," Harlie assured him. He gave Howie a crooked grin. "Some ol' soldier probably got you in his sights right now, boy."

Howie made a face. "How come the scouts ain't seen anything, then? There's nothing out there but flat, and you can look 'bout a thousand miles everywhere."

Harlie studied the lone bite of beans left on his plate. "Ol' Kelsey didn't see that snick, neither. But *it* seen *him*." He shook his head. "Ain't no use wishin' for what isn't goin' to be. They're out there, and they're goin' to hit us—because they got to.''

Howie figured he was right, but it just didn't make sense, everyone settin' around eating and talking and knowing what was going to happen. They ought to be doin' something, shouldn't they? The more he learned about war and fighting, the less he understood.

He had his own reason for risking his neck out in the middle of nowhere. He'd promised himself a long time ago he wouldn't get far from Pardo until things were settled between them. But what about Harlie, and the rest of the riders? And Hacker's troops, for that matter. Some of them wouldn't be coming back from this business. They all knew that, and thought about it plenty, but they went right on putting their necks in a noose for a day's pay and rations. Even if they came through all right they wouldn't gain much. The Rebels would just go on fighting somewhere else until they got themselves killed or all shot up, and the riders would keep making money for Pardo, or someone else who didn't care whether they lived or died. Why, Howie wondered? Maybe they had reasons for doing what they did, same as he did. But what they were, he sure couldn't figure.

All the fires were out by the time the sun dropped through low clouds in the west. The Loyalists might know where they were, but there was no use in making targets. A few men slept, but most huddled in small groups against the cold. Both Pardo's men and the Rebels kept to themselves. They had no quarrel with each other, but there was bad blood between their leaders, and you didn't get real friendly with a man you might be fighting later. That seemed like a damn fool idea to Howie, when they all had plenty on their hands with the Loyalists. But as Harlie or someone at supper had pointed out, ''even if Monroe ain't climbing our backs 'fore morning, what you figure is goin' to happen when we meet the rest of Hacker's troops? There's twenty-four of us, and about twenty of them if I'm countin' right. There's no trouble in a match like that. But what about tomorrow, when the odds ain't so good? You figure Hacker's goin' to worry about *paying* for those guns—when he's got maybe a hundred or so troopers to back him? Hell no, he ain't!''

No one could think of a good answer for that, and it didn't make sleeping any easier thinking about maybe getting through one fight before morning, so you could take on the Rebels by noon.

''That's plain silly, is what it is,'' said Kari. They stood together out of the wind. The high spires of rock looming above looked like dark fingers against the night.

''You don't like Pardo much,'' she said flatly.

He looked at her. ''What's that got to do with anything. No, I don't like Pardo at all. If...''

''What?''

''Nothing.''

Kari grinned without looking at him. ''You let what you feel get in the way of your head, Howie. You hate Pardo so you don't mind thinking he's stupid. He isn't.''

''I never thought he was, Kari. I didn't say that.''

''You do, or you wouldn't listen to stuff like that, or come talking to me about it. Pardo knows what he's doing. Or he wouldn't do it.''

''Well godamn,'' he said irritably, ''I can figure out things like that, too. I sure don't need you to explain it to me!''

She faced him in the dark, the pale starlight showing him the deep, curious eyes, the tiny frown above the bridge of her nose.

''All right. What would you do?''

''What do you mean?''

''If we get past Monroe,'' she said patiently, ''and meet more Rebels than we can handle, Howie.''

''Well hell, I don't know. And I don't figure anyone else does, either.''

''Pardo does,'' she said simply.

Howie's ears burned. ''You've sure taken a sudden liking to him. I reckon I should have figured.'' He knew what he was trying to say and was immediately sorry. But Kari didn't take it that way, or didn't care.

"No," she told him, "that really isn't true, Howie. I don't guess Pardo's better or worse than any man. He just wants more than some and goes after what he wants."

"Meaning what?"

Kari gave him a questioning look.

"You mean something," he pressed her. "What did you mean?"

"Nothing, Howie. I didn't mean anything at all. Why does everything have to mean something?"

Howie bit his lip. "You're *always* doin' that. Saying something and then saying you didn't *say* anything. Or that you don't care one way or the other anyway!"

"I don't, Howie."

"Come on. Kari..."

"No. *You* care, Howie. I know you do and I know a lot of other people do. Maybe I'm just different. But I don't. And I don't think I want to." She studied him a long moment. "I don't want to be like you. Or anyone, if that's what I have to do...care so much I can't think straight."

Howie didn't know what to say, so he didn't say anything. Kari wrapped her arms around slim shoulders and shivered. "I'm cold, Howie. I'm going to wrap up and try to keep warm and get some sleep. If you want to come and bring your blanket you can, but if you're thinking about feeling around and stuff like that I don't want you to."

She turned and disappeared around the stone pillar and Howie stared after her. He didn't know whether he hated himself more right then, or Kari. Why did it always have to end up the same way, every time? Why did she have to say things like that? It wasn't true, anyway. People *had* to feel things—whether they said they did or not.

Someone laughed softly in the darkness, right behind him. Howie went cold, then jerked around quickly. Pardo grinned up at him. He was stretched out on a flat rock, his hands behind his head. Howie felt sick. Lord, he'd been there all the time and heard everything!

"Sure is an interestin' night, ain't it?" Pardo cleared his throat, sat up and spat into the dark.

"Guess you got yourself a earful," Howie said soberly. "Sure hope you enjoyed it."

"Couldn't much help doin' some hearing," said Pardo. "It's a natural thing if you got them little holes in the sides of your head."

Behind Pardo, the pack animals stirred as one of the beasts brushed his hide against stone. He'd brought his valuable cargo to the highest, safest point on the rise, then.

Howie wanted to leave. He was embarrassed, and angry. "I reckon I'll get myself some sleep," he said.

"You do that," said Pardo. He grinned at Howie. "Go an' get yourself under your blanket an' dream about your true love..."

Howie bristled. "Listen, Pardo..."

Pardo laughed. "Shit, boy, you might's well poke it in that big old rock there. Do you 'bout as much good as sniffin' after that one. You ain't goin' to get any."

"I suppose you tried!" snapped Howie.

"I got more sense than that."

"Well, I ain't."

"Uhuh."

"And...and I reckon that's my business!"

"Sure is. You can't tell nobody nothin' they don't want to hear." He paused a moment, chuckling to himself. "She ever tell you 'bout Sequoia?"

"What?" Howie tried to see the man's face in the dark.

"High Sequoia." Howie caught his grin.

"Well, what's that?"

"Just ask her sometime. See what she says."

"Maybe I don't want to," Howie said stubbornly.

"Suit yourself..."

"Maybe I don't care nothin' about High...whatever it is!"

Pardo laughed. It was a deep, whiskey laugh that started in his belly and came rumbling out of his throat. Howie knew he was going to kill him, right then and there. He knew it and felt it rising up to happen. His hand went right to his pistol like it already knew what it was supposed to do.

He knew something was wrong, because he hadn't fired a shot yet and everybody in the world was shooting at him.

25

The fight lasted no more than a good quarter hour, though it seemed much longer than that. The Loyalists sent every man in camp scurrying for cover under a deadly hail of gunfire. Pardo and the Rebels recovered quickly enough and returned the favor with a vengeance. For a while, a small part of the mesa was nearly as bright as day. Then, the government troopers suddenly broke off the attack and disappeared into the night.

"I don't like it," scowled Hacker, "it don't taste right to me."

Hacker was a big man, with a fat belly and thighs round as oaks. He'd spent all his life outdoors, but his face refused to take the sun. That, and the raw corn he consumed in great quantity, left his beefy features puffed and florid. He sat his horse between his two lieutenants and eyed Pardo against the faint smudge of dawn. All three soldiers were clad alike in pale blue uniforms and black Rebel caps. They kept their mounts a respectable distance from Pardo. Klu, Jigger, and two more of the biggest men among the raiders were close behind their chief.

"The thing is," said Hacker, "I've fought them fellers before and they ain't no fools. Monroe and Conner is smart as whips, and I figure one or both of 'em was out there last night. Why, hell . . ." He spat contemptuously into the dirt, "we was all shootin' at nothing in the dark and so was they. If Monroe'd wanted to take us he'd of been halfway up that rise 'fore he let off a round." He looked hard at Pardo. "There sure wasn't nothin' stopping him."

Pardo let the remark go by, but he met Hacker's gaze straight on. There wasn't much he could say, without starting a small war right there. It had been his men on outrider duty when the government troopers attacked. Instead of cutting a wide patrol so they could warn the camp in plenty of time, they'd hugged the base of the rise like birds on an egg. The government soldiers had sliced an extra mouth in four of them before they knew what was happening. They'd been the only casualties in camp except a Rebel trooper who couldn't keep his head down. If the Loyalists suffered any losses, they'd taken them with them. There wasn't a sign on the mesa that anything bigger than a snick had been there.

Pardo looked back over his shoulder at the first streaks of morning, then faced Hacker. "I reckon that's real interestin' if you got time for it," he drawled lazily. "But it appears to me we got a sight more to do than sit here talking 'bout yesterday. I figure today'll be excitin' enough for everybody." He grinned at the riders around him and they laughed with him.

Hacker didn't smile. "I think yesterday's got a lot to do with today," he said stiffly.

"Meanin' what?"

Hacker shook his head irritably. "Godamn, Pardo, don't sit there and tell me you figure there wasn't nothing *wrong* with that business last night!" He leaned forward on his mount, his face growing redder than ever. "I don't think much of you and I sure don't trust you no further than I can throw you, but I don't figure you're an ignorant man, either."

Pardo shrugged wearily. "Hacker, I got no damn idea why we wasn't all killed up there or what Colonel *Mon*roe's got up his ass. Maybe he figured we'd scare easy. Maybe he knows more about that column of yours than you figure he does. Might be he just wanted to spook us a little 'til he can catch us in the open." He grinned crookedly, and winked at the Rebel leader. "Reckon he done a fair 'nough job of it, too."

Hacker gaped at him.

"Now just hold on," Pardo threw up his hand, pushing air before him. "Ain't no need for us to get all riled up at one another. We're both still sittin' in the same stew."

"And you're stirring it with a knife, Pardo," warned Hacker. "I ain't goin' to sit here and—"

Pardo jerked his horse abruptly, and galloped off down the rise. His men followed, leaving Hacker swallowing dust. Howie, a few mounts behind, heard the whole thing. He figured Pardo was likely right; one way or another, it sure was going to be an exciting day.

HACKER DISPATCHED six of his riders out across the mesa. He was plenty anxious, now, to meet the strong Rebel forces. Monroe had shown he was close by and ready to fight. And he'd sure as hell hit the column again before the Rebels got there, if he could. And there wasn't anything stopping him.

A scout returned just before noon. He hadn't found the Rebels, but he'd seen signs of Monroe's troopers. He swore he'd read the tracks right and that there hadn't been more than fifty mounted men in the force that hit the camp. More than that, after they'd broken off the fight they'd headed northwest for a while, paralleling Pardo and the Rebels, then suddenly veered off to the southeast.

Southeast? That didn't make any sense at all, thought Howie. Why would they head away from the column, back toward Roundtree? Even if they were part of a larger force, which they pretty well had to be, why drag along behind somewhere?

No one even slowed down for the noon meal. Every rider grabbed what he could in the saddle. Pardo and Hacker kept the column tight and sent men on scout duty to all points of the compass.

Low clouds had formed in the north just before midday and now a strong, high wind pushed them to the south. A wide band of darkness rushed down to meet them, shutting out the sun. Ordinary colors turned peculiar shades of brown and blue, and everything on the mesa seemed strangely sharp and distinct—as if something in the storm had finely etched the world below. White veins of lightning searched the ground far to the north and men counted the seconds it took the sound to reach the column.

"Ain't never been in a storm up here, have you?" grinned Harlie. He watched Howie sniff the air.

"I been in storms before," Howie told him.

"Not up here you ain't."

"What's different about here?" Howie wanted to know. "It's goin' to dump all over us and get everybody wettern' hell and I seen that once or twice."

Harlie shook his head smugly. "What it's goin' to *do*, boy, is come down like *rocks* instead of water. So fast and hard you can't breathe without near drowning. It'll drive you to the ground, pound the flesh off your back, and after it's over you'll think you been beat with a godamn stick." He looked over at the other rider beside him. "Now, ain't that the truth, Bo?"

Bo nodded grimly at Howie. He was a short, stout man with sad eyes and wiry hair matting his head and face. "Likely to," he said solemnly. "'Course if it comes down hard enough, we won't be findin' them Rebels, an' we'll be sittin' out here without no help when ol' Monroe gits us."

"Bo..." Harlie looked pained. "If we can't find them Rebels, Monroe sure as hell ain't goin' to find *us*, neither."

"Well, maybe," Bo said glumly.

Klu trotted by and glared at the three of them; reminding them that they were being paid to keep their eyes open, not to sit around jawing like whores out of work.

The wind picked up, stirring cold sand in the air. A few drops of rain splattered the ground and it was hard to see what lay more than a few hundred yards away. The column slowed, and Howie saw the ground ahead was getting rough and choppy. Shallow gullies cut the mesa like wrinkles in an old man's face. The land was the same as far as he could see; there was no place else to go unless the column turned back on itself, and he didn't figure either Pardo or Hacker were about to do that.

Hacker didn't like the gullies. It was a surprise he hadn't counted on and he looked accusingly at Pardo, as if he might have put them there. "That's goin' to be just real fine," he said acidly, squinting against the sand. "We get ourselves caught in one of them things with Monroe on top of us and there'll be nothing else for it." He ran a quick finger past his throat to make the point.

"I ain't as worried about Monroe as I am about that," Pardo said flatly, looking at the sky.

"What? The rain?"

"Rain and what comes with it in this country, if you don't know. The land up ahead is some higher. If the storm hits up there it'll fill them gullies like a floodin' river 'fore you know it. Monroe and them bastards can sit back and watch us *float* by."

Hacker bit his lip. "There's high ground ahead. We got scouts out. They'll see water coming."

"Naw, I don't much like it," Pardo shook his head.

"And I don't much like sittin' up here plain as day, either." He looked darkly at Pardo. "I guess I feel better worrying about water than I do thinkin' about Monroe hitting us 'fore we find the column. He sure ain't goin' to see us down there."

"Hacker..." Pardo frowned painfully and turned in his saddle to face the Rebel. "I'm telling you, it's too godamn risky. I ain't goin' to lose my head *or* them guns in no gully-washer—an' that's just what'll happen. We come too far for that."

Hacker yelled something at him but his voice was lost to Howie on the wind. Pardo leaned over and said something to Jigger that sent him trotting to the rear of the column.

The wind was moaning over their heads like a banshee and the black clouds were so low Howie could watch dark tendrils reach down to touch the earth. He jerked his mount around out of the wind, and moved over to help Harlie quiet the pack animals. He'd stayed clear of Kari all day, but now he squinted back along the column to find her. She's crazy as a damn owl, he told himself crossly, and doesn't care any more about me than a stone, but if the whole world is going to come to an end out here there isn't anybody else going to help her but me.

A shout ahead brought him around. A Rebel rider came curling through one of the gullies, waving his arms wildly. Howie reached for his pistol, then relaxed. The whole column broke into a ragged cheer. Behind the scout Howie could see the first riders from the Rebel detachment. Hacker and his officers broke from the column and galloped down to meet them.

It was a strong force. Howie tried to count them as they trotted out of the gully into the wind. There must have been two-hundred riders in all, more men on horses than he'd ever seen at one time. The Rebels mingled with the raiders and shouted at one another. A soldier no older than Howie rode up to him and leaned out of the saddle to shake his hand. Howie grinned and the soldier said something he couldn't hear. He looked past the Rebel to the north, at the black clouds pushing solid sheets of rain before them. Dark torrents pounded the ground and tossed dry dust in the air. The whole horizon was a veil of black clouds, gray rain, brown dust. And—what else? Howie leaned into the wind and studied the broad band where the earth met the sky. There was—something. More than just dust running before that rain.

Suddenly, his stomach turned upside down and he was sure he was going to lose everything he'd ever swallowed. There were men in the dust. Riders! Coming right at them, and stretching from one end of the horizon to the other, as far as the eye could see.

26

The battle on the mesa was decided long before the first shot was fired. There was killing to do and men to be buried if you were on the winning side, but there was never any doubt about the outcome. Hacker knew it, and most of his men, and even Pardo's raiders, who had no experience with this kind of fighting. They were dead men. It was just a question of when and how it would feel when it happened.

Hacker rallied his troops above the storm. There was only one defensible position on the flatlands and he took it. Troops to the front and mounts to the rear—soldiers hunkered down in a broad circle with the gullies at their backs. Hacker's horses wouldn't help him here and he knew it. Not against the thunder bearing down from the north. Nobody could say how many they were, but it was clear the enemy dwarfed his own two hundred.

It was an awesome, terrible sight. Howie could see their faces, now, and even the bright feathers in their caps. War cries sang above the shriek of the wind. He sat frozen on his mount and stared, his mouth full of sand, until Harlie galloped by and dug his boot in the horse's rump and sent it flying.

A shot whined past. Then another. A rider went down ahead and he saw the frightened white eyes of the mount, hooves clawing air. The Rebel forces scrambled for cover and died getting there. Their officers tried vainly to form orderly fire lines they knew wouldn't stand against the first Loyalist charge.

Howie glanced back, searching wildly for Kari. But there was nothing back there anymore, only black clouds and destruction. Monroe had swallowed the rear of the column without slowing down.

He thought he saw Pardo, snaking his pack horses down a sharp ravine, Klu or Jigger beside him. The rain hit, burning his flesh and closing his eyes. His horse slid down the sides of the gully, pawing frantically for footing in the wet earth. He saw what was coming and clutched his rifle and jumped, praying the animal fell the other way. The ground came up to meet him. The rifle cracked hard across his brow, bringing blood.

He was up, then, and running. There were dead men in the water beneath him, men crying out on every side. He could see nothing, but he knew he had to keep running. The gullies were filling fast. He stumbled, fell. A hand clutched his shirt and jerked hard. Howie yelled and swung his rifle blindly against whatever it was. The man cuffed him sharply, drawing his face close to his own. Howie stared. He knew the face. One of the raiders. The man shouted but Howie didn't hear. The raider pointed back behind him and Howie nodded and followed. There were four others, bunched together atop a muddy bank, sending fire back at the troopers. Without thinking, he took up his own position and began shooting in the same direction.

It was a crazy, senseless thing. His eyes were filled with mud and water and he could see only vague shadows past the end of his barrel. Who was he shooting at? Rebels? Loyalists? He realized, suddenly, that it hardly mattered who was out there. As long as he was slamming cartridges in the chamber and watching the fire flash from the end of his muzzle the fear stayed a respectable distance away. The time was marked for killing and maybe something more terrible than dying would meet the man who didn't take his share.

The rain parted briefly, letting awesome sights and sounds fill the world. Howie was appalled to see he'd run no more than thirty yards or so into the gully. He was sure it had been a good mile.

A veil of acrid smoke masked the heart of the battle, but he could clearly see the Rebels at the edge of the ravine had broken. Still, stragglers quickly reformed their ragged lines a few yards back. They were dead men, but they made the Loyalists pay for every inch of ground. The rain had been Monroe's ally in that first, terrible charge, but now his own mounts were as useless as Hacker's. The dry ravines had turned to a thousand water-filled trenches, and it was one man against another.

A great cry went up from the mesa as a fresh wave of government troopers swarmed into the fight. The Rebels held a brief moment, then crumbled.

The fighting was over, but there was still killing to be done. Troopers roamed the trenches firing point blank at anything that moved. The cries of the wounded were quickly stilled with the butt of a rifle or the edge of a blade. As Howie watched, a great, dark figure rose up out of nowhere and nearly cut a Loyalist soldier in half with his axe before a dozen shots brought him to ground. Klu. Or Jigger, maybe. He couldn't tell. The rain swept in again on a roll of thunder and covered the sight.

"Go*damn*!" rasped the man next to him. He turned his muddy, rainstreaked face to Howie, eyes weary with fear. "I seen enough. I sure don't want to see no more." He scrambled down the muddy bank, leaving his rifle where it lay, and disappeared into the rain. His companions looked blankly after him a moment, then quickly followed.

Howie suddenly felt terribly alone and vulnerable. Not that the raiders could have done much, but they'd *been* there, anyway. He slid down into the cold water, searched through the rain, and moved off to his right. A volley of shots brought him up short. He crouched low, squinting into the storm. The shots had been so close he'd seen the red blast of a muzzle. A man cried out. Another shot stilled him. A soldier called out cautiously and another answered. Howie knew immediately what had happened. The raiders had run right into a Loyalist patrol. A cold ball of fear knotted his belly: *They're behind me, now. In front and behind and me in the middle!*

A figure rose out of the rain right on top of him. Howie brought his rifle up and fired. The man's face disappeared.

Howie went down beside him and searched blindly through the water. He found the Loyalist cap with its sodden feather, tossed his own hat away and replaced it with the soldier's. Then he stripped the jacket off the man and forced his arms through wet sleeves.

"Mark, you all right?" The voice was no more than three yards away.

"Yeah," Howie mumbled, "I reckon." He stood and moved quickly down the water-filled gully, away from the body.

27

The storm swept over the mesa an hour before sundown, leaving a dull, leaden sky behind. There were men among Pardo's band and the Rebel army who would never curse bad weather again; only the raw power of the driving wind and rain had enabled them to escape the Loyalist slaughter. Even then, pitifully few got away and fewer still once the storm abated. Monroe's troopers meticulously combed the gullies for survivors, taking no prisoners.

Howie watched them and waited for darkness. He had stayed alive by moving with the troopers under cover of the storm. It was an unnerving experience. What if the rain let up, and the soldiers saw him there and knew he didn't belong? He shook with relief when an officer called them back to the mesa. When the others answered, he hung back and let them pass him, then turned and started running as fast as he could. He had no idea where he was going. All he could think about was putting as many miles as he could between himself and the Loyalists. They'd be back. And he didn't plan to be there.

He stumbled more than once, choking on muddy water that was waist-high in places. The last time he fell, something groaned beneath him. He shrank back, startled. A face looked up at him and grinned feebly.

"Harlie!"

He could see his friend was badly hurt. Only his head and shoulders were above the water. Howie started to move him further up the bank but Harlie shook his head painfully.

"I ain't goin' nowhere and don't want to, boy."

"Harlie. Where you hit?" Howie asked him.

"Belly. 'Bout twice, I figure. Godamn if once wouldn't have been enough."

"Is it . . . bad?" Howie didn't need to ask.

"I ain't walking out of here, if that's what you mean," said Harlie. He studied Howie, trying hard to focus on his face. "It ain't too bad, boy. The water's good and cold and I haven't felt nothin' for a while." He tried to grin again but couldn't. "Dyin' don't mean a lot, but hurtin' sure does."

Howie took off his trooper's cap and draped it over the man's head. The rain was letting up a little and the cap kept some of the water from Harlie's face. He told Howie he'd been hit right at the beginning of the fight, when Monroe's soldiers had overcome the Rebels and poured into the gullies.

"Tam got it, and then Gus," he said. "Gus was right beside me when they come over. I tried to get him out but there wasn't no use in it. There was 'bout . . . six of us. We left him there and kept firin' and moving back from one damn mud hole to the next an' then I got hit and someone . . . got me to here. Wouldn't let 'em . . . take me no further." Pain swept over Harlie's face. His body arched, then relaxed into the water. "Wasn't any of 'em fit to . . . anyway. I think Mac and that kid Raney got on out. And . . . maybe some others. I don't know. Not many of 'em, for sure . . ."

He closed his eyes a minute and took a deep breath.

"Harlie . . ." Howie bent low to his face. "Did you . . . did you see the girl anywhere? Kari? Did Kari get out?"

Harlie opened his eyes and shook his head. "Didn't see her." He looked hard at Howie. "I wouldn't count on it, boy."

"Did you see her anytime? After they hit us?"

Harlie looked off into the distance, somewhere over Howie's shoulder. "She was . . . back in the column. Wasn't nobody got out of there."

"Harlie . . . you don't know that!" He knew, though, it was true. But he wouldn't let himself believe it.

"I . . . seen Jigger go down," said Harlie distantly. "And then Klu. Though that took some doing. They was all together, them two and Pardo." He forced a terrible grin.

"Same as ever. Monroe's got him, now. I seen that. Pardo, and them godamn pack animals in the bargain...."

Howie straightened. "They *took* Pardo?" He put his face against Harlie's. "He ain't dead? They didn't *kill* him?"

Harlie didn't answer.

"Harlie!"

Howie looked at him a long minute, then closed the empty eyes and covered them against the rain. For the first time, he noticed the storm was easing up, passing swiftly to the south. *Pardo. Alive.* Only that couldn't be. Maybe Harlie only thought he'd seen him taken.

With the rain moving out, the troopers would be back. And soon. If they found him.... They wouldn't, though. He'd keep one step ahead of them until the dark. They sure couldn't search every hole on the mesa. And when the sun was down, they wouldn't look anymore.

THEY HAD SET UP the camp half a mile to the south, away from the site of the battle. It was a big army. Howie couldn't even guess how many men had pitched their tents on the tableland, but there must have been a hundred or more big cookfires going.

He was tired, hungry, and shaking with cold. Lordee, he could smell meat cooking—fresh meat! He didn't know anything about armies, but it had to be a big one if they carried their own live meat around with them.

Edging up through the gullies he got close enough to see there were few guards posted along the perimeters. One or two every hundred yards or so and maybe a dozen outriders on horseback, patrolling the dark. They weren't expecting trouble. Not after today.

It would be easy enough to get in, then, once things settled down for the night and the fires burned low. But...then what? If Pardo was still alive, how would he find him? In a camp of over a thousand men—and he was sure there were that many—where would you start to look for one?

It took him a good two hours to circle the camp. Most of that on his belly to avoid the guards. It was easier when the fires burned down some, but harder to see what was going on. In the end, though, he decided he had a fair idea of how the camp was put together. The mounts were roped off away from the men, and well guarded. He'd have a time stealing one, but that wasn't something to worry about yet. The supply tents and wagons were bedded down near the small herd of stock. The regular troopers were grouped together and the officers to one side.

He decided that was where Pardo had to be if he were alive, near the officers. If Monroe was with the army, he'd sure have Pardo close at hand. Howie couldn't think of anything that would please the Loyalist officer more.

From the stars that peeked through gray tails of cloud he decided it must be two in the morning, or later. Something would have to be done soon. He watched the officers' tents, trying to figure what they were doing. One tent seemed to be busier than the others. It was all lit up inside by an oil lamp. Men wandered in and out every few minutes, and he watched to see where they went.

Another hour went by and he learned nothing. If anyone in the camp had anything to do with Pardo, he couldn't figure it. Maybe Pardo wasn't even there. Maybe Harlie was wrong; Pardo could have escaped. Or he could be dead in the gullies. . . .

Suddenly, Howie sat up straight. Two men came out of the lighted tent. Instead of walking past the front of it and going to the left or right, they moved out *behind* it.

That was important. Because it was different. No one had done that before.

They went straight to a smaller, darkened tent some thirty yards away. Howie had noted it earlier, figuring it held supplies or something. If it did, though, why would the men be going there now? In the middle of the night?

When the two officers came out, Howie crawled past the guards and straight into the camp. There was no time to worry about whether he was right or wrong. If the sun came up and caught him there, he wouldn't have to wonder about Pardo or anything else.

The tent was old and the cloth parted quickly and silently under his bone-handled knife. He stopped where he was and waited a long moment. It was dark inside, but the other end of the tent facing the officers' area was still open. Pale yellow light spilled over the bare ground. There were dark patches above where the tent had been repaired, and a rent that let the stars through. Howie froze. To the right, in near darkness—something else.

At first he thought it was a trick of the night. There was nothing in the tent but a few sticks of firewood—old, dried branches with the bark peeled off. Like wood you found on the river bank. Howie looked again. Bile rose up from his empty stomach. It wasn't wood at all. It was Pardo. He was staked out naked on the ground and someone had neatly stripped all the skin from his body.

Howie bit his lip until blood came and crawled closer. You could hardly tell who the man had been. There was no hair on the head. The scalp had been carefully peeled away from right above the eyes. The nose and lips were gone and the rest of the face had been carved away. There was bone showing on one cheek and under both eyes.

Howie started and almost cried out aloud. The hollow eyes suddenly opened and looked at him. The terrible, ruined mouth parted like a raw wound and tried to talk!

"P-Pardo?" *God help us all. Ain't nothing like that ought to be alive!* "Pardo? It's me. Can you . . . talk?"

The mouth opened and a noise came out. It wasn't a voice at all. It was a horrible, rasping thing. Sound scraping against bone. A chill crawled up Howie's spine.

"You?"

"Yes, Pardo."

"You . . ." The sound tried, failed, then tried again. *"You . . . doing here . . ."*

Howie looked at the terrible face. "I had to know, Pardo. They...Harlie said you was taken. I had to know if you was alive. I promised myself that." He stopped a minute. It was hard to look at the man and make the words come. "It was . . . for Cory, Pardo. I come to kill you. Like I said I would."

It seemed a useless, empty thing to say. But he made himself say it. The eyes stared up at him a long moment.

Then the head tried to nod understanding. The effort, though, was too great. The mouth-thing started working again, dark teeth looking hideous and unearthly without lips to cover them. It was costing Pardo everything he had to talk. Pain spread over the awful face and rippled in a great wave down the ruined body. Howie brought his face close to hear.

"Do it ... boy ..."

Howie jerked up and stared at him. Understanding came and he shook his head angrily. *"No!* No, godamn you, I ain't goin' to *give* you that, Pardo. Not me!"

No, he told himself flatly. I won't. It's too late for that. Cory had to hurt. And Harlie. And everyone else who's touched him. Everyone's hurt but Pardo.

"It's your turn, now," he said aloud, "and by God it's a long time coming!"

The eyes pleaded with him.

"No!"

The mouth twisted pain into words again.

"No," Howie cried, "I *won't*, Pardo. You can just quit asking!" His eyes filled with hot, angry tears. He could hardly see anymore.

"You got no right," he said. "You don't, Pardo."

The eyes refused to let him alone. They reached out, holding him.

Howie forced a laugh through his tears. "You can just hurt, 'cause I sure ain't goin' to help. I'm ... not, Pardo."

He felt the bone-handled knife in his fist. It burned, like there was fire in it. His arm was heavy as iron. He remembered the first time he'd seen the knife in the window of the store in Bluevale, and how Papa had said if the meat sold good maybe there'd be enough for the knife, and some sweet sugar candy....

"Well, now."

Howie straightened, blinked back his tears. The bright torch blinded him a moment. Then he saw the gaunt face above yellow light, the thin smile. He knew the face. He blinked again. Roundtree. The skinny man in the alley in Roundtree.

The man's eyes moved down and fell on the knife. The smile faded. "That was a bad thing to do, Howie. We wasn't through with him."

Howie wondered if he could make it out the rear of the tent before the man shot him, and decided he couldn't. He was too tired to try, anyway. Then he saw the smaller figure behind the man, outside the tent. Slim, with a wide mouth and Kari's curious eyes.

28

His name was Lewis, or so he'd told Howie. He didn't wear a uniform, just plain clothes like anyone, but you could tell he was important by the way the guards treated him.

Howie didn't look at him. He gazed past the man across the empty room to the window with the thick wooden bars. It was a bright, clear day outside. White clouds sailed by like big, lazy beasts and he could hear people talking and moving about in the busy street below. If he got up and went to the window he could look down and see them; merchants hurrying from one place to another, women going to market, and soldiers—plenty of soldiers. Beyond were the high walls of the city where swarms of workers labored all the day, and at night under torchlight. And past that, far on the horizon, the dim blue shadow of the mountains.

The skinny man smiled at him and blinked watery eyes. "Sure a *nice* day, ain't it? Reckon a boy like you'd enjoy being out there takin' in the sunshine. Maybe squiring a pretty girl 'round or something."

Howie looked at him curiously. "Well that ain't real likely, is it?"

Lewis shrugged. "Now you don't know that."

"Uhuh."

"Things can happen," Lewis assured him. "They sure can."

Howie laughed out loud. "I figured that's why you brung me here," he said dryly, "so you could round up all them pretty girls. That's it, ain't it?"

Lewis looked pained and disappointed. "Howie, Howie..." He shook his head and let a shallow breath through his lips. "Remember what I told you back in Roundtree? How you had friends and didn't know it? How they could help, if you wanted them to? That still goes, Howie."

Lewis was perched on the only piece of furniture in the room, a three-legged stool. He'd brought it with him and Howie figured he would take it with him when he left. They sure weren't leaving him anything he could tear up, or get his hands around.

"Why you reckon I'd believe that?" said Howie. "You lied to me about knowing Cory. You never even *seen* Cory."

Lewis looked thoughtful a moment. "All right. That's true enough. I didn't know him, but I knew all about him, didn't I? I knew about Cory, and what happened to him, and I'm dead right in saying Pardo killed him—and everyone else who wasn't in on that deal with him. Is that true or ain't it?"

"Sure," Howie shrugged. "I reckon it is." And what difference did it make, he wondered? The whole business was over and done with. Talking about it wasn't going to bring Cory back. And they sure weren't going to hang Pardo for it.

"You see?" said Lewis. He held his hands open wide. "Answering questions ain't all that hard. I'm an easy man to get along with. You don't have to be scared or nothing, Howie."

"I ain't," Howie lied.

Lewis grinned and winked at him. "Well, you *might* be. Just a little. Couldn't blame you for that. But you sure don't have to be. Howie, we know a lot more about Pardo's business than you think we do. We know that he promised to see that meat through, and how he sold us out to the Rebels. We even know how he did it—gettin' everybody all worked up and scared over false rumors 'bout the Rebels coming down from the north, or up from the south and all. 'Course he planned all along to lead the herd right *to* the Rebels, before we could get there. And we know somethin' else, too." He pointed a long finger at Howie. "We know you wasn't in on any of that. You didn't have no use for Pardo, and we know that, too. You was just doin' what you had to do.'' He sat back and folded his arms and gave Howie a secret grin. ''We even know you tried to kill him . . . took out after him with your knife, when you found what he'd done to your friend Cory.''

Howie didn't say anything. Lewis leaned forward. ''You see? That's what I been tryin' to get across, boy. That we ain't after *you* for nothing. There's just things we want to check on . . . kind of tyin' up loose ends and all. You got no reason not to talk about what's over and done with, do you? There ain't nobody it's goin' to *hurt*, is there?''

''Don't reckon there is,'' said Howie, trying to sound like he meant it.

The skinny man was good at what he did. After listening to him awhile you caught yourself almost believing he was your friend, and didn't mean any harm, and sure didn't want you to say anything that'd get you in trouble.

Howie knew better. And he was certain Lewis was aware of that. If he'd really known everything about Pardo's operation, like he said he did, he wouldn't be wasting time talking about it. He wanted something, and figured Howie could tell him. What, though? If the man was as smart as he seemed to be, wouldn't he know Howie was about the last person Pardo'd tell his secrets to?

He even told that to Lewis. Lewis just smiled and said they knew that and didn't expect him to have that kind of information. Like he'd said, they were just checking. They really already knew everything they needed to about Pardo.

When he left, he took the stool with him, and said they'd be talking again soon. Howie wasn't sure of too much anymore, but he was certain that was so.

It was a four-day ride from the mesa to the city. No one spoke to him the whole time. He didn't see the skinny man. Or Kari. He had plenty of time to wonder, though, what Kari was doing there—alive and well, with nearly everyone else in the column dead and gone. The more he thought about it, the worse he felt. Finally, he tried to put her out of his mind. She was alive, and he was glad of that. He wasn't sure he wanted to know much more.

He didn't know the name of the city and no one told him. They put him in the bare room and left him, and gave him water and a little food—not so much, though, that he wasn't always hungry.

He kept count. No one came to see him for eight days. It was peculiar, he thought, but that scared him more than anything. No one was hurting him, or bothering him at all. But every night he figured they'd come for him in the morning. He couldn't forget what they'd done to Pardo.

Every day was worse than the one before, until finally it was hard to keep from banging his fists against the door or tearing at the heavy bars on his window.

No! he decided. That's what they *wanted* him to do and he wouldn't give them the pleasure. Only it was a lot easier to say it than do it. To really keep the fear inside. Finally, he even stopped looking out the window. Nothing out there belonged to him anymore. There was only the room. It had a gray, dread finality about it. Like he had come there to stay.

He almost cried openly when the skinny man came to see him. Whatever happened was better than waiting for it. Even if they killed him, or did something terrible to him, it would be over sometime. He'd know.

He tried not to show the man his fears, but he knew, all right. Why, that's why they'd left him here—so he could *get* good and scared! The thought made him angry and the anger made him feel a lot better. They could only get to him if he let them, he decided. Only, that wasn't so, and he knew it. All you had to do was remember Pardo.

LEWIS WAITED three days after his first visit. Just long enough, Howie decided, to let him worry a little.

This time he wanted to talk about Pardo himself: what he was like, what he did, what he said about this and that. He asked Howie where he'd come across Pardo and how he'd gotten mixed up with him. Howie told him, figuring there was no reason not to. He told about getting caught by Klu and Jigger, but didn't mention Old Chattanooga or the river.

"And before that," asked Lewis, casually enough to bring Howie fully alert, "what in the world was you doin' out wandering around in the wilderness?"

Careful, Howie told himself. Careful now...

"I ran away from home."

"I see," said Lewis. "And whereabouts was that?" He shook his head and showed his palms to Howie. "It don't matter, if you don't want to say."

"No, it's okay," said Howie. "It's down south. On a farm. Only I didn't want to be no farmer."

Lewis grinned sympathetically. "Don't much blame you. Where down south? Near a town or anything?"

Howie tried to think of some of the places Aimie had mentioned, but couldn't. "There wasn't much of anything around there. 'Cept Harlie. It's a little ol' place. Maybe 'bout a hundred people."

"Harlie."

"Uhuh."

"And your folks is farmers."

"They raise a little stock, too."

"And their name is...what? I don't think you ever said."

Howie felt the knot tighten up in his belly. Did they know? The soldiers had known about him at the river, when he'd first joined the meat herd with Pardo. But that was way back east, right after it happened. Did Lewis know about him? Was he just pretending that he didn't? Bluevale was a long way off. But a story like that, what he'd done to Jacob...

It was a moment he'd dreaded for a long time. He had put it carefully aside, in the back of his head somewhere, hoping maybe it wouldn't come. Now, he silently cursed himself for growing careless and using his real name in Roundtree. He'd thought the world was a lot bigger than it was—that a man could just disappear if he was halfway across the whole country. It came to him, suddenly, that if Lewis already knew who he was, his *first* name would be enough to hang him. He wouldn't even need the rest!

"It's Kover," he said, remembering a neighbor near Papa's farm. "My father's name is Joseph, and my mother's is Kate."

"No brothers or sisters," said Lewis.

"Just me," Howie said evenly.

Lewis made a note, and if his expression changed at all, Howie didn't catch it. He allowed himself a small breath of relief.

The questions went back to Pardo. What had Howie done for Pardo in Roundtree? Exactly how had they put the gun shipment together for the Rebels? Lewis had him name the places in Roundtree where the weapons had been put together. He had a list in his hand and checked things off on it, but Howie had no way of knowing whether anything was really on it.

"You helped load up the guns, then," Lewis asked, "the night before you took off with Hacker to meet the Rebels?"

"Yes. Everyone did, just about."

"You helped put 'em on the pack horses."

"Uhuh."

"There was...what? About twelve loads. Twelve horses?"

"Sure, there was twelve." Now what was he asking a thing like that for? Howie wondered. He'd know how many horses there were. His troopers had taken them when they got Pardo.

"I suppose Pardo guarded them horses real careful," said Lewis. "I mean, once they was all loaded and everything. That was right valuable cargo."

"Well, sure he did."

"Was you part of that?"

"What? Guarding the guns? Yeah, I took a watch."

"You recall who else did?"

Howie tried to remember who had pulled guard that night, and Lewis took it all down. Then he picked up his stool, told Howie he'd been real helpful, and that maybe they'd be talking again.

For a long time, Howie sat where Lewis had left him, looking at the bare walls and the barred window and the locked door. He thought about the things Lewis had asked him. Most of it was like the man said—stuff everybody already knew, that wasn't important to anybody. Only, Howie sensed that it had stopped being unimportant right near the end. When they'd started talking about the guns. And why, he wondered, was that? The Loyalists already had everything they wanted: Pardo, the weapons, and a whole troop of Rebels besides. Why did they want to know damn near everything about something that was over and done with?

29

Whatever else his room might lack, it offered a good view of the city. The building he was in was five floors high, higher than he'd ever been before in a town. And there were several others nearby, just as tall. He knew they had to be left over from the War, which made them hundreds of years old. No one could build things like that anymore. They'd been patched and mortared all over. There was no building he could see that didn't have half a dozen different kinds of bricks and stones checkered up its sides, but they were still standing.

Clearly, the people out here didn't have any fears about living in the old places, like they did back east. But then, this city wasn't anything like the ruins of Chattanooga, either.

The more Howie watched, the more he learned. No one had told him anything, but it was easy to see something was going on outside. The work on the city walls continued night and day. There were more laborers on hand than ever—laying stone, carrying big baskets of mortar, and hauling great carts of rock to the wall. It was two floors high in most places already. From the way colors in the rock changed, you could see there had been a smaller wall there all along, but the army clearly wasn't satisfied with that. They wanted it higher and they wanted it fast.

It seemed like more soldiers swarmed into the city every hour. They swelled the streets and finally overflowed outside the walls, their campfires ringing the city. There was a constant flow of farmers and merchants through the big wooden gates. The farmers hauled wagons loaded with grain and vegetables, their wives and children bouncing along atop the cargo.

You didn't have to know a lot about armies to figure what was going on. Sooner or later, the war was coming right here. If it wasn't, the city was sure going to a lot of trouble for nothing. And what would happen if the Rebels did attack and take the city? Not much, as far as he was concerned, Howie decided soberly. *They* didn't like folks who'd worked for Pardo any more than the government did.

Lewis came back the next morning. He asked Howie everything he could think of concerning the guns, from the time they left Roundtree until the troopers attacked the column. Howie told him everything he knew, which he didn't figure was much of anything.

The skinny man was all business, this time. There wasn't any fine talking or sugar smiles, or how Howie was a good boy and not to blame for anything. He did what he'd come to do, picked up his stool, and left. Now what was all *that* about, Howie wondered?

Right before noon, shouts and cheers brought Howie to the window. He watched a great meat herd coming through the gates, drivers cracking their whips above a sea of sundarkened backs. The crowds parted to let them through and the herd moved under his window nearly an hour before the last animal was by. It was a lot of meat, he decided, even for a large city. If he'd had any doubts before, he was sure enough now. The army figured they were all going to have to live behind those walls for more than a little while.

Later, he watched a detachment of troopers leave the city to meet a column coming in from the south. There was nothing unusual about soldiers on horseback, but these caught his eye. Most of the troopers he'd run across on either side were just as shabbily dressed as anyone else, with parts of their uniforms missing or patched, the colors in their trousers and jackets faded by the weather. This group, though, was just as smart as it could be, every man sporting bright parade jackets with white wooden buttons and new feathered caps. He couldn't see who they were meeting, but it had to be someone special—a big government man, or maybe a general. He didn't know how many generals you had in an army this size, but he didn't suppose it hurt to have several.

THE SUN was just falling behind the mountains when they came for him. The door opened quickly and before he could turn around the two soldiers were there, pistols raised and ready. Howie's heart sank. That's why Lewis wasn't even pretending to be friendly anymore, then. They were going to kill him—right then and there!

Instead, one of the troopers motioned him out of the room and into the hall. There was another man waiting outside. From his markings, Howie knew he was an officer.

They took him down the long flights of stairs clear to the main floor, then one more, below ground level. Howie could smell his own sweat before they got there. They weren't going to shoot him, then. It was going to be something worse.

Lewis was waiting for him inside the room. It was a cold, damp-smelling place with stone-gray walls, floor, and ceiling. It wasn't real stone, but the artificial kind they used so much in the old cities. There were no windows. Torches lit the somber walls.

"Howie," Lewis said without smiling. "I want you to sit down. Right there."

Howie saw the chair for the first time. He went cold all over. Lewis nodded at the two troopers. They grabbed his arms on either side and slammed him down roughly on the hard wooden seat.

"Listen," Howie said hoarsely. "I didn't do nothing! What you *want* with me down here. I told you everything you wanted to know, didn't I? *Everything!*"

Lewis looked at him. "Probably so, Howie."

"Huh?" Howie stared. "Then you don't have to do nothing, do you?"

"I said probably, Howie." Lewis shook his head, like he felt bad about it. "Thing is, we can't be real sure, can we? 'Bout all we can do is go over it some down here, and see."

Howie prayed silently that he'd die before they did anything. That God would just kill him right quick and not make him be there when they started doing to him what they'd done to Pardo.

The chair was heavy oak, bolted to the floor so it wouldn't move. There were tight straps around his arms, chest, and legs. He watched, frozen in fear, as Lewis directed the two soldiers. A round log, thick as a barrel and flat on both ends, was set up in front of the chair. There were straps nailed to one end of the log. A trooper squatted down beside Howie's left leg and started taking off his boot.

"No!" Howie yelled, and kicked the man square in the chest. The soldier glared at him. His companion came to help and Howie's bare foot was strapped firmly to the log. An extra torch was brought over and set in a bracket close by.

Lewis leaned over and put both his hands on Howie's shoulders. "I want you to know what's goin' to be happening here, boy," he said firmly. "Just *listen*, now, and don't start no screamin' or hollering until you have to. What we're going to do is make a little cut in the bottom of your foot— not a big cut, just enough to get a flap of skin loose. After we do that, we're going to take hold of that flap with these."

Lewis reached back and took something from one of the soldiers and held it up for Howie to see. Howie shrank back from it and closed his eyes. Lewis leaned down and gently forced them open. The tool had wooden grips and metal ends. The metal ends curved in upon themselves to form two ugly pincers.

"Y-you're goin' to *skin* me, aren't you?" Howie said desperately. "Like you did Pardo. I know that's what you're goin' to do!"

"Just a little, Howie," Lewis assured him. "Just a little on the bottom of your foot."

"But *why*!" Howie moaned. *"I don't know anything I ain't told you!"*

"I know you say that, Howie."

"It's true, damn it . . . I ain't lying!"

"I don't figure you are."

"Then . . ."

"But I got to be sure, Howie." Lewis moved away from him.

"Just listen," Howie cried, "*listen* to me!"

Lewis turned and faced him. "Howie," he said patiently, "I done told you this once. It's something that's got to be done. I don't think you know nothin' and I told you that. I don't figure ol' Pardo told anyone *any*thing 'bout what he was up to—an' I think he told *me* just about everything that ever come into his head out there on the mesa. I don't reckon there's a little tiny *piece* of Pardo I don't know about." He looked evenly at Howie. "Now we ain't goin' to do anything like that to you, but we're going to have to do some. Just yell all you feel like and it'll be over right soon. Then you and me'll do some more talking, and see where we go from there."

He turned away then and joined the two soldiers by the big log. In a few minutes he felt them start to work on him.

He was expecting something terrible.

But he'd never imagined how bad it would be. . . .

30

He was awake when the door opened. Dead tired, he was afraid to shut his eyes, even for a minute. He'd decided that if he went to sleep, they'd come in and kill him. It was downright crazy, he knew. If they wanted to kill him, they would. He couldn't stay awake forever waiting for it.

The figure moved toward him across the darkness. He shrank back in the corner, trying to squeeze himself out of the room.

"*Howie?* Howie, where are you?"

He let out a breath. "I'm over here. What do you want, Kari?"

Kari felt her way along the wall, then let herself down beside him. "Are you all right, Howie?"

"Sure," Howie told her. "I'm just fine. I'm having a real good time here."

"Is your . . . foot all right?"

"It feels swell," he said. "All they done was peel a bunch of skin off the bottom, kinda slow like so I wouldn't miss nothing. I'm sure sorry you didn't get to see it. But I reckon Lewis give you all the details."

"Howie . . ."

"Listen, Kari." He sat up as well as he could. "I don't know what you come for, but I'm sure it don't have nothin' to do with my foot and how it's feeling. I told your friend everything I know, which ain't nothing at all. If he doesn't believe me, he can come on up and work on the other one."

Kari looked at him in the dark. "You think Lewis sent me."

Howie gave her a harsh laugh. "Now why'd I think a thing like that?"

"Well, he didn't."

"Uhuh. You just ambled on up here an' told the guard 'hey, let me run on in there and see old Howie.'"

"Of course not," she said crossly. "I asked Lewis if it was all right. He said it was."

"You admit it, then."

"I don't *admit* anything, Howie," she said evenly, "except that I wanted to talk to you. If you don't want to see me, I'll go. Is that what you want? If it is, say so."

"Kari..." He tried to make her out in the dark. She was no more than shadow against a greater blackness that swallowed the room. "I'm tired, Kari. I'm tired and I'm hurt and I don't mind sayin' it—I'm plain scared. You can go or you can stay. It's all the same to me. I don't figure we got much to say to each other. Not anymore."

"Why not anymore? What does that mean?"

He couldn't see her, but he didn't have to. He could read her in the dark. Head cocked slightly, the little pinched line between the wide, curious eyes. She didn't see it at all. She really didn't. It was something he could never really make himself understand.

"Kari. You're out there and I'm in here. Ain't that enough?"

She was silent a moment. Then, "You're mad at me? Is that it? Because the troopers didn't torture me like they did you and Pardo. Because you're locked up in here and I'm not."

"No, it's just..."

"I think that's exactly what it is, Howie. You're locked up and hurt and you think everybody else ought to be if you are. Only that's not so and you can't make me feel bad that it's you instead of me."

"That *ain't* it and you know it," he said wearily. "I'm glad you got away. I didn't think you was alive. I didn't think anybody was. It's just...well, you showin' up like that with Lewis. Out there in the tent with Pardo...like he was."

"I didn't exactly get away," she told him. "I mean, I got caught, just like you did. I can't go or anything. I've got to work on guns for them, but that's all right, I guess. I like to do it and I'm good at it." She was silent a moment. "Howie. Maybe you could work with me. If you want to. I could talk to Lewis."

"Kari..." He reached out in the dark and found her hand. She jerked quickly away from him.

"Listen," she said flatly, "I *asked* you because I can use the help. It doesn't have anything to do with you touching or feeling or anything like that. I shouldn't have ever let you do that...see me naked and everything back at the Keep. That was a big mistake."

Howie stiffened. "Well don't worry your godamn head about it," he snapped angrily, "it ain't likely you got any big problem with me! Lewis sure isn't goin' to let me get close to no guns."

Kari didn't seem to notice his anger. "Oh, I don't think that's true, Howie," she said seriously. "He knows you told him everything."

Howie snorted. "He does, huh?"

"Yes. He told me so. He said he just had to make sure."

"That's what he kept telling me," Howie said darkly, "all the time he was slicing away at my foot."

"I think he meant it, though," she said. "They were pretty mad about Pardo. Losing all those weapons when they thought..."

"Hey, wait, now..." Howie stopped her. "What do you mean, *losing* the guns, Kari? They got the guns. I already know that."

"No," she shook her head in the dark. "They were supposed to. I mean *really* supposed to. Pardo made a deal with the Loyalists. He was going to deliver the guns at a higher price than Hacker would pay. Monroe was to wait until the column met the big Rebel force and get them all at once."

Howie was shaken. "Pardo was double-dealing Hacker? And he trusted the Loyalists, after what he'd done to Monroe?" He let out a short whistle. That didn't sound like

Pardo. Only it did—Pardo figuring he could outslick any-one, no matter what.

"That's just it," Kari explained. "He *didn't* trust them. Not really. Any more than they trusted him. They'd al-ready decided to kill Pardo and everyone else in the attack and just take the guns. Only, Pardo didn't have them."

"He did, though," Howie protested. "We all packed them on horses at the Keep, I saw them. So did you!"

"He had them *there*. Lewis figures that's why he made such a big thing out of letting everyone know what he was doing. He didn't have them on the mesa, though, when the troopers attacked us."

Howie was bewildered. "He didn't? Then..."

"He told Lewis what he'd done with them. After Lewis...did those things to him. It was the second night we camped, Howie. Up on the rise with the big red rocks? Pardo had arranged to have the government troopers stage an attack there. He said it was to make Hacker nervous and throw him off guard. It wasn't, though. What he wanted was a few moments of confusion to hide all the guns, and fill the packs up with rocks. He and Klu and Jigger had it all planned out."

Howie groaned. He could finish the rest. Pardo had fig-ured Monroe would try to trick him, somehow. If he didn't have the guns *with* him, though, he'd have Monroe over a barrel. Monroe would have to come across with the money, and leave Pardo alone, or he'd never find out where the weapons really were. Only Pardo had outsmarted himself, this time. He'd never had the chance to put his deal to Monroe. The Loyalist officer had been hurt bad on the meat deal with Pardo, and he had never forgotten. He'd kill Pardo first—then take the guns.

Howie searched out Kari in the darkness. "If that's so," he frowned, "why'd Lewis have to put me through all that? If Pardo told him where the guns are, why, he can just go out an' get them. He don't need to cut a man all up for nothing!"

"He knows where they are, Howie," she said patiently, "and he knows Pardo told the truth. Only...he can't *really* know for sure until he sees them, can he? And he can't very well do that right now."

"Why not?" Howie wanted to know, "what's stopping him?"

"Well, the Rebels, of course," she told him. "Don't you even know what's happening, Howie?"

"Only to me," he said dully. "You want to tell me, or not?"

"Lewis says it's the biggest Rebel army ever. And that they've chased the Loyalists clear out of the west, nearly. Everywhere but here. So there's no one who can get through to find the guns. Maybe nobody'll ever get them."

That's what it was all for, then, he thought grimly. Two-, three-, maybe four-hundred men had died out on the mesa. And neither side had one gun more than they'd had before. And when the Rebels attacked the city—how many more would get killed over that? Someone would win. Then what?

"Kari . . ."

"I got to go, Howie." He could see her shadow stand and move away from him, and hear the rustle of her clothes. "I'll try to get back, maybe."

"Kari, I want to know something. Did you . . . were you there when Lewis got all that out of Pardo?"

She was silent for a minute. "Did I watch? Is that what you mean?"

Howie didn't answer.

"Some," she said absently. "Why?"

31

The first skirmish of the battle began just before midnight. It wasn't much of a fight and it seemed to Howie there was more shouting than shooting. Mostly, it was a chance for the Rebels to let the city know they were there, and itching for trouble.

He watched from his window as long as he could, following the winks of gunfire out into the night. Now and then he caught the tail-end of a command, or a traded insult. When his foot hurt too much to stand on anymore he limped back to his corner and curled up on the hard floor.

Sleep didn't come easily. His foot throbbed something awful. It ought to be getting better, but it wasn't. It was hot to the touch, now, and pounding all by itself, like a small heart. The pain was starting to move right up the back of his leg, past the ankle, and he didn't like that at all. The poison from a bad wound, if it wasn't clean, could go right up through your body. You could lose your whole leg before you knew it. Unless he got some help, that might just happen. Only, where the hell was he going to get any help in here?

On the edge of pain he wondered how the battle would turn out and whether the Rebels would take the city or not. If they did, then what? Suppose they swept the Loyalists clear out of the west, and then pushed them all the way back east, too, and took over the government?

To keep his mind off the pain, he tried to list in his head what was good and bad about both sides. He sure couldn't think of much difference. One was about as bad as the other. He'd heard Lathan wanted to make things better for folks, but that didn't mean anything—just saying it. As near as he could see, it was Lathan he wanted to better.

Things hadn't been too bad, really, before anyone had even heard of Lathan. Most people had enough to eat and clothes on their backs. And the government *had* been trying to do things. Why, if there hadn't been a war, they might've even gotten to where farmers and ranchers could get horses. When would that happen, now? No matter who won, horses were going to be scarcer than ever.

He hurt too much to keep up with the list. It didn't make sense, anyway. All he could figure for sure was that people had been better off when there wasn't any fighting going on. And you had to say one thing about the government, they *wanted* to do things for the country. You couldn't forget there was still Silver Island. And that was something. Maybe it was even one thing worth fighting to keep. As long as you had something like that, you had the *hope* of something better, anyway.

Whatever happened, he couldn't forget that. Even thinking about what the government was doing to him right now. Hell, the Rebels would have done the same. And they didn't have any Silver Island for folks to go to, either. It was, truly, the only thing he could think of that was really right with the world. He thanked the Lord that Carolee was there and didn't even have to know anything about this.

He dozed, finally, thinking about her. Only he saw her now like he remembered her, on a warm, lazy day floating down the canal on the way to the fair at Bluevale. It was a good thing to think about, and for a while his foot didn't hurt anymore.

PAIN BROUGHT HIM UP again in the bleak, dull hour of dawn. His eyes were pasted together and his throat was dry. He couldn't stand the smell of himself. He tried to recall when he'd had a bath in clean, hot water.

There was food again, and a jug of water. He wolfed down the cold bread and meat, and saved most of the water. His foot was worse than ever. The skin was red and swollen and hurt just to touch. He couldn't stand on it at all without near passing out from the pain. Crawling over to the window, he pulled himself up and ran his fingers over the surface of each of the thick wooden bars. They were smooth and slick with age, and there was nothing rough enough to pull loose. For an hour he dug his fingernails into one tiny split in the wood, standing on one foot and prying at the spot until his hands bled. When the piece finally came free it was no more than a splinter, but it would have to do.

He crawled back to the wall, exhausted, clutching his prize. There was no use putting it off, he decided. It wasn't going to get any easier. Using a little of the water, he cleaned off the top of the ugly wound as best he could, wincing at his own easy touch. Lordee, if it hurt that much just to gentle the thing....

He knew what was coming, so he stuffed his shirt in his mouth and bit down hard. Then he dug the sharp splinter right in the middle of the fester. He swallowed the pain and ground his teeth into the cloth. Sweat stung his eyes and red and black suns swam before his vision. The ugly yellow poison poured out of the wound and he forced it through the angry red skin until no more would come. Then he washed the whole area clean with the rest of his water and bandaged it as well as he could with a strip from his shirt. When he was finished, he was drained clear down to the bone. His hands trembled and he couldn't hold back the tears any longer.

PATROLS HEADED OUT from the city in the afternoon, but they didn't get far. There were more Rebel cookfires on the horizon than a man could count.

In midafternoon, with the sun behind them, the Rebels attacked in force. They swarmed down on the city like a river in flood, until there was no bare ground beneath them. They shouted as they came, one mighty voice that swept all sound before them.

In the vanguard was the cavalry with green banners flying and hooves sending thunder over the city. There were more mounts before the wall that day than any man alive had ever seen. Behind them came the foot soldiers armed with swords, clubs, long ugly pikes, and every weapon imaginable. The Loyalists poured over the walls to meet them. When the two armies met, the din and cry was a terrible thing to hear.

Howie watched, his foot forgotten for the moment. Nothing could match the pain before his eyes. He felt strangely uneasy, seeing the battle and having no part in it. Men were fighting and dying a few hundred yards away, while he stood at his window and watched. Somehow, it didn't seem right. You ought to be able to die without people watching.

For a while, the rumor spread about the city that Lathan himself was there, leading his army. But no one could say whether or not this was so.

Just before this sundown the Rebels withdrew, and, less than an hour after that, attacked another side of the city. The battle there raged for nearly an hour. Then the Rebels withdrew to their camps, now bright with nightfires. No one cheered their retreat; everyone knew they had broken off the fight of their own will. The two terrible battles had been little more than probing actions to test the strength of the Loyalists. They would be back again, and soon.

HOWIE WISHED KARI would come to see him again. He hated to admit it, but it was so. There was no way to forget what she did to him. He knew what would happen if she came. She'd start talking nonsense again and he'd get mad and blow his stack. But he wanted her there, anyway.

His foot didn't feel so bad now and he could rest a little. He tried to stay awake, though, thinking she might come. She hadn't come until late, last time. For the first time in longer than he could remember, he felt a little like himself again. Like he could sit back and think, maybe—without worrying whether Pardo was going to get him into something where he'd get killed; or Klu or Jigger or someone would put a blade in his ribs just for fun.

He laughed softly at his thoughts. It was sure a funny time to get feeling good, locked up with his foot all swollen and hungry and thirsty half the time. All that would pass, though. A couple of good meals and a week or two off his feet would take care of those problems. He wasn't really too worried about Lewis anymore. Kari wouldn't make up something like that, crazy as she was. Lewis could torture him some more, or kill him—but what'd be the point?

Lewis and everyone else had plenty on their hands right now. He didn't think they'd be worrying over one prisoner who couldn't help or harm them, one way or the other.

And if the Rebels broke through.... He'd given some thought to that. When it happened—and he figured it would—he sure didn't intend waiting for an invitation to get away. Just how he'd bring that off he couldn't say. But there'd be a chance. And he'd take it.

And after that? He wouldn't even let himself think about it. He wasn't even sure he knew how. He couldn't remember a time when he'd just done whatever he liked, or gone wherever he wanted to—without someone saying what he *had* to do.

When they came for him it was in the early hours of the morning. He didn't even know they were there until they'd jerked him up off the floor and set him on his feet. The first jolt of pain shot all the way up his leg and set him howling. He tried to pull away and tell them he couldn't walk; that it was all a big mistake, but they wouldn't listen. When he fell they just picked him up and started him off again. Or gave him a quick boot in the ribs to show they meant business. He couldn't go down the stairs so they dragged him most of the way; the bad foot hitting every step until it hit so many he couldn't feel it any more.

Before they strapped him in the big oak chair they stripped him naked, not bothering to look for buttons, just ripping and tearing until everything was gone. There were two big logs this time and they strapped his ankles to both of them, stretching his legs wide and leaving a big open space in between. His senses were near drowning in pain, but exposing him like that brought him up again quickly. He was suddenly struck by a cold, terrible fear worse than anything he could remember.

He called out again and again, telling them he didn't know anything, that he shouldn't be there. If they'd just listen to him they'd know that. Where was Lewis? All they had to do was ask Lewis. He'd tell them it was all a mistake.

But they were gone, then, and there was no one in the room to listen. All he could hear was his own heartbeat. All he could feel was the pain coming back into his foot again, and the awful coldness of the room that went all the way to his bones.

32

The waiting. That was it, he decided. The waiting was supposed to be the thing. Make him sit there naked and cold with his legs spread out and plenty of time to think about what they were going to do to him. So when they did finally come he'd be begging to tell them what they wanted to know.

That's what scared him more than anything. Knowing that Lewis had lied about all of it—and maybe Kari, too—just to get him thinking everything was all right again. They'd set up the whole business just for this *and he didn't know anything to tell anyone....*

His mind raced. Maybe there was something. Maybe he could *make up* something! Tell them he *did* see Pardo hide the guns. That Lewis was right—they were back there at the rise where they'd camped. He had watched Pardo and Klu and Jigger put them there when the troopers attacked. He'd seen the whole thing, but he was too scared to tell them before because he'd figured they'd think he had something to do with it, and that wasn't so.

Would they believe that? They'd have to! Lordee, *there wasn't anything else he could do!*

They wouldn't stop. Not right away. He might as well get used to that. They'd keep it up for a while, just to make sure. But they wouldn't do it *too* long. It wouldn't be as much. He'd keep telling it over and over and they'd—

His heart stopped. The door opened behind him. Footsteps on the damp floor. More than one man. Two. Maybe more. The cold swept through him. He shook all over. Lewis, then. And the others. They'd start, now. What would they do first? The other foot? The same one? *Oh God, not between his legs please don't let them do that!*

One of the men walked around in front of him. Howie had never seen him before. A soldier. Heavy brows, short hair, and a wide mouth. He stood perfectly still, studying Howie carefully. He squatted down and inspected the bottom of his foot. Howie winced, but the man didn't hurt him. He got up, left, then came back with a torch. Howie blinked in the sudden brightness. The soldier stood there another moment, holding the torch high. His face was like stone. Then he put the torch in a holder and went away. Howie heard him say something but couldn't hear what it was.

"What!" The voice behind him roared. Howie jumped against his bonds.

"Major Lewis...you responsible for this?"

"Sir..."

"Just *answer*, godamn you!" It was a harsh, rasping voice, like a man with something caught in his throat.

"Sir..." Lewis hesitated. "I explained that. We questioned the boy about the guns..."

"You did more than that, Major."

"Sir, we had to establish—"

"You had orders!" the man snapped. "The boy was not to be *touched*!"

"Yes, sir. I'd like to point out..."

"Don't you point out nothing to me, Major. What you do is get yourself out of this room. Fast. You hear?"

The door opened, then closed again. Howie let out a long sigh of relief. He could have hollered out loud. He didn't know who the man was and didn't much care. He'd given Lewis pure hell for what he'd done, that was enough! They'd let him go, now. At least, there wouldn't be any more business with the pincers. Maybe he could....

The soldier moved around in front of him again. This time the other man was with him. The soldier was helping him, like he couldn't walk well by himself. When they got in front of Howie, the soldier set a little stool down right between Howie's legs and helped the man down on it. The man looked up at him and smiled.

"Hello, Howie Ryder. It's been a long time, boy."

Howie stared. A little cry caught in his throat and died there. He knew it was really all over, now. He'd come all the way around again and there was no place else to go. He wasn't even scared anymore. He knew exactly who the soldiers had gone out to meet in their fancy uniforms and why he was there and what was going to happen.

Jacob just sat there and smiled, with the terrible, ragged thing that wasn't a mouth anymore. His face was crossed with ugly white scars, and there were empty black holes where his eyes ought to be.

"You know me, then," said Jacob, "that's good. I've been a long time looking, Howie. And I've thought about you. Reckon you've thought some about me, too."

Jacob waited. His smile faded and his face went dark. "I want to *hear* you!"

"I..." Howie found his voice. "I don't guess there's nothin' to say."

Jacob looked pleased. "Dory here says you growed some. I guess you have. Don't *sound* like a boy anymore." He shook his head thoughtfully. "A lad sure fills out fast 'bout your age. Just springs up like a young tree..."

Jacob stopped. Pain seemed to crawl quietly over his face, making the white scars move like live things. After a moment, the features relaxed again. "Dory remembers how you was, though," he said finally. "Got a good look at you when we was up to your Pa's. Not many seen you then...besides me. They was mostly loadin' up wagons down at the trees. You remember all that, boy?"

Howie swallowed. "I remember it."

"Lordee," said Jacob, "there's a awful lot I remember about that day, and the ones that come before. I can just sit back sometimes and let things come into my head, and see what color the sky gets at morning, and how a fine column of troopers looks riding up a draw on good horses."

He savored his thoughts a moment, then leaned toward Howie. "You really growed up, have you? Gettin' to be a man." Jacob's hands searched out blindly and found Howie's legs. Howie shrank back from the touch. Jacob grinned at that. He let his hands slide up Howie's legs and over his thighs and come to rest between them. He squeezed lightly, and Howie's heart stopped. *Now, he thought, oh God it's going to be now...!*

Then Jacob let him go and leaned back on his stool. "You sure ruined me there," he said soberly. "You tore me up somethin' awful, Howie. I think about havin' a woman, and how it is, and then I think about you..."

"Godamn you!" Howie blurted. He couldn't stop himself, no matter what. "Just what'd you *figure* I'd do...walk up and...and shake your hand or something? After what you done to my mother and Papa!"

Dory started swiftly forward, one hand whipping down in an open fist. Jacob felt him move and waved him back.

"Howie..." The empty eyes reached out for him and he was sure they could see him, right out of nothing. "I reckon you're kinda scared, ain't you, boy?"

Howie almost laughed. "Yeah," he admitted, "I kinda am."

"What you think I'm goin' to *do* to you?"

"Just about anything."

Jacob nodded thoughtfully. "Well, I can see how you might figure. What would you think if I was to tell you I ain't goin' to do nothing at all? What'd you say to that?"

Howie did laugh this time. "I ain't that dumb," he said. "I don't figure you come all this way for talkin'."

"Well," said Jacob, "like I say, I can sure see how you might figure. I'll tell you something, though, and you can believe me or not. Talking's 'bout all I *did* come for and that's the truth. You done some bad things to me, Howie. But there's no taking them back, and I don't *blame* you for 'em. I'd have done the same thing if it was me."

"I...don't reckon I'm goin' to believe that," Howie said warily.

"Don't blame you for that, either," said Jacob. "All I really figure on doing, though, Howie, is telling you what we done to your mother. I think that's something you ought to hear. I want you to know how we stripped her down naked and wired her to that bed. And how every one of them troopers of mine had her. And while we're talking, Dory," he said quietly, "I'd be pleased if you'd get that knife of yours and take out one of this boy's eyes. I don't reckon I got to tell you not to go too fast..."

33

A lazy sun dappled the forest floor with shifting coins of gold. He stretched and stared up at the dazzling brilliance, then lay back and closed his eyes. He could hear the drone of bees circling the big oak, and smell the cool crushed odor of fern....

Without opening his eyes he reached over and let his hands slide down Kari's soft nakedness. His fingertips brushed the tips of her breasts, wandered past the flat curve of her belly, and came to rest between her thighs....

Papa looked down at him, his big shadow covering the sun. "That's wrong, Howie," he said sternly. "I taught you better, boy. The Book says that if a man do consort with the beasts, then he shall become as the beasts...."

"No, Papa, it's Kari. She's a girl. She ain't meat! Honest!"

"Howie, I done everything I could for you. I took you into Bluevale and let you see the stuffed nigger and got you a bone-handled knife. And then you go and do a thing like this."

"No, Papa, it's Kari. She..." He turned to look at her and the big mare grinned up blankly and reached out to grab him between his legs. Howie shrank back in horror....

"You can look all you want, Howie," she told him, "but just don't go feeling around or anything."

"Kari?"

Papa's arrow dug into her face, just above her mouth. Another quivered in her eye....

"Don't, Papa!" Howie cried. "Please don't!"

Papa was trying to ready another arrow, but he was having trouble with it. His eyes were black and empty and he couldn't wipe the dark away without dropping the bow. With his other hand he struggled desperately to keep his belly together, but they'd split it bad and the guts kept falling out in soft puddles to the ground....

"Just look is all," said Kari. "Don't go trying to touch something...."

WHEN HE WOKE UP he knew right where he was and what had happened and just what they'd done to him. He heard his own scream somewhere and then the pain came down hard and put him under again.

The next time, he prayed for sleep or death or anything, but nothing happened. The hurt was unbearable, but he couldn't leave it. He knew there were places to go that were dark and soft and quiet where you couldn't feel anything at all, but he didn't know how to get there....

He could see, with his good eye. The gray wall. A spiderweb crack like a tree branch winding up past the dim torch. Without moving his head he could look down and see his arms strapped to the chair and his legs spread over the flat logs. Everything seemed all right between his legs. They hadn't done that yet. They would, though, Howie knew. Jacob was going to take it all.

There was a dull, rumbling sound somewhere. Like thunder. Or a faraway drum. He listened a minute and it came again.

He tried to look around the room but the slightest movement of his head sent pain ripping like a knife through his skull. It ... Wait, now. That was something worth knowing wasn't it? He thought a minute. It was hard to think with the pain.

Pain was bad.

And good.

Bad and good at the same time. Could that be so? It was, if he could do it.

And he could. Because he had to. He couldn't stay there. He had to get away from the pain. Get away—or give himself to it. Let it take him and put him in that place again. If *he* couldn't do it, maybe the pain could do it for him.

He cried out and cursed himself and begged himself to stop. He shook his head as hard as he could and opened and closed the empty eye again and again and again and it seemed like it took an awfully long time, but he made it.

IT WAS COLD to the bone and Carolee took all the covers. That was just like a little sister—let you freeze your butt off and then next morning sure as light she'd be telling mother it was him that—

"GOD, *nooooooo!*"

"Hey, easy now." The big hand clamped his head hard against the back of the chair. "It's goin' to hurt, but it's going to get better. Just sit still, if you can."

The man poured something cold as ice into his empty socket. Only it wasn't cold for long. It was a hot, fiery coal and it burned all the way through his brain and out the back of his head. He couldn't even get the scream out before the darkness pulled him under.

He wasn't gone near long enough.

When he looked up the man was still there. "Who..." He tried, but couldn't make the words.

"I ain't anyone you know, and no one you're goin' to," said the man. "Is the hurt some better? Don't try to say nothing. You sure ain't fit to. That stuff won't last forever, but it'll dull the pain some and give you time to rest. Whatever good that'll do you."

He came down close to Howie and he could smell the faint odor of sweat and the strong smell of whiskey. "You know he's comin' back, don't you? Reckon I don't have to tell you that. Son of a bitch! Godamn son of a bitch..."

The man stumbled in the half light and caught himself on the chair. Howie moaned.

"Oh, Lordee, I'm sorry about that! I sure didn't mean to hurt you none. Don't *need* that, do you? Know what that bastard's doing? Well, shit, 'course you don't. He's *killin'* us all, is what. It ain't just you. Son'bitch goin' to have us *all* dead 'fore it's over, 's what he's goin' to do! If old Monroe wasn't coldern'n a stone out there someplace we'd... Listen, boy, if I could I'd be more'n glad to cut your throat for you an' I know you'd thank me for it. Only I...ain't got the heart for it no more. Or the stomach, neither. I just *can't*, is all. I wish to hell I could...."

When he came out of it again he wasn't sure whether he'd dreamed the man or not. The hurt was some better, so maybe it was real. The pain was still there, though—simmering just below the screaming point.

He wondered how long he'd been in the room. He had no feeling for time anymore. An hour? Two? Longer than that. A day or so, maybe. Or a week, for all he knew.

His throat was parched dry, the sides sticking together making it hard to swallow. He tried to work some spit into his mouth but the motion warned him. It wouldn't be too hard to wake up the pain again.

The thunder was closer now. He dully remembered hearing it before. Once, it came so close the room shook and a veil of white dust trickled down the wall in front of him. He watched it, following the slow path with interest.

"HOWIE? Come *on*, now, Howie..."

"Wh... Papa? Is that you?"

Jacob's harsh laughter exploded in his face. Howie came fully awake.

"By God, boy, you ought to *be* up there! It is *life*...it is what a man was *born* for!" Jacob's whole body trembled. His voice was near ecstatic. "A soldier don't need eyes for that. He can feel it and smell it all around him. The *world's* bein' shaped up there. God's voice is in the heavens!"

He stopped, like he was coming back from some far place. "Don't guess you care much 'bout that, do you?" He showed Howie his terrible grin. "Reckon you got other things on your mind. We got a little time for that, too. We will *take* time, Howie. We surely will."

Jacob's hand reached out. Howie saw what was coming and tried to pull away. A long finger slid over his chest and up his face. He screamed when the finger found what it was looking for, and when he felt himself slide under again, he hoped maybe this time he'd just die and not come back any more...

THE COLD WATER hit his face and set him gasping for breath. It ran down his forehead and hurt terribly when it hit the empty place. He tried to suck in the stray moisture with his tongue.

The thunder came again, closer than ever, shaking the room and sending gray stones rattling to the floor. Jacob cocked his head and listened. "We ain't got much time, boy, and I'm sorry for that. Got to get back *up* there. Got to." He came close to Howie. So close Howie could smell the sweet odor of death that seemed to cling to the man like an extra skin. "Had to come here, though. There's things between us that has to be. And I know you understand what I'm saying. Things that's got to be set right, Howie, or it just ain't no good for either of us. You know that..."

The empty eyes jerked away from him. "Dory, they need us up there. Get on with it."

The blade seemed to come out of nowhere and find itself in Dory's hand. It flashed torchlight as Dory squatted down and reached out to grasp Howie between the legs.

Howie's heart stopped. *"Oh, my God please no please no...!"*

"Best think about girls real quick," Jacob said gravely, "if you ever had any, now's the time to run 'em all through your mind, boy."

Dory pulled him out tight so the blade would slice easy. Howie went rigid and screamed—

—thunder slammed down like a big fist and sucked the scream right out of him. In a brief instant he saw Dory look up, surprise starting on his face. Then something dark came down, turned his features red, and he was gone.

Howie gasped for breath and choked on dust. Warm blood filled his ears. The torch was gone. But there was another light up above. Daylight, from a ragged hole in the gray ceiling. He was covered with white powder and small bits of stone. There was blood, too, already clotted with dust, but he decided most of it wasn't his.

The thunder had come in from behind and above, driving great chunks of rock before it with a terrible force. The back of the heavy chair had saved him, then; but Dory and Jacob were nowhere to be seen. He supposed they were buried under the rubble at his feet. Blinking against the dusty light, he could see something white against the wall. Dory, maybe, or—

Howie started. Something cold grasped his leg. He looked down and found Jacob's empty eyes. His head was covered with dust and blood and he was trying to work his mouth, but nothing came out. Kari was standing beside his chair. She gave him a curious glance, then kneeled down, put the pistol against Jacob's ear, and pulled the trigger. Jacob's head jerked. His hand let Howie go.

"Howie, we've got to get out of this place," she told him. "We can't stay here any longer."

34

Howie tried to see her through stone dust that clouded his good eye. He wanted to say something, but didn't know what. He had the peculiar feeling he ought to explain it all to her, that it was important she understand what he was doing there, stretched out naked in a cold cellar.

He caught her looking at his face, and what they'd done to it, while she tore the straps from his arms and legs. She just looked, without saying anything.

"Kari...."

She shook her head. "Don't talk, Howie. Just sit there a minute. Can you move? Your arms and legs are probably going to be stiff, but we don't have much time to warm 'em up. You think you can stand?"

Howie thought sure he was going to laugh, but knew how much it would hurt if he did.

"Come *on*, Howie." She grabbed one leg and started slapping it hard. Howie sucked in a breath and grabbed the arms of his chair.

"Go*damn*, Kari!"

"Feeling coming back, huh? Good. Try to get up."

Howie shook his head. More thunder rumbled outside. Close, then far away, then close again. Without warning, Kari ducked her head under his arm and pulled him up. Blood rushed to his legs and he let out a yell and collapsed, taking her with him. The fall jolted his head and he thought sure he was going under again.

"*How*ie..."

"I flat can't, Kari." He tried to look at her. Her face was swimming and it made him dizzy.

"You've got to," she told him firmly. "We can't stay here."

"Why not?"

She looked at him, then got up and ran quickly out of the room. He tried to sleep but she was back again.

"Here." She raised his head. "Try this." Howie tasted water and clutched at the jug, trying to get his own hands around it. She pulled it away.

"That's enough for now. You're going to get sick." He pleaded with her, but she wouldn't listen. "When we get out. Okay? When we get *out*, you can have some more. Now. Try to get up again."

With Kari doing most of the work, he made it past the door and halfway down the long hall. He took one look at the steps and shook his head.

"Kari. I can't."

"Yes you can. You haven't even tried, yet."

"Give me . . . some water."

"At the top, Howie. Up there. You've got to get up *there*."

He tried to think of something that would make her give him the water. His head was pounding hard and he knew he wasn't going anywhere at all, but he wanted the water. He looked at the steps again. They were nothing but a blur. Kari's face was melting again. He closed his good eye and started crawling. . . .

"BETTER?"

"I don't know. Some. Nothin's swimming 'round no more."

"Good. We can't sit here all day, Howie."

"Maybe you can't," he told her. "I don't figure on goin' anywhere soon."

He drank a little more of the water and decided maybe she was right. His mouth and throat thought it was the best stuff ever, but his belly didn't think so. Instead, he tipped the jug and splashed it in his face.

Down the narrow alley past the door where they'd come up from the cellar, the street was full of people. Some were running, or hauling carts full of their belongings, or clutching things they'd stolen from the shops. Some just stood and stared at nothing. A woman was crying somewhere. Soldiers clattered by on horseback, one man carrying a tattered pennant that said '2nd ARKANSAS.' His shirt had been burned away and there was blood on his arm. The air overhead was thick with smoke, turning the sky pale orange. Howie could smell wood burning. There was gunfire, some of it close.

Thunder struck again nearby. Howie winced. The ground shook beneath him. He turned to Kari. "Listen...what the hell *is* that, anyway?" Until now, it hadn't even occurred to him to ask.

"Boomers," Kari said shortly. "'Least that's what the troopers call 'em. It's powder and stone all wrapped up tight in barrels. The Rebels sling them over the walls from big machines. Same thing as a cartridge going off in a chamber, sort of. Only these go off *out*side. I heard about 'em before, only nobody ever made one work. Look, Howie..." She gave him a hard, stern look. "We simply can*not* stay here any longer. Don't you understand? If the Rebels get over the walls...and they will, too...*no*body's going to get out. Can't you just try, Howie? Just try?"

He closed his eyes and leaned back against the wall.

"Howie!" She was on her feet, glaring down at him. "You can't go to *sleep*, Howie!"

He tried to listen to her. It was so easy not to do anything. She was probably right, too. They *ought* to do something. Only, it didn't seem real important anymore. And if they did something, what would it be? He couldn't think of anything very helpful.

"Kari," he said wearily, "If Rebels are comin' in, how are *we* supposed to get out? And where's there to go, anyway?"

"We can get out," she said stubbornly, "because we'll have horses. Nobody can stop us if we have horses."

"Horses?" He decided that was worth waking up for. "Kari, what's the matter with you? Ain't nobody goin' to give us *horses*."

"Of course not," she said crossly, "you'll have to shoot someone, Howie, and take them."

He laughed, even if it hurt. But Kari wasn't laughing. "If you ain't had a good look at me, you better look again. I don't much feel like shootin' nobody."

"You could if you wanted to. If you had to."

He wasn't really sure that was so. What if he did, and missed? He hurt too much to think about getting hurt again.

Kari seemed to guess his thoughts. "I know you don't think you could be any worse off than you are," she told him. "But that's not true, Howie. You sure *will* be if you just keep sitting there."

He looked up at her. A Boomer hit somewhere down the street and shook the earth. "I owe you, Kari. I can't tell you how I feel 'bout what you done. Coming down and getting me out and all. But I don't *feel* like doin' nothing about it, Kari, and I don't figure you got no need waiting around for me any longer."

Her eyes showed shocked disbelief. "What do you *mean*?"

"I mean if you want to go shootin' someone and stealing horses, just get on about it."

"I won't, either," she said fiercely, "not without you!"

The words wrapped around him like something warm and easy, for a moment, pulling the hurt right out of him. Why, she *felt* something for him! She honest to God did. It had taken a whole war to pull it out of her, but there it was.

"Kari..." He pulled himself up, fighting off the nausea that came with standing. "I'll...try, Kari. I'll give it the best I got, and I can't do no more than that." He looked at her. There was dirt on her face and her hair was tangled and powdered with dust, but he'd never wanted her more.

"I couldn't let you down," he said. "I just couldn't. Not now."

"Good," said Kari. "I knew if you just thought about it you'd see it."

"See...what?"

"Well that you *owe* me, Howie. Like you said. I wish we hadn't had to waste so much time talking about it."

35

He felt some better with pants on. The man had been killed when one of the Boomers exploded right beside him; there wasn't much left of his head and the shirt was half torn away and blood-soaked, but the pants were all right. He didn't care about the shirt, and boots were out of the question.

Kari held the pistol and kept an eye on the street while he changed. The way things were in the city, Howie didn't figure anyone'd understand why he was stripping a dead body in the alley.

"I hope you don't expect me to shoot anybody," Kari complained, "because I told you I don't know how to do that."

"You did all right back there," said Howie, trying to get his bad foot through a narrow trouser leg. "Just keep watching, okay?"

"That was different. It's not the same when you can go up and just . . . touch somebody with it."

"Kari . . ." He stood and took the gun from her. "Just shut up, all right?" He tucked the weapon in his pants and limped out of the alley.

"I don't know what you're so mad about," said Kari. "You do that all the time. You want me to be like you, and I'm not, Howie."

"You ain't like anybody," he said darkly, "you don't need to worry none about that." He stopped, glanced up at the sky, and pulled her back in a doorway. A Boomer arced high overhead. He followed its wobbly path; the big barrel hit beyond them and exploded. The ground shuddered. Black smoke roiled into the street.

Howie moved out of the doorway. "What I'm mad about is I don't like bein' *used*," he told her. "You think someone's doin' something 'cause.... Shit, you find out it ain't that at all."

"All right, Howie."

"No!" He turned on her. "It *ain't* all right. Comin' down there and gettin' me is one thing. *Why* is somethin' else. Don't you see that?"

She brushed hair out of her eyes. "Didn't we talk about this? Do we have to do it again? We don't have time, Howie."

Howie glared down at his foot. It was throbbing again and starting to hurt something awful. "You wanted someone who could shoot and catch horses. That's about it, ain't it?"

"I told you," Kari sighed, "I know everything there is to know about guns. But I don't know how to *use* one. Is there anything wrong with that?"

Howie stopped and looked right at her. He could see her and hear her and touch her. But she wasn't really there. Nothing had changed at all, and nothing ever would. He could see it, plain as day, and he wondered how long it took to get from seeing to really knowing.

THE REBELS were in no hurry to occupy the city. Their great catapults were well out of range of government riflemen, and well-placed sharpshooters discouraged heroes from leaving the walls. Earlier, the Loyalists had mounted a desperate attack to put the Boomers out of action, but the Rebels were too much for them. The fields before the city were dark with the dead and dying.

Rumor had it that the troopers were dropping their weapons and fleeing the city through the north wall, leaving it to Lathan's marauders. It might be true, Howie decided. You didn't have to know too much about battles to see this one was lost. He wondered how many soldiers would get by the Rebels if they tried. Not many. It was pretty clear Lathan was determined to make this fight count for something.

The noise wasn't so bad anymore. The Rebels had shifted their hail of destruction toward the center of the city. In the eastern sector, anyway, the streets were practically empty.

That was fine with Howie. He guided Kari past an alley choked with debris from the start of the battle. The broad avenue beyond was nearly impassable. The Boomers had hit buildings on both sides of the street, and the ancient structures had collapsed without a will. Howie took one look at the mess and turned back. They'd have to find another way.

"Wait," Kari stopped him, "over there."

He followed her gaze. Through a veil of black smoke was a portion of the wall. One section, a good five yards wide, had collapsed nearly to ground level. The stone on either side of the hole was dark with black powder and the fire that had come after. Kari started toward it without even looking back. Howie caught up and grabbed her arm. She frowned and jerked away.

"It's a way out, Howie. You don't have to come if you don't want to."

"It's a way out if you want to get killed bad enough. Kari...you got the idea in that stubborn head of yours that you're goin' to get *out*, even if you get dead doing it."

She fixed him with big, curious eyes. "You want to stay, Howie? I can see how you would, considering you had such a fine time here."

"I got my eye took out," he said sourly, "only it was a knife that done it. It wasn't no Boomer or a rifle bullet. You ain't making any sense, as usual."

"I am to me."

"Well you're—" The noise turned him around quickly. He took one look behind him and jerked her back around the corner.

"What is it?"

He didn't answer. He limped back over the short block, crossed the street, and angled down a narrow alley toward the wall.

"Howie..."

"Just shut up, and listen. The way we come back there's filled with Rebels. They must've got through another break further down." He muttered under his breath. "They're goin' to be all over the damn place in about a minute. They see us wanderin' around out here they ain't goin' to stop to talk."

The little crease between her eyes started working. "Then we'll *have* to go out through the wall."

"And meet 'em comin' in that way, too?"

"All right. What do you suggest, Howie?"

Howie ignored her. He imagined he could hear boots scraping on cobbled streets. They could stay where they were and get caught—or keep moving, and run right into more Rebels, for certain. Either way.... He stopped, sniffing the air. There was sure something besides smoke and black powder in the air. Something a lot stronger than that. He moved to the end of the alley and risked a look. The smell was overpowering, now. A man didn't even need one eye to track down an odor like that.

There were maybe a couple hundred head—bucks, mares, and even colts. They'd broken out of their pen somewhere and nobody'd bothered to round them up. They were scared stiff, cringing together against the high wall, eyes glazed with fear. From the look of them, they hadn't eaten in days.

Howie watched another long minute, then turned back for Kari. She was full of questions, but he wouldn't talk to her until they were back around the corner from the herd.

"Kari..." He took a deep breath. The next part wasn't going to be easy. "Kari, I want you to take your clothes off."

Puzzlement, then anger, started at the corners of her eyes. He waved her off. "Now it ain't what you think. I want you to take your clothes off 'cause we're goin' to drive that meat out of here through that wall, with us right behind 'em. Now don't *say* nothing, just do it. There's no other way and I figure them soldiers ain't going to kill no stock. It's 'bout the only thing they're not shootin' at."

Kari found understanding. Her mouth dropped open and her big eyes widened. "You are crazy as you can be, Howie. If you think I'm going to run around naked out there...with *meat*..." Her mouth closed with revulsion around the word.

"They ain't goin' to look," he said wryly. "I don't like it no more'n you do, Kari, but we're goin' to do it. 'Less you got something better in mind."

She stared as he dropped his trousers and stepped out of them, keeping only the pistol. He searched around and found two blackened sticks. He handed one to her. She shook her head.

"You won't go without me, Howie. You know you won't."

He didn't look at her. He took his stick and hopped down the alley as best he could and out into the sunshine. He waved his stick at the frightened stock. They'd probably never seen people without clothes on, he decided, but there were a lot of unusual things happening in the world, and even meat was going to have to get used to them.

36

There was no problem getting the herd moving. They were glad enough to have someone tell them what to do next, and didn't much care what it was. Once the point got turned in the right direction, the others followed—right through the shattered wall and out of the city.

There was noise and confusion out there and plenty of things to frighten an animal. But stock was like that. Howie's father had always said meat felt a lot better being led to slaughter than having to think of something else to do.

The land rose up slightly outside the walls and the Rebels had placed their siege engines on small hillocks some two-hundred yards from the city. There were only three of the big catapults close by and a few troopers milling around them. That was one break, anyway, Howie decided. The real fighting had evidently shifted to the north wall and the bulk of the soldiers had followed it there. The Boomer crew would be taking a care where they dropped their missiles, with their own men entering the city from the east.

"Howie," Kari moaned, "I can't take this anymore. I mean it."

He glanced over his shoulder. She had stopped a few yards back, standing with her legs rooted to the ground, hands stiff against her sides in tight little fists.

Howie was horrified. "Go*damn*, Kari!" He ran back and jerked her roughly forward. She pulled away and he smacked her soundly on her bare bottom.

Kari let out a little cry. Her eyes turned black. "Don't you ever do that again, Howie. Not *ever*."

"I won't," he told her, "less I have to. Just stick right up here where you belong... with the rest of us meat."

Kari went white. He thought for a minute she was going to hit him. Instead, she gave him a dark look and stalked off ahead.

He had to grin at the red brand of his hand across her shapely rear. Kari's slender, almost fragile figure stood out like a sore thumb against the sun-darkened, dirt-encrusted stock. He felt just as bad about the whole thing as she did. But he wasn't about to tell her that. It made him feel queasy all over. It wasn't right, people mixing with stock. It was against just about everything. It was some better than getting caught by the Rebels and maybe getting shot on the spot, but that didn't make him feel any more comfortable doing it.

Someone fired a shot on the rise ahead and he hobbled off to the right for a look. He couldn't tell what was happening, but troopers were swarming all over one of the big machines. The whole business made him nervous. What he'd like to do was swing the herd further to the left, as far away from the soldiers as possible. To do that, though, he'd have to move out of the rear and shout them over, putting him in plain sight of anyone watching.

Kari was up beside him, looking scared. "Howie, what are you doing? Don't go off like that."

"I'm not goin' anywhere," he told her, pulling her back into the protection of the herd. "I was just checking."

"What is it?"

"It's nothing, Kari. I was looking, is all."

There was a heavy, thudding sound and one of the dark Boomers whistled over their heads toward the center of the city. The herd grunted in fear and jerked as one away from the noise. Howie grinned. By God, he couldn't ask for better help. There was high grass up ahead. Another fifty yards or so. All they had to do was stick with the herd until they could lose themselves out there. Then, stay low for a mile or so until the city and the troopers were far behind.

"I'm getting sick, Howie. I mean it."

Kari sounded like she was strangling on something. "You don't look too good," he told her.

Her eyes blazed. "This is a terrible idea. I never should have listened to you."

Howie shrugged. He sympathized, but there wasn't much he could do. It was bad enough being naked with a bunch of stock. Besides that, it was never any fun trailing behind 'em. Especially on foot. They smelled bad enough all the time, but when they got underway they were likely to leave new stuff for you to step in. Anyway, it was working. They were leaving the big engines behind and the grass wasn't far. It was a good thing, too. He wasn't sure how much longer he could keep Kari from just sitting down and throwing up. He didn't feel too damn wonderful himself. His head was aching something awful and his foot hurt every time he stepped on it.

A big buck turned and stared at him, the blank eyes trying to figure what kind of creature he might be; knowing, in it's small mind, that something was wrong, that Howie didn't belong. Howie waved his stick threateningly and the buck flinched and turned away.

He glanced over at Kari, and cursed under his breath. Godamn it, she'd dropped back again, keeping as far from the herd as she could. He turned and started back for her, then stopped. His heart came up in his throat. The trooper was almost directly behind her. No more than thirty yards off and riding hard.

There was no question that he'd spotted her. Maybe he knew right off there was a naked, long-legged girl walking behind the herd. Or maybe he was one of those men who didn't much care whether she was meat or not, if she looked as good as Kari.

Howie felt a moment of helplessness. If he called out to her she'd turn and look at the rider and scream or something and they'd both be spotted for sure. He couldn't warn her, then. All he could do was let it happen. He held the pistol up tight against his chest and nudged himself in between two big mares. God, they smelled awful! One stared at him with glazed eyes, spittle hanging out of her open mouth.

He kept one eye over his shoulder. The rider was right behind Kari. He could see her close now and he was grinning from ear to ear. Howie stepped out of the herd and turned. The trooper looked at him, a question starting on his face. Howie fired. The man shuddered and fell heavily to the ground.

He'd figured Kari would scream or run or faint dead away or all three at once. But Kari fooled him. She stopped in her tracks and stared at the dead man, then at Howie. Suddenly she turned and ran as fast as she could after the trooper's horse. The animal was trotting dutifully back to wherever it had come from, but Kari wasn't having any of that. Her long legs flew over the open ground. It was the prettiest sight he'd ever seen. She leaped for the reins and brought the mount to a stop. Howie ran to meet her, not thinking about his foot any more. He started to tell her what a great job she'd done and then the bullet sang right between them. Another dug up dust. He jumped on the mount's back and pulled her up behind. He yelled at the horse and it bolted, nearly tossing them both.

He glanced to his left and saw the two riders. They were throwing dust and coming up fast. He knew what they had in mind, they wanted to drive him back past the stock to the Rebel siege engines. Ahead was open country and no place to go. They'd sure never make it to the distant line of hills. Not riding double.

"Howie," Kari moaned behind him, "I'm getting sick."

"Not now, damn it!"

"I . . . can't help it."

She clutched him tighter and he heard an awful noise and felt something warm on his back.

"Aw, hell, Kari . . ."

There was no use running, and he knew it. He reined up hard, jerked Kari off the mount, and shoved her into high grass. "Just hold the godamn horse," he shouted, "and keep your head down!"

Seeing him go to the ground, the riders came on harder than ever. One had a rifle, the other a pistol. They kept shooting and yelling war cries at him as they came. Howie ignored the shots and the shouting. Pardo had told him more than once that you might scare a man to death bearing down on him from a mount, but it took more than a fair shot to hit anything that way.

He got the first rider square in the chest. The second had more sense. He reined in and bore down on Howie with his rifle. But he was breathing hard and madder than hell about his partner; the shot went wild. Howie wasn't mad at anyone. He was just bone tired and anxious to get as far away from soldiers as he could.

WHEN HE GOT BACK to the narrow draw under the hill Kari was hunched up in a tight little ball, her knees up to her chin and her hands wrapped around her ankles. She had the blanket they'd taken off the horse draped over her shoulders but it didn't help much.

"We're going to freeze to death," she said flatly, without looking up. "If you'd gotten clothes off those soldiers we'd have something to wear, anyway. You should have, Howie."

Howie let out a long breath. "We been all over that. More'n once. Ain't any sense goin' over it again. There wasn't no time, Kari."

Kari muttered something he didn't hear.

"Okay," he told her, "we might have gotten the clothes. An' we might've gotten killed, too. I don't reckon you thought about that, did you?"

But Kari wasn't listening. She'd curled herself up tighter than ever and pulled the blanket over her head.

It was going to be a miserable night, he knew. It was plenty warm during the day but when the sun went down in the shadow of the big peaks to the west, it sucked all the heat out of the earth. There was still maybe half an hour before dark and he could feel the promise of a chill in the air. Howie had decided he wasn't going to start a fire, even if he could. No matter what Kari said. The city was behind them, but it couldn't be far enough, as far as he was concerned.

After he dug the shallow depression in the ground, he lined it with as many dead boughs as he could find. There weren't many, but they'd have to do. They could get under the blanket and out of the wind, anyway, and maybe pull in dirt and more boughs to keep out some of the cold.

Kari gave the sleeping arrangements a dubious eye. The little crease between her eyes started working and Howie could see it coming. On top of everything else, it was just about more than he could take. He didn't even give her a chance to get started.

"It's goin' to be pretty godamn awful, Kari," he said sourly. "You're going to have to *touch* me without no clothes on, and you're goin' to have to get 'bout as close as you can to keep from freezing. 'Course, if you think it'll make you sick or somethin' you can always sit up naked all night and talk to the horse. It don't make no difference to me."

She studied him warily. "Couldn't I just keep the blanket and stay up here, Howie? I think that'd be a better idea. Then you could have the hole all to yourself."

Howie didn't bother to answer. He got up and walked over to her and jerked the blanket off her shoulder and left her sitting bare on the ground. Then he got into his bed and started pulling dirt and leaves in after him. She watched him a long moment, scowling, and shivering in the chill air. Then she got up and moved in beside him, keeping as far away as she could. He could feel her shaking, but she made no effort to touch him. The sun went down and the cold wind swept out of the mountains to frost the earth.

"Howie?"

"What."

"If I turn over and get close you won't . . . feel anything or do anything, will you?"

"If you do that," he said wearily, "there won't be no way I can help feeling you, Kari."

"You know what I mean."

He didn't answer.

"Howie. *Please* turn over and h-hold me. I'm freezing to death!"

He turned and took her in his arms and she came to him, pressing herself against his body, burrowing into every hollow she could find.

"Howie," she said after a minute, "I'm sorry. I know the things you want to do to me and I guess this makes it a lot harder not to do them, doesn't it?"

"There ain't nothin' I want to do to you, Kari," he lied, "go to sleep."

"Yes you do. You like to see me without any clothes on whenever you can, but I know you want to do more than that. You want to now, Howie."

Howie ground his teeth. "Kari . . . just shut up and go to sleep. I don't want to talk about it." She's got to know what's happening to me, he thought helplessly. There ain't no way she couldn't!

Kari suddenly went rigid. "You're . . . going to, aren't you?" He caught the small edge of fear in her voice. "Even if I don't want you to. I can feel that and *I don't want you to do anything!*"

Howie shuddered and moaned to himself. He jerked roughly away and turned his back to her. She stayed away a long moment. He could hear her breathing, and thought she'd fallen asleep. Then she moved up against him again and her flesh was like fire.

"Howie. I'm sorry."

"You always been like this?" he asked harshly. "You didn't ever feel nothin' . . . with anyone?"

Kari hesitated. "Some . . . I guess."

"Where was that? In High Sequoia?"

She stiffened at his words. "What do you know about High Sequoia, Howie?"

"I don't know nothing. Pardo mentioned it once."

"Pardo did. About me." She sighed against him. "Pardo always knew things you didn't figure on."

"What is there to know, Kari?"

"There isn't anything."

"All right . . ."

"Howie, it's a place is all."

"And you come from there?"

"No."

"But you said you'd...felt something for someone. I thought maybe..."

She gave a sad little laugh. "Not there, Howie. You don't *feel* things there. You feel everything and not anything. You're supposed to, anyway."

"That don't make much sense."

"I don't want to talk about it any more, Howie. Not any at all. Okay?"

Howie shrugged. He lay still and listened to the wind. He felt her heart beat against him and smelled her hair crushed up on the back of his neck. The cold ate into the place where his eye had been and made him want to bite his tongue with the pain.

He tried to think about something else. What they'd do the next day. They'd go south, maybe. Where it was supposed to be a lot warmer all the time. They'd get food, and clothes, and there wouldn't be any soldiers anywhere. He'd take them so far nobody there would even know about the war. He wondered if there was a place like that.

He was puzzled over what Kari had said—or hadn't said, really. Something pretty bad had happened to make her like she was. She hadn't always been like that. She just couldn't have been. And people didn't *have* to stay like they were, did they? They could change, and be something different. And Kari just had to. Because whatever she was, there wasn't anyone else he wanted. Not anyone.

"Kari?" he said softly, "you awake?"

"Uhmmmm," she said sleepily.

"Kari, I think we ought to circle around real wide tomorrow, 'til we get pretty far from the city. Then I want us to head south. Real far, where it's warm. That all right with you?"

"It's fine with me, Howie," she told him. "Whatever you think."

She pressed warmly against him and wrapped one arm around his chest. In the half darkness he could look down and see the dim whiteness of her fingers on his shoulder. He knew it didn't mean anything at all but he could imagine that it did. "What happened to you, Kari," he said suddenly. "Damn it I'm sorry, but I got to know that. I got to know what it was."

She stiffened slightly but didn't move. "You can't leave anything alone, can you Howie?"

"Not that I can't."

"Pardo didn't tell you."

"He didn't tell me nothing but High Sequoia. I don't even know what it is."

Kari was silent a long moment. "It's a place where you can get whatever you want, Howie. That's what it is. Whatever you want if you got the goods to pay. The best whiskey and food and everything else." Her voice was distant, as if someone else were talking and not Kari at all. "My daddy taught me how to fix guns. He was the best there was till the sickness took him. A man from High Sequoia saw me shopping in the market. I was going on twelve. I didn't get away for four years. A man bought me and took me off. Me and a horse and two guns that didn't work. I fixed one of the guns for him and killed him and ran off."

"Oh, Lord, Kari..." He wanted to turn over then and hold her but knew better. "I'm sorry. I didn't know it was something like that."

"Why are you sorry, Howie? You're always sorry about something, or thinking how you ought to feel. Don't feel anything at all and you'll be just fine. That's something you've got to learn. I'm cold. I want to get some sleep. I don't want to talk anymore."

Howie tried to think of something to say, but knew there was nothing that would do either one of them any good. He felt her against him. Felt her there like something hollow, as if she'd died and didn't know it. He knew this was close to the way it was.

WHEN HE WOKE in the gray dawn he was stiff with cold. He sat up and saw he was lying naked on the ground with nothing over him at all. The pistol was missing. Kari wasn't beside him anymore. The horseblanket was gone; so was the horse.

EPILOGUE

By the end of spring he left the foothills of the high range behind. One day he turned, looked to the north, and saw that the distant peaks that had watched his path so long were only thin blue shadows on the far horizon. Ahead, the land stretched flat and hard. He knew he had reached the edge of the great southern desert.

The heat felt good. Sometimes he just stood and let the sun fill him. Bake him clear to the bone. He didn't think he'd ever get too warm again.

He loved the desert and marveled at the strange, spiny green things that grew there. He wasn't afraid of the land, but he respected it. He sensed that it could be cruel to a man who didn't know its ways. He never tried to cross that great, barren space, but kept it beside him, so he could know that it was there.

The region that bordered the desert was nearly as dry and empty, but there was life there, too. Besides the green spiny things there were purple-gray bushes that hugged the earth and filled the air with dusty smells. Sometimes, there were stunted trees that looked like lean old men. He saw snicks and rabuts, and other things he couldn't name. The further south he walked, the more creatures he saw.

There was water, usually from muddy streams no wider than his hand. He found a great, wide riverbed that stretched a mile or so from side to side. It was nearly as dry and parched as the desert, but there was water near its center, a foot or so beneath the harsh red soil.

He had little to eat. But he got used to that....

HE COULDN'T REMEMBER when he'd last seen another person. There had been some earlier, in the foothills. He'd sometimes stolen from them. Food and clothing and, once, a knife. But he hadn't tried to talk to anyone. He didn't want that. Not soon.

He followed the dry riverbed down the long, endless miles, always keeping the desert in his sight. He decided the riverbed was a kind of border, separating the land where a man could live from where he couldn't.

He lost count of the days. There was warm sunlight, and there were cold stars. There were days with food and water, and days without. Each day began and ended much the same as the one before. Until the morning he woke, sat up, and saw the man.

He was walking just on the edge of the horizon to the south, moving from east to west across Howie's path. Behind him trailed a small herd of stock. One, two, three, Howie counted. Four, five, six, seven...eight. Hardly even big enough to call it a herd.

He was greatly surprised to see a human being. Why should that be, he wondered? Another man could be out here in the middle of nowhere. *He* was.

He wasn't sure how he felt about the man. He was sure he didn't want to talk to him. If he just sat where he was, the man would disappear in a little while and he wouldn't have to worry.

He didn't want that, though. He wanted to see the man, but he didn't want the man to see him. He didn't understand why this was so, but it was.

IT WASN'T HARD to follow a man in the wastelands. He couldn't get away from you. All you had to worry about was getting too close. If you could see forever out across the desert, so could he.

Howie kept out of sight during the day. After dark, he'd wait until the man built a fire and then he'd move in some. He never got too close. He just sat quietly in the dark watching the man's shadow move about the fire. After a while, he'd crawl back to his place, pull his blanket about him, and go to sleep.

Before he slept, though, he thought about the man. What kind of man was he? He'd never gotten close enough to tell. What did he do? Did he live out here? He sure wasn't making any kind of living hauling eight head of stock around. Maybe he was just trying to get away from other folks, too.

He'd think about things like that, or guess what the man's name might be, or how old he was. And then he'd go to sleep.

ONE MORNING, about a week after he'd first seen the man, Howie woke up with a start, knowing something was wrong. The man stood right above him, big boots spread wide and a heavy, long-handled axe in his hands.

Howie didn't move.

"That's right," said the man. "Just stay quiet like." He nodded toward Howie's belt. "Slide that knife out slow and toss it aside."

Howie did as he was told.

"You got anything else on you?"

"No."

"What's in your pockets?"

"Some nuts. And a couple of them green fruits."

The man looked at him. "What kind of fruits?"

"The kind that grows on the end of sticker plants."

The man almost grinned. "You eatin' cactus buds, are you?"

"I eat whatever I can get." Howie couldn't hold back any longer. Ever since he'd opened his good eye he hadn't been able to take his gaze off the man. Strong, wide chin, dark eyes, a broad nose, and—he was *black*! Just as black and shiny as pitch!

"Something botherin' you?" asked the man.

"You, I reckon," said Howie. "Damn...you ain't a *nigger*, are you?"

The dark face didn't change. He motioned with the axe. "Get on up."

Howie did. "What you goin' to do with me?"

The man slung the axe over his shoulder and scratched his belly. "First I'm goin' to ask you why you been sniffin' my heels for 'bout a week. Sittin' behind bushes and watching a man eat his supper." The man made a face. "You got to have some reason for doin' somethin' like that."

"I just wanted to, I guess," said Howie.

The man shook his head. "Not good enough."

"It'll have to be, mister." Howie looked right at him. "'Cause there ain't no more to it than that."

The man seemed amused. "You're not much afraid of this axe, are you? Don't you figure I can use it?"

"I figure you can. But I ain't goin' to stand here shaking, if that's what you're waitin' for."

"How'd you lose the eye?"

"A feller cut it out with a knife."

"You fight him back?"

"There wasn't much way I could."

The man nodded. He dropped the axe down to his side. "You can come and have some breakfast if you like. I don't have no *cactus* buds, but I reckon you'd eat somethin' else if you had to..."

THERE WAS a big flat pot of beans in the fire and loaves of hard bread that looked like they'd been baked in ashes. There seemed to be plenty. Howie dipped his cup gratefully. The taste of real food almost made him cry.

The man watched him, eating just a little himself. He motioned for Howie to take more, if he liked, but Howie nodded his thanks. His stomach had been empty too long.

He had a lot of questions he wanted to ask the man. Mostly, he wanted to know about niggers. There weren't supposed to *be* any since the War. But he guessed there were, all right. Did they live out here, in the desert? Was that where the man was going?

He kept the questions to himself. The man probably had plenty of questions about him, too, but he hadn't asked much, considering.

When he was finished, the black man took his own cup and Howie's and set them aside. Then he took the rest of the beans and the ash-colored bread and carried everything away from the fire and out of the camp into the brush.

Howie watched, more than a little puzzled. The man sure didn't strike him as the wasteful sort—throwing a whole good meal away when food was hard to come by. He walked on, making his way over the flat, and when he finally stopped he just set the beans and bread on the ground. *Right down on the ground where his stock was bedded!*

Howie was horrified. He couldn't believe what he was seeing. The meat jumped right in and fell hungrily on the food, dipping it out of the pot with their hands. Howie's stomach turned over. He could taste everything he'd eaten in his throat and he could have gotten up and killed the black man on the spot. There was no use hoping it hadn't happened before. This was clearly the man's regular habit, which meant *he'd* been scooping up beans, big as you please, right where stock grubbed their filthy hands the meal before!

"Something wrong?" The man stood watching him across the fire.

Howie was too angry to hold back. "Maybe I got no business saying it, mister...but I sure never seen a man feed good beans and bread to his stock. An' off of pots meant for people, at that!"

The black man's face didn't change. He squatted by the fire and squinted far off like he was chewing something over in his mind. "They ain't exactly stock," he said finally. "They just kinda 'pear to be."

Howie didn't look at him. He just sat real still where he was. If he'd learned anything at all about people there was one thing certain as night: You couldn't ever really figure a man inside, even a man you knew some. And he sure didn't know this one. He wondered if he could get up and out of there on his bad leg before the man could grab the big axe again.

The black man read him easy. "I'm just telling you." He eyed Howie squarely. "You was the one asking." He poked a stick in the fire. "They was wandering 'round half starved when I come on 'em. Picking up leaves and bugs and whatever. Looked more like a bunch of bones than anything. Got all this far, though. Halfway 'cross the damn country."

Howie considered. "Just how you figure that?"

"Figure what?"

"Where they come from."

The man stopped his poking and looked up. "One of 'em *told me*, is how. Rest of them got their tongues cut but this one talks so you can understand him some. You don't believe none of this, do you?"

"About meat *talking*?" Howie studied his hands. "Mister, I ain't arguing with a man that's feeding me breakfast. But I'm saying if one of them...if something talked to you, it sure ain't meat."

The man gave him a humorless grin. "Well, that's what I'm saying too, ain't it?"

While the black man gathered up his things Howie kicked dirt over the fire, though there was nothing on the land to burn away. Neither spoke about it, but when the sun blazed up and turned the land hard as brass they started out together. Howie didn't ask any more about the others. They trailed along behind, always keeping a distance. The black man didn't seem to notice they were there.

They walked the long day, together and not together, neither pressing the other, taking their company for what it was. When they did talk, Howie found the black man knew surprisingly little about the world beyond the desert. Was there a war? He hadn't heard about it. The name Lathan meant nothing to him. He did know men came down to the desert more than they used to, moving to the south and then coming back with horses. He knew what the horses were for, but wanted nothing to do with them himself. A man'd be a fool to get on the back of such a thing.

When the night came and they stopped for the evening meal, Howie ate sparingly. He told the black man he was much obliged but didn't want to deplete another man's rations, when there was nothing he could contribute himself. The man said nothing, but understood it was mostly because of the stock.

They'd stopped for noon under the sparse shade of a mesquite. It was the highest point on the flatlands as far as the eye could see, no other object being more than a foot off the ground from one horizon to the other.

"If I'm askin' something I maybe shouldn't, just say so," Howie said. "What I'm wondering is where all this goes, and what's after it." He caught the black man's eye, and the little touch of caution there. "I wasn't askin' where *you* was headed," he added quickly. "That's sure no business of mine."

"Didn't figure you was," the man nodded. He snapped a dry twig and worked it around in his mouth. "North you know better'n I do. And east too, I reckon. I never seen either and don't want to. South is nothing at all. Just more of this. You start calling it Mexico somewhere down the line. Only it don't change the land none to call it something different."

"What's down there?"

"I said nothing. Or nothing I know of."

"There's horses."

"There's horses. Nothin' more than that."

"And west?"

"West is California. There's plenty there...none of it much better'n where you come from, I don't reckon. There's cities. And people." His eyes brightened some. "And ships. There's an ocean there, blue as it can be. And once in a while a ship comes in to port. Long and dark, with big bright-colored sails. And people that don't look nothing like me..." He grinned, "...or like you, either."

Howie was curious about that. "They ain't from here, you mean?"

"No. They sure ain't from here."

"Where, then? There isn't anyplace else."

"Well, I guess maybe there *is*."

Howie thought about that the whole day and part of the next. He tried to picture what one of the big ships with colored sails would look like. And people that weren't the same as either him or the black man. What kind of people would they be? And where did they come from? There were other places in the world before the War. Everybody knew that. But there weren't supposed to be any now.

The business of the black man's stock was on his mind, but it wasn't a subject Howie felt like bringing up again. Where the man was taking them—whatever they might be— sounded too much like asking about the man himself. And that was clearly something the man didn't want to get into. Howie couldn't much blame him. If there weren't supposed to *be* any black people, and no one figured there were, there might be a good reason to keep quiet about where there were some more.

Once, he'd let the man know real plain about that. "I can take off some other way. Whenever it pleases you. I figure you got places to go that ain't the same as mine."

The black man looked at him a long moment, then said he'd sure let Howie know.

HOWIE DIDN'T HAVE to bring up the stock again. The man did that on his own, coming back to the fire one evening after staying a long time in the brush. "One of 'em is pretty sick," he announced. "Don't figure he'll make it for long." His dark eyes got hard and thoughtful. "Reckon he's been through enough for anyone, without crossing a place like this. Don't know as I done 'em a favor taking them on."

The man's face, which always seemed to hide a great and silent strength, was suddenly drained and weary. He squatted by the fire, big hands on his knees, and watched the popping coals.

Howie felt he ought to say something, but didn't know what. Maybe the man didn't want to hear anything just then.

"Is he the...one that done the talking?" he finally asked.

The man shook his head without looking up. "No. 'nother one from that."

"He still talk to you some?"

The black man raised his eyes. "He don't like to do a lot of talking. If he talks, he got to think 'bout where he's been."

Howie thought about that. "He ever say where that was? Where they came from?"

"Said he didn't talk a lot, now didn't I?" The man tossed a stick in the fire. Howie got the message, but couldn't bring himself to stop.

"Look," Howie said, "I'm not saying it isn't so, or that this feller don't *talk*, just like you say. But it don't make sense. If he *talks*, he ain't *meat*. And if he's *people*, then someone treated him and the others like they *wasn't*. Why'd anyone do that?"

The black man looked pained. Like *nothing* people did surprised him much. "Why'nt you just get up and go *ask* him?" he told Howie. "Reckon he'd be the one to answer that." He stood and gave Howie a brooding look, then walked off out of the light until Howie couldn't see him anymore.

It doesn't make *sense*, Howie thought, and decided he was tired of thinking and saying it all the time.

THE BLACK MAN didn't talk to him in the morning. Howie followed him across the flat hot land that didn't seem to end or begin. Then, when they stopped to share sparse swallows of water, the man stoppered his clay jug and looked right at Howie. "Look. My name's Earl. You can tell me yours if you want." Howie did, and the man said it once to himself. "I can't take you where I'm going, Howie, but you can go along some, then I'll show you how to bear north and west. It's where the ships come in I was tellin' you about. You might want to see 'em."

It was a fine thing for Earl to do, and it made Howie feel better than he had in a long time. "Why, I might just do that," he said.

IT WAS PECULIAR how it started, because he was thinking about ships, and the funny-looking fish Earl told him he might see. It came to him slowly, like he was watching the dark surface of a lake for something rising up quietly from its depths. He couldn't say what it was, but he didn't feel good about it at all.

When the night came again and supper was done, he made himself walk back to where the others always stayed, a little away from the camp. They looked at him cautiously, but didn't run. He knew at once that Earl was right. They were dirty and looked like stock, but their eyes told him better. He wanted to turn and go. Until now he could tell himself that Earl was maybe crazy, or making it all up. He couldn't do that anymore.

"Which one of you is it that talks?" Howie said. They all looked at him. One of the girls was tending the boy who was sick. They were all younger than Howie. "I don't mean any harm. Earl'll tell you that."

"What do you want, mister?" The boy who spoke had pale blue eyes and a nose that had been broken and had healed bad. His voice was thick, but Howie could understand him.

"Who treated you like this?" Howie said. "I want to know that, I want to know who did it."

"Who are you?" the boy said.

"I'm not anybody at all. My name's Howie Ryder."

The boy looked down at his hands. He didn't face Howie again for a long time. "You're not one of them, I don't guess," he said finally.

"One of who?"

"The guv'munt. One of *them*."

"It was the gover'ment give me this," Howie said flatly. He pointed at the scarred flesh covering his bad eye, then squatted beside the boy. "Is that who it was? Why the hell for?"

"They can do whatever they want," the boy said simply, as if that explained it all. "Whatever they want to do."

Howie waited. The boy looked at the others and something seemed to pass between them.

"I want an answer," Howie said. "That's all."

"I don't have any of those," the boy said. He stood, walked back to the others, sat with his back to Howie, and pretended to be doing something else. Howie couldn't do anything but leave.

EARL WAS ASLEEP, or didn't want to talk. The sky seemed alive with stars. The boy hadn't told him a thing. The government, which likely meant troopers, had treated him like meat. Or so he said. It wasn't something Howie wanted to believe, but he couldn't put it aside. They were there and he could *see* them.

The desert night was chill and he rolled up in his blanket. He wished there was a way you could turn off your head when you liked. When you didn't want to think anymore. Something like that'd be a blessing.

He wondered about Kari. Where she was; what she was doing now. He guessed the war would go on until it quit. Until one side or the other got tired of dying and gave up. Maybe that's what had happened in the War way back when. Maybe there was no one left who wanted to fight, nothing left to burn.

He turned over with a start, suddenly aware that he had slept, that the night was nearly gone, that something had brought him abruptly out of sleep. He reached for his knife, then recognized the shadow. The boy was just sitting there, watching, not moving at all.

"Whatever you was thinking, it ain't that," the boy said. "You couldn't know it. Not 'less you been there, you couldn't. Hadn't anyone *ever* got out of that 'cept us. What they do there is use you like they want. You ain't meat, but you're by God close enough to it."

Howie's throat seemed constricted. "Use you how? What is it you're talking about?"

The boy worked his mouth funny. "They do it 'cause stock gets weak and don't breed good anymore. Meat don't care if it's humpin' its sister or its ma, and that makes the blood go bad. You can't stop 'em doing it, so they put good blood back in the herds. Only it ain't *meat* blood. It's people's. The boys got to serve the best mares. The girls are put in with healthy bucks an'..."

"Godamn, you're lying!" Howie exploded. He sat up and stared at the boy. "No one'd do a thing like that! *No one!*"

"They can do whatever they want," the boy said.

Howie was shaken. Supper starting to crawl up his throat. "Someone...someone'd find out. They couldn't do it without someone finding out."

"Isn't anyone going to do that," the boy said. There was no feeling at all in his voice. "It's down in the old Keys and you don't get close unless you belong. It's a lie, the whole damn thing, and they can't take a chance on anyone finding out."

The boy looked away from Howie, north, or nowhere at all. He seemed to be somewhere else. Howie thought he was simply turning away, like he did when he didn't want to talk.

"Look," the boy said finally, "Earl said it was up to me, but that I probably hadn't ought to say anything at all. Only I *got* to do it. Maybe it ain't right, but I got to do it. See, the thing is, I *knew* her. They don't always cut your tongue right, and she could talk as good as me. She talked a lot about you. I knew who you was right off when you said your name. I tried to act like I didn't but I did. You was the..."

"*Huuuuuuh...!*"

Something tore at Howie's heart. Food came up and he couldn't stop it. "You're...talkin' crazy stuff," he said harshly, his voice as thick as the boy's. "D'wanta...hear g'damn crazy stuff!"

"Listen, I'm sorry." The boy's eyes seemed to plead with Howie. "I wanted *someone* to know. You see that? I wanted someone to know what they do. That's all it was..."

Howie cried out with all the anguish and loneliness that was in him, and knew it was a cry caught up inside him that no one else could hear. The sun rose out of the desert and he was lost in its terrible light. He wondered why there was no hurt at all. If he could make it hurt bad, someone would take it all back and do it over. But there was nothing in him now. It had been there once and it was gone. He couldn't make it happen anymore...

"You all right?" Earl touched him gently. "You want a little water or something?"

Howie shook him off.

"I can get you some water if you like."

"I got to go," Howie said. "I'm...obliged for your help and all. I can't stay here no more." The desert was a blur. He looked at Earl and didn't see him. The others were there somewhere in the sun, the boy who talked and the rest.

He started walking. Just walking away. He saw Carolee as he always saw her—a small flash of laughter in a bright flower dress on the boat down to Bluevale, a comic miniature of her mother. He held on to that picture as long as he could. When it turned to something else, he shut that corner of his mind and never looked at it again.

"There ain't nothin' up that way you can do," Earl called after him. "You know there ain't, boy."

"I got to go see if that's so," Howie said.

He wondered if he'd said it aloud or just thought it.